hollywood bliss
My Life So Far

Also by Chloë Rayban

Hollywood Bliss: My Life Starring Mum
Hollywood Bliss: My Life So Far

hollywood bliss
My Life So Far

Chloë Rayban

BLOOMSBURY
CHILDREN'S
BOOKS

First published in Great Britain in 2007 by Bloomsbury Publishing Plc
Published in the United States in 2007 by Bloomsbury U.S.A. Children's Books
175 Fifth Avenue, New York, NY 10010
Distributed to the trade by Holtzbrinck Publishers

Library of Congress Cataloging-in-Publication Data
Rayban, Chloë.
Hollywood bliss : my life so far / by Chloë Rayban.—1st U.S. ed.
p.   cm.
Summary: Thirteen-year-old Holly moves to New York with her superstar mom but
finds trouble in the form of her father, a new pet, and especially a boy named Shug.
ISBN-13: 978-1-59990-093-3 • ISBN-10: 1-59990-093-9
[1. Mothers and daughters—Fiction. 2. Celebrities—Fiction.
3. Children of celebrities—Fiction. 4. Singers—Fiction. 5. New York (N.Y.)—Fiction.]
I. Title. II. Title: My life so far.
PZ7.R21026Hol 2007   [Fic]—dc22   2006029302

First U.S. Edition 2007
Typeset by RefineCatch Ltd
Printed in the U.S.A. by Quebecor World Fairfield
2 4 6 8 10 9 7 5 3 1

All papers used by Bloomsbury U.S.A. are natural, recyclable products
made from wood grown in well-managed forests. The manufacturing processes
conform to the environmental regulations of the country of origin.

For Leo Bear
my personal LA correspondent,
without whose dedicated attendance
at parties, premieres and other random A-List events
this book could not have been written

Monday 19th May, 6.00 p.m.
First Class cabin, Flight KHA 19

The flight attendant is in tears. I think it must be her first day – like she's just been moved up from Club Class or something. But she clearly didn't know that Mum's in-flight beverage preference is (and always will be) 'still spa water, no ice'. And Mum doesn't need to be bothered with a menu 'cos all her in-flight food is prepared, sealed and delivered to the airline by Thierry, her own personal French chef.

Perhaps I should explain, you see, my mum is Kandhi. Now you're doing that wide-eye, no-way thing. KANDHI! Yep, Kandhi's my mum (UN-fortunately). Superstar pop idol, tenth richest woman in the world – if I'm up to date, that is.

Anyway, being Kandhi's daughter is NOT the bundle of laughs, luxury and long shopping afternoons you'd think it would be. No, as a matter of fact it's a total PAIN. Because MY mum seems to think my life is hers to do whatever she likes with. SHE wants to move to New York? WE move to New York. The fact that I've had to part company with my best friend, the best great-grandmother ever and the most adorable lop-eared angora rabbit in the world doesn't matter. Remembering Thumper makes me really miserable. In fact, I don't think I'm ever going to be able to enjoy anything again as long as I live. Hang on, my little linen tablecloth is being laid out ready for my First Class meal . . .

'What?'

Mum has hauled the earphones off my head and I was SO-OO into that film.

'Your meal's been prepared by Thierry as well, babes.'

'But can't I have . . .?'

No. It seems my in-flight meal choice is a starter salad, followed by a main salad, with fruit salad for dessert, accompanied by still spa water. Great!

Mum's still on her 'only raw foods' diet. And so am I when she's around. ('You are what you eat' is one of Mum's favourite sayings. I reckon one day I'm going to wake up with *roots* in place of feet.) However, rebelling at this point is going to entail a long, tedious lecture and I want to get back to the film. So I dutifully munch my way through my meal, hoping that I'll be able to get the flight attendant to snaffle me some of those little chocolate squares they serve with the coffee when Mum's not looking.

So why are we moving to New York? Mum says she's sick of being 'a five-star nomad' and that 'you can only take so much of hotels' – even if they are the world's most exclusive and extortionately expensive ones. She wants to settle down and get 'a home of our own'. My choice would have been to settle in London but does anyone listen to me? No way.

Mum's *had* London – period. She's looking for somewhere new to dump me because she's currently involved in this massive world tour, The Heatwave. She's had a smash hit launch in Europe and now she's got the States, the Far East and the Rest of the World to do. She said this whole 'settling down' thing came to her in the middle of a long-haul flight. For The Heatwave she has five continents and thirty-five countries to cover, so she checked out the American Airlines in-flight world map and found New York was the obvious choice because it was 'right in the middle'.

10.00 p.m.

The flight attendants have closed all the shutters and dimmed the lights and I've sent my seat through so many manipulations it now thinks it's a bed. Mum's been laid out with her eye mask on and her earplugs in for a good hour so I guess I better try and get some sleep too. But somehow my body can sense that it's still really light outside and refuses to feel sleepy.

I lie awake going through my Ultimate Wish List – giving it a spring clean, update and tidy.

1) Boobs (any size beyond AA). This wish seems to be resolving itself, so maybe I can afford to drop it. I replace it with:
1) An email from Rupert

Rupert is the tutor Mum hired to teach me when she snatched me out of boarding school without so much as asking my opinion on the matter. It turned out for the best really, because Rupert was the most perfect tutor any girl could have. I'm lost for a moment picturing the way the little smile lines play around his perfect lips. (I know I shouldn't be having such illicit thoughts about a teacher and one that's way older than me, but I am growing up. And Rupert's only four years, two months and three days older than me. He's just got to hang on in there and wait.) And besides, Rupert isn't teaching me any more because he was most cruelly dismissed by Mum and is now in Tanzania doing Voluntary Service Overseas in a highly dangerous location where he could be stung by a poisonous spider or swallowed by a boa constrictor or snogged by some rampant female VSO worker. Rupert has been replaced by my new tutor Mr Wallace (of the nose hair), who is currently travelling with us, but back in Economy. Ugghh!

So back to the list:

2) A trip to Ranthambore National Park in Rajasthan to visit what's left of the Royal Bengal Tigers (v. important. This can stay)
3) Dad to record a hit – or maybe sell more than 100 white labels

I consider this for a while. Perhaps I ought to explain – my dad is Pete Winterman, lead guitarist and vocalist for The Icemen. I don't expect you to react to that, because The Icemen sank into oblivion before I was born and Dad isn't famous any longer. He doesn't actually do any recording any more. In fact, he doesn't even go out much these days. He certainly won't be at JFK Airport to meet us, because he can't stand publicity or anything to do with the press. All the time Dad was with Mum he was hounded by them, and so was I. I featured on the front of every major media publication before I could walk. The only peaceful part of my life was when I was at a convent boarding school in England and nobody knew who I was. Which brings me to wish number 4 on my U.W.L.

4) Teeth that fit for Sister Marie-Agnes. I can drop this one as I've heard this has been dealt with by something called Dent-u-Fix, so No. 4 is now: Hair that doesn't frizz when damp (this MUST stay)

5) To pass Maths GCSE with a Grade C or above (might have to change the qualification if I go to an American school)

6) That Gi-Gi (my great-grandmother) lives for ever and ever, or a long time at any rate (this definitely stays)

7) That beetroot had never been invented (hmm . . . might think on that one)

8) That caged birds are banned (definitely still in)

9) That Becky, my best friend and ace violinist, gets the Stradivarius she'd give her right arm for (well, maybe not her right arm)
All of which means I can now have a new number 10.

I was pondering on choices for U.W. No. 10 when I must have fallen asleep. Because the next thing I know all the cabin lights are on and they're serving breakfast – or is it tea, because it's *still* light outside and we're told to put our watches back because it is now 4.00 p.m. New York time.

As I eat my tea/breakfast of fresh fruit salad and yogurt, I ponder over whether if I continued to fly in this direction I would start to get younger and younger. And if not, why not? I decide to set this as a problem for Mr Wallace. *That should give him something to think about.*

4.00 p.m., JFK Airport

Mum is breezing towards Immigration Control, saying what a comfortable flight that was. I am tagging along behind her, watching out for the rest of the entourage who have been forced to slum it with Mr Wallace in Economy.

'Well, there are so many of them,' Mum always says. 'I can't be expected to pay First Class for them all.'

Mum and I sit waiting for them, separated from the world of ordinary mortals by the VIP Lounge glass doors.

They start filtering through one by one. First comes Sit, Mum's religious adviser (and devoted fan). Poor Sit – he's drying his eyes on his saffron robe. He holds his hands together and bows his head low before he heads off to the Transit Lounge. He's on his way back to LA because Mum's *had* Buddhism – period. She's currently checking out other religions to find one that might fit her personal profile better.

Sit is followed by Vix (Mum's personal assistant), Daffyd (her personal hairstylist), June (her personal make-up artiste), Thierry (her personal French chef), Gervase (her personal

trainer), Abdul and Sid (her bodyguards) AND, not for-
getting of course, my tutor Mr Wallace. At that point
Mr Wallace's nose hair comes into view, closely followed by
Mr Wallace.

We join them as they go through Passport Control.

Mr Wallace is moaning about the fact that he didn't sleep
a wink on the flight. (A lucky break for all on Flight KHA 19,
I note. Mr Wallace snores for Britain.)

Daffyd is already on his mobile to his fiancée Bronwyn
in Bangor. June is having trouble hauling along the trolley
bag containing Mum's emergency make-up supply. Sid and
Abdul are doing their 360-degree head-turn-and-eye-
swivel-thing – after all, this a public place and they are
bodyguards.

Once our passports are checked, Mum takes a deep
breath, raises herself to her full height and turns on her
Winning Press Smile. I follow her through the automatic
doors and I'm blinded by camera flashes. There are only
about fifty or so photographers present. That is nothing –
you should see it when she draws a crowd.

I try to creep by in the wake of Mum's incredible popularity. Maybe if I stay really close, the press won't notice I'm
there. But no such luck – they're snapping me too. I know my
hair has stuck flat to my head, my eyes have diminished to
slits and I've lost the ability to coordinate lips, tongue and
cheeks. How does Mum do it?

Sid and Abdul escort us along at a trot and before we know
it we're out through the concourse and sliding into a waiting
limo. Phew!

'Are we going straight to the apartment?' I ask Mum as the limo heads out past the long rows of nice homey suburban houses that skirt the airport.

'It's not ready yet, babes. The designers are still in there. But I've booked us into a nice little place overlooking the Park. You'll love it.'

Still Monday 19th May, The Wessex Hotel – and still only 6.00 p.m.

Mum's 'nice little place' isn't homey at all. It's so interior designed that everything is black and spiky and shiny. Even the plants have been tortured into weird, unnatural shapes.

Mum's all wide awake and ready to give a press conference in her suite. My jet lag has kicked in with a vengeance. I feel so disoriented that the floor seems to be doing odd wavy things beneath my feet, so once in my room I fall into bed and sleep until . . .

It can't be only midnight, can it?

It's ominously dark outside. I climb out of bed and stare down at the car lights sweeping in a never-ending arc around the park. I'm in 'the city that never sleeps' and it certainly looks like I'm going to fit in, 'cos sleep is the last thing on my mind. In fact, I feel ready to get up, go out and run round the park.

I decide to call Dad.

'Dad?'

'Holly-Poppy! You've landed!'

'Hi, Dad. How are you?'

'I'm just fine. How are you, baby?'

'Wide awake.'

'Oh, it's that jet lag thing.'

'I guess.'

'Hmm. You want to come over?'

'Aren't you about to go to bed?'

'No way! Who goes to bed at midnight?'

'Mum does.'

'Well, I guess your mum has to get her beauty sleep.'

'I don't like to wake Sid or Abdul.'

'I'll get a cab sent over for you. Bulletproof to keep your mum happy.'

The cab turns up ten minutes later. I leave a long message for Vix, telling her I've had to go over to Dad's because he's really been missing me and is terribly hurt that I hadn't gone to his place straight from the airport – and asking her to *cover for me*.

Tuesday 20th May, 12.30 a.m.
Apt 12, 1794 South Mercer

Dad has this massive loft space in SoHo. He's had it for ever. Like *before* SoHo got on the cool-and-stylish bit of the New York city map. And now his block is surrounded by top designer boutiques and restaurants, but you still go up to his floor in this grotty goods elevator. But when you arrive, it's like this space filled with massive paintings and sculpture and stuff done by friends who've dropped by and stopped over.

Most didn't have any cash to pay for food or anything so they've given Dad all these pricelessly valuable artworks instead.

I used to live here with Dad while Mum was too busy being famous. When Mum and Dad divorced, Dad got this massive settlement from Mum which meant he didn't have to work any more. So he stopped doing virtually anything. I mean, even things like getting his hair cut sent him into trauma. Living with Dad was like being part of a big and rather weird family. There were always friends hanging around doing deep arty things – like painting people purple and letting them roll around on canvas. Or making movies in which nothing actually happens, which win awards in film festivals nobody's heard of. Or writing really serious music which goes on and on and on, repeating noises like the way the elevator door screeches and the throbbing sound a fridge makes when you leave the door ajar.

Then, one day, someone from the Social Services Department dropped by and asked where I was going to school. Dad looked kind of vague because by the time I was six or so he'd already taught me to read and write and pick out tunes on his keyboard. And I could do all the sums needed to check if they'd overcharged us on the takeouts.

But the Social Services lady was SO NOT impressed. That's when Mum stepped in and took charge of my education and sent me to boarding school in England. But back to the present . . .

The wheezing and clanking of Dad's elevator brought back happy memories of my carefree days before I lived with Mum. It arrived with a screech and a sigh at the eighth floor and I climbed out.

As soon as I was out of the doors, I was enveloped in a big close hug from Dad. Then he held me at arm's length.

'Wow, Holly-Poppy! What've they been giving you? Growth hormone?'

'Hi, Dad!' I noticed he was getting a bit of a paunch. And he had a lot less hair than last time I'd seen him. What was left was tied in a ponytail that was starting to go grey at the sides. My heart did a little lurch. Parents should most definitely NOT be allowed to grow older.

'Come on in. Let's hear it all. How's life been treating my favourite daughter?' Because of Dad's preferred form of communication (he refuses to communicate by anything but postcard) there's quite a lot to catch up on.

'I'm your *only* daughter, Dad!'

'That doesn't stop you being my favourite.'

I cast a glance around the loft. Nothing much had changed: there were more artworks on the walls and some new stuff standing around which I guess must've been sculpture. Not much in the way of furniture apart from a load of Afghan cushions and sagging beanbags.

'So? Where is everybody?'

'Oh, they're around. Be back sometime soon.'

We went and settled on a pile of cushions.

'Hey, what you been doing to your nails?' asked Dad.

'Nothing. I mean, I've stopped biting them.' (At least, I haven't bitten them *much*. I was too scared of June getting hold of them and insisting I wore stick-ons.)

'No, those white bits – cuticles. You should push those down, you know. When you're in the bathtub. Or after a shower. Doesn't your mum tell you to do that?'

I stared at him lovingly. Dad really cared about me. He cared about my *cuticles*. How many daughters can say that?

At that point (saving you from a totally gooey sentimental bit) there was the sound of a key in the front door.

'Da-dah! There she is! The fabulous, the one and only . . .' came a voice I recognised.

'Fred's *still* here!' (Fred's a painter friend of Dad's, although he doesn't actually use paint – he more like finds stuff and frames it.)

'He's just about to move out,' Dad reassured me.

'Hi, Princess!' Fred exclaimed as he grabbed me round the waist and swung me round. 'Are you still going to marry me?'

My answer was drowned out by cheers and whoops as more people came flooding into the apartment.

'So who's this?' said a big guy looming out of the doorway. 'Pete, are you going to introduce me to this beautiful lady?'

'Marlowe, this is Hollywood Bliss Winterman. Holly-Poppy, this is Marlowe.'

'You can call me Holly – everyone does.'

'Oh boy! I don't believe this. You're Kandhi's daughter!' said Marlowe.

18

I glanced at Dad. I wish people wouldn't do this. They used to call Dad Mr Kandhi, which was so hurtful. Like he was *nothing* compared with Mum.

So I kind of shrugged off the comment, saying, 'I guess so.'

But I couldn't help staring at Marlowe. He looked like he'd stepped out of a movie. All perma-tanned and stubble-faced.

'Haven't I seen you somewhere before?' I said.

Marlowe tipped his head on one side and raised an eye-brow.

'Just add a ten-gallon . . .' he said with a wink.

'Oh my God, I have! It's you on all those hoardings . . .'

'That's me. Ten yards high . . .'

'Wow! You're really famous,' I said. He was the guy from the Hustler jeans ad. The posters were up worldwide.

'Not as famous as your mum.'

'No one is as famous as her mum,' commented Dad drily.

I slipped my arm through his. 'Come on, Dad. Introduce me. Who are all these other people?'

Suddenly I was getting hugged and kissed by people who seemed to know me. I was trying to match them to the hazy memories I had of shadowy figures coming and going from my life. I couldn't help noticing that a lot of them seemed ominously at home. They were raiding the kitchen and beers were being cracked open and bottles uncorked.

'Hey,' called out a voice. 'Is there anything to eat?'

Dad shrugged and nobody moved, so I went and peeked in the fridge. Nothing had changed there either. It was empty apart from a bottle of ketchup, a jar of peanut butter with fuzz on the top and a tin of anchovies.

1.00 a.m.

A delivery boy arrived weighed down with takeout cartons. As soon as he set foot in the loft, people descended on them like a flock of vultures. There were little scuffles and shouts like: 'Hands off! That's mine – it's got double pepperoni.' 'Who's the pasta salad for?' I don't like to think how Mum would have reacted. Her carb-counter would have gone into burnout.

'You want some, Holly?' asked Dad.

'No thanks, I ate on the plane.'

People were settling down to eat.

'Dad,' I said, drawing him to one side. 'Are all these people like living here?'

'Oh, not all of them,' he said between plastic forkfuls of food.

'How many?'

'Errm, well, it's a shifting population.'

'How many, Dad?'

'Well, there's Marlowe. And Max, of course,' he said, indicating a guy who was drinking from a bottle of wine. 'He's just here while he finds a publisher.'

'You mean the guy with dreadlocks?'

'Yeah . . .'

'What does he do?'

'Oh, he's a poet. His stuff's really good. And there's his girlfriend, Juniper.'

'That's already five including you,' I said, keeping count on my fingers.

I turned off while Dad droned on about Max's imminent breakthrough. I didn't even care to look in the back rooms. If I knew Dad, they'd still be furnished in classic roadie style – bare mattresses and well-strewn clothes.

'Honestly, Dad, you're too good to these people.'

'Well, you know what they say, Holly – if you've got it, share it. But there's still space for you, honey. I've kept your little room just as it was – in case you ever want to come back.'

My little room was so small it was what most people call a cupboard. I wasn't absolutely sure I could fit in there any more. Well, maybe I could, just, if I kept my knees bent. But it was high up and looked out over an epic view. You could see the buildings of New York stacked as far as the eye could see and at night, when they were lit up, it was like Christmas all year round.

'Thanks, Dad. I nearly did come back once, when Mum and I had a row.'

'How is she? The *mega-star*!'

'She's fine.' Reacting to Dad's tone I found, unaccountably, I was leaping to her defence. 'She's making a real effort. To be a mum, I mean. She's even bought an apartment. It's having a makeover right now so we're still in a hotel, but –'

'They came and interviewed me about her film, you know.'

'*Supernova*?'

Supernova is this big-budget bio-pic that they're currently shooting about Mum. Mostly they're using footage from her videos and concerts, but she's still got some link sequences to shoot in New York.

'They didn't want me to play me though,' continued Dad, putting himself down as ever. 'Wanted a younger guy. Cast some unknown. But they're using some of my music.'

'But that's brilliant, Dad!'

'Yeah. But they don't want any new stuff.'

'Are you writing any new stuff?'

'Just about to get down to it as a matter of fact.'

I sighed. I'd heard this before. Over and over again. All the things that Dad was *about* to do. It made me feel kind of hopeless. If they gave awards for being laid-back, I reckon Dad would've got one.

Things had calmed down somewhat now everyone had eaten. People had stretched out and the air was filling with smoke and the comfortable hum of voices. Someone was picking out an old blues tune in Dad's music room. Suddenly the sleep that had seemed so impossible back at the hotel started to overcome me.

'I might just go and take a nap,' I whispered to Dad.

'You do that, Holly-Poppy. Great to have my baby back,' he said, giving me another big hug.

'Great to be back too, Dad.'

Like Dad said, my room was just as I'd left it. I checked out the view. I could see the Chrysler Building, which Dad used to pretend was the Emerald City. He said they'd changed the colour so that nobody would know, and that we'd go there sometime, but of course we never did.

I climbed in under my *Jungle Book* comforter and found

there was just enough room to stretch out. The jungle mobile Dad had made for me, with balsa wood animals he'd cut and painted himself, was still hanging from the ceiling. I blew at it and they started to dance the way they used to do. When I'd lived at Dad's this was how I'd always fallen asleep.

9.30 a.m. (New York time). Oops!

I'm woken by my phone vibrating like a furious wasp under the covers.

I answer it.

'Where on earth are you?' It's Vix.

'It's OK. Keep your hair on. I'm still at Dad's. I left you a message.'

'You're meant to be at a breakfast meeting with your mother.'

'Nobody told me about it.'

'We didn't think we'd have to. We imagined you'd be in the hotel. I'm sending Abdul round for you right now.'

'OK.'

'And by the way . . .'

'Yeah?'

'I covered for you.'

'Thanks, Vix.'

I stumbled out of my cupboard. The interior of Dad's flat looked like a scene from the nastier side of hell. There were bottles and glasses and paper plates full of cigarette butts and the lumpy shapes of people who must've fallen asleep where they were sitting. I crept through the debris and quietly let myself out through the front door.

I paused on the threshold. Shouldn't I leave a message for Dad? No need. He'd just assume I'd gone back to the hotel. I'll give Dad one thing – he isn't paranoid about security. He was already a roadie by the time he was fourteen. As far as he's concerned, at thirteen and three-quarters, I'm old enough to look after myself.

10.00 a.m., The Wessex Hotel – breakfast meeting

If Mum's laid on some interview with a journalist, I'll kill her. On the other hand, if she knows I've been out of the hotel for the night, she'll probably shoot first. But luckily Vix's cover-up has worked and I make for Mum's table in the Wessex Dining Room.

'Babes, did you sleep well?' she says. 'Meet Anthony. Anthony, this is Hollywood.'

Anthony doesn't look like a journalist. He's wearing a crumpled white linen suit with a black polo neck.

'Have the grapefruit sorbet,' says Anthony by way of introduction. 'It's awesome.'

I go and help myself to a plate of awesome sorbet and return to catch Mum say, 'Burnished pewter . . . What does that look like, exactly?'

I slurp sorbet, assuming that Mum's planning some new look for a video or something. But no, Anthony turns to me.

'So, Hollywood, have you decided how you want your suite done?'

'My suite?'

'You're old enough to have ideas of your own, babes. I

want you to plan your whole decor for yourself. Just tell Anthony what you want and he'll fix it.'

'You mean, I can have anything I like?'

Anthony spreads his hands expressively. 'Anything . . .'

'Errm . . .' Why is it that when you can have *anything* your mind goes totally blank? I thought back over my dream decors of the past. The princess phase, when I wanted a bed draped in gauzy stuff and crystal chandeliers. The punk phase, when I wanted walls covered in graffiti and curtains full of rips. The eco-phase, when I wanted fake grass and a fish pond and banks of real growing flowers where Thumper my rabbit could roam free . . . But all of these sounded far too childish to suggest to Anthony.

'It's really difficult to imagine until I've seen the place,' I say to stall him.

'She's right,' said Anthony. 'Why don't I take you both over and we'll take a look at the site?'

10.30 a.m., the site

We don't have to go far to 'the site'. They've gutted this building that used to be an all-time beautiful hotel and it's just a few blocks down from the Wessex. We have to wear hard hats to go into the building but once inside we're taken through passages of billowing canvas to an elevator – which is still covered in polythene and Scotch tape – and whooshed up to the forty-fifth floor.

As we emerge my hopes of somewhere 'homey' are totally dashed. We're in a massive penthouse which has glass walls all round and the most awesome view of Central Park.

'This is your mother's salon and her state room leads off,' says Anthony, leading the way.

The apartment's huge. Anthony's virtually disappeared into the distance, opening doors, saying: 'Bureau, kitchen, TV room, gym . . .'

'Heaven, isn't it?' says Mum.

'Umm . . .' It's so stark and cold and white.

'And this, Hollywood, is your suite,' says Anthony, throwing open a final door.

I walk in. The room is huge. Ceiling-to-floor windows open on to a balcony. The interior walls are made of mirror so the whole place feels twice as big as it is – endless, in fact. A further door leads to a massive mirror-walled bathroom. This suite gets 100 per cent for style. Ten out of ten for view. But homey-ness is not on the menu. I think of my little room back at Dad's with longing.

'Well?' says Mum.

'Well, maybe it needs some plants – palms and things,' I suggest. (Or screens or blinds or drapes, or something to make it feel more like a place you could actually live in.)

'Plants?' repeats Anthony, sounding so unimpressed by this. 'Just plants?'

'Hollywood's really into nature. Plants, animals, things that grow – all that kind of stuff,' says Mum.

'What about furniture?' asks Anthony. 'Any ideas?'

'Well, I guess I'll need a bed . . .'

'A bed! But what kind of bed?'

'Are there kinds of bed?'

'Kinds of bed? Are there *kinds of bed*? Hollywood Bliss,

there are Italian baroque, French provençale, British four-posters, Victorian brass beds, sleigh beds, hung beds, testers, half-testers . . . or there's hi-tech – steel and glass, circular, blow-up, a water bed . . .'

'No, listen, honestly – for me, anything. A hammock would do.'

Anthony pauses. 'Stop! I'm getting pictures in my mind. Could you give me a free hand here? Oh, this could be stellar!'

I look at Mum and shrug.

'Anthony is a genius,' says Mum. 'Trust him.'

11.00 a.m., The Wessex Hotel

On the way back to the hotel I check my mobile and find I have a text from Becky.

She doesn't communicate much for a best friend. I mean, not ten times a day like most best friends. But she has a pretty good excuse. She's transferred from the convent boarding school where we met to a specialist music school in London. So now she has like double the workload. She does music all morning and has to cram all the other study into the afternoon, not to mention practising.

The text reads:

Hi Holly
you know
that cute boy Jamie I told you about
who plays third trombone?
he's asked me out!
Bx

27

Becky! Becky has a date. Immediately I want a date. He doesn't have to be anything very grand. Just a boy. Practically any boy will do.

But where would I meet a date?

a) In the hotel lobby? I haven't spotted anyone under fifty staying at the Wessex.
b) In our luxury penthouse? Not unless a passing helicopter drops one on the terrace.
c) At Dad's? Any boy I met at Dad's is bound to be weird.

Back at the Wessex, we find Mr Wallace waiting for me in Reception with his battered briefcase. They've hidden him behind a bank of tortured bamboo so he doesn't get mistaken for a guest.

'Aha! Hollywood!' he says, leaping to his feet. 'Now, in theory this is still term time – you should be doing school work.'

'But I've only just arrived.'

'We have the requirements of the syllabus to fulfil all the same,' he says. 'Now, I've sorted us out a workspace. Not ideal for our purposes, but –'

Mum nods. 'I know how important your schooling is to you, babes. You don't want to fall behind, now do you?'

I eye Mum suspiciously. Since when has she taken an interest in my schooling? She clearly wants to be rid of me.

Mr Wallace and I have been given this horrible stark conference room to work in. It's freezing cold because the air
conditioning has to be on full blast since it doesn't even have
a window – it's underground. We're sitting at this endless
table that can seat at least a hundred people and I'm trying
to concentrate my mind on my work. I can almost feel the
other ninety-nine people who aren't there, looking at me in
disapproval because of what Mr Wallace is saying about my
books so far. He's not at all happy about my progress in
science subjects.

'Take Chemistry, for instance. Where exactly did your last
tutor leave off?' he's asking.

I explain that my *last tutor* (Rupert, sigh!) didn't really leave
off anywhere. In fact, we barely got started on Chemistry.
I think I knew more than he did.

'But Chemistry is really important, Hollywood. It is the
key subject if you want to realise your ambition.'

My ambition is to become a vet. I know it may sound a
little *over*-ambitious for someone like me, who is kind of
challenged on Maths and Chemistry and stuff – although I
did get an A+ once in Biology for my drawing of the life cycle
of the frog – but it's what I desperately want to do. And it
must be easier than becoming a superstar like Mum because
there's only one Number One and there are loads and loads
of vets.

Mr Wallace has put down my Chemistry book and is
looking through my Maths book, making little grunting

noises through his nose hair. He is SO NOT impressed by that either. In fact, he's saying in a rather cross voice that if I don't 'pull my socks up' the nearest I'll get to treating animals will be clipping nails in a poodle parlour. And I'll be lucky to get that.

'Mr Wallace,' I say, looking him straight in the eyes, 'have you no faith in the powers of education?'

He pauses there. 'Well, yes, I suppose where there's a will and the dedication to put in some hard work –'

'Exactly. I mean, where would Einstein have been, or Churchill . . .' (From what I've heard, neither of them got off to a very good start.)

Mr Wallace and I spend an intensive two hours working on something called bonding. The bonds have little oblique lines going in all directions. By the end of the morning my exercise book looks like it's had a bad attack of cellulite. I'm told to memorise all these bonds by tomorrow.

1.00 p.m., lunch hour (at last!)

When I'm let off for lunch I go to the dining room to see if Mum's there. She's not. And neither are Vix or Daffyd or June or anyone I know. There are all these smartly dressed people having ultra-smart lunches. I just can't face eating there on my own. The only other option is to have lunch with Mr Wallace. The thought of eating face to face with his nose hair is more than I can bear.

I take refuge in the restroom and consider the alternatives. A room service lunch alone in my room? Or no lunch? I stare at my reflection. I'm in jeans and a grey polo top. I look like any other teenager. Without Mum or a limo or two six foot seven bodyguards, how would anyone recognise me? All I've got to do is behave like a totally ordinary person and no one will give me a second glance.

So I walk out through the hotel lobby with a relaxed stride.

I was right! Nobody took the least bit of notice of me. Once in the street I'm struck by the total euphoria of being ALONE. This may sound odd to you, but you haven't had the life I have. I've had to live under threats of kidnapping. I've been hounded by the press. Normally, I'm driven everywhere in an armoured car with tinted windows. Being out alone I get my first heady taste of freedom. This must be what ordinary people feel like all the time!

I wander along the sidewalk that skirts the park, checking out the horses that pull the carriages for tourist rides. I'm happy to announce that all the horses look well fed and well groomed and most have their noses happily stuffed into their nosebags and are having a peaceful munch on their lunch. This makes my tummy rumble enviously. What I need is a burger or a hot dog. And then I realise I don't have any money. Here I am, daughter of the tenth richest woman in the world, and I don't have a dollar in my pocket. I consider going back into the Wessex and borrowing some cash from the concierge, but I'd be bound to be spotted by someone from Mum's entourage.

No, if I want an hour of freedom I'll have to ignore my hunger pangs. I turn my back purposefully on the ice-cream vendor who is parked down the street. (Oh, what I'd give for a choc chip vanilla!) and head away from the park.

After twenty minutes or so of purposeful walking the welcoming doors of Bloomingdale's beckon to me.

Inside, all is warm and light and glossy. I stroll along nonchalantly, for all the world like any other normal teenager, browsing through the yummy-smelling perfume department and sampling all the samplers till I smell like some horribly clashing mixed floral bunch.

Then I take an escalator up to check out the fashion department. I find there are loads of girls a bit older than me searching through the racks of evening dresses. They all seem to be with their mums and they look as if they have something pretty important on their minds. And then I realise what they're doing. *They're choosing prom gowns!*

I lurk behind a rail of full-length sheer chiffon and watch.

You wouldn't think a person like me, who has everything she could possibly want, would be *envious*, would you? But I was. I was envious of all those girls who would shortly come whooshing down the family staircase dressed for the prom. Each of them with a dad taking photos and a mum standing there tearful with pride . . . and some nice ordinary boy to escort them to the car.

But I'd never go to a prom if I didn't go to a school.

That's when it came to me. I should stand up for my rights. I was not going to put up with Mr Wallace (and his nose hair) any longer. I had a right to schooling like any other girl my age.

2.30 p.m. Oops! I'm a bit late back

I'm in trouble. Mr Wallace, assuming I had lunch with Mum, has rung her to ask where I am. Mum was none too pleased at being interrupted during what she called 'a very important lunch appointment'. She wants to see me at the end of the day, which suits me because I want to see her too – about school.

Mr Wallace and I spend the afternoon catching up on Maths. Or at least half my mind is doing Maths, the other half (or maybe three-quarters) is fantasising about which of Bloomingdale's prom dresses I will wear when I'm elected Prom Queen of the real American School that I'm about to persuade Mum to send me to. Mr Wallace seems to sense the fact that my mind is not truly on my work and piles on the pressure.

He sets me three whole algebra exercises to do for homework.

4.30 p.m.

As soon as I'm released from classes I go up to Mum's suite.

'So where did you have lunch?' she demands.

'Nowhere,' I reply truthfully.

'No one has lunch nowhere,' she says.

'OK, if you really want to know – I went for a walk. Then I looked round Bloomingdale's.'

'You went for a *walk*? You mean *alone*?'

'Yes. In broad daylight, along with a million or so other people.'

'Holly! *Anything* could have happened to you.'

33

'Like what?'

'Like *anything*.'

'In *Bloomingdale's*?'

'Wherever!'

'I was only taking a *walk*. Other kids my age are allowed exercise.'

'You're not just any kid, you're my daughter. And you are not to go out alone. Do you hear me?'

'That's not fair.'

'Life's not fair, Holly. You'd better get used to it.'

'No. I won't get used to it. I have a right to some personal liberty. *And* education! Why can't I go to a school like other girls my age?'

'Holly, you are prey to all sorts of people – kidnappers, extortioners, muggers, murderers! There's no way you can go to an ordinary school. It's simply not safe.'

'I know Dad would let me.'

'Hollywood, don't you side with your father against me.' Mum was really getting angry now. But so was I.

'It's my life. I've got two parents. I shall side with whom I like,' I snapped back.

8.00 p.m., Apt 12, 1794 South Mercer – siding with Dad

Dad opened the door to me: 'Hi, Holly-Poppy! Your mum's been on the phone. What's this fight about?'

I peered past him into the apartment. 'Where is everyone?'

'Fred's making a suspense movie. He's got them all hanging off Brooklyn Bridge.'

I walked in and slumped down on one of the beanbags.

'So what's up?' asked Dad.

'Mum is trying to keep me prisoner. She won't let me go to school. She won't even let me out on my own.'

'Well, maybe she's got a point. This is New York, honey.'

'Dad, I don't believe it! You're on her side.'

'Now, I wouldn't say that.'

'Other kids my age go out alone.'

'It's only because we care about you.'

'You weren't much older than me when you left home for good! You had your own band by the time you were sixteen!'

'Yeah – well, maybe. But things were different back then and besides, I was a boy.'

'So it's one rule for boys and another for girls?'

'It's not because you're a girl, Holly. It's because you're Kandhi's daughter.'

'If anyone says that again, I shall scream!'

'Come on, ease up. Look, we're going to have a great evening. I've ordered up all your favourites.' He pointed to a stack of DVDs. Oh great! He'd got *The Jungle Book*, *Mary Poppins* and *Chicken Run*. Didn't Dad realise I'd grown out of stuff like that?

'And I've got popcorn and Doritos *and* . . .' He shook the packet. He'd bought me Barnum's Animal Crackers.

'Oh thanks, Dad. Cool.' He missed the sarcasm. He was too busy sorting out the DVD. He put on *The Jungle Book* and plonked himself down beside me.

I sat fuming while Dad tried to get me involved in the movie. He was fooling around, making silly animal faces and swinging his arms like Baloo, even singing along to some of the numbers. As he shoved the box of Animal Crackers under my nose for the fifth time, he caught sight of my black expression.

'It's OK. I've saved you the giraffes . . .' he tried.

That's when I grabbed the remote control and put the DVD on Hold and said: 'Dad, do you think we could talk for a bit?'

Dad settled back in his seat and said, 'Sure. What do you want to talk about?'

'*Me!*'

'There's no need to shout.'

'Dad, neither you nor Mum seem to have noticed that I, Hollywood Bliss Winterman, am *growing up*.'

'Yeah, I noticed. You're up to my shoulder.'

'Listen, Dad. You've got to realise I'm not a child any more. I need to get out and meet people.'

'Holly-Poppy, you're meeting people all the time.'

'Not people my own age.'

'Oh . . .' said Dad, looking thoughtful. 'Like boys and stuff?'

'Maybe.'

'Uh-huh,' he said. 'Now, Holly, a girl in your position has to be careful.'

'Careful? Why?'

'You can't date just any boy.'

'Why not?'

'Guys are going to be after you because of your mum. Because you're rich. Even maybe because they want to sell

36

their story: "My Date with Kandhi's Daughter" – all that kind of stuff . . .'

'The way things are, boys won't be going out with me at all,' I said grumpily. 'I'll never get a chance to meet any if I don't go to school.'

'You'll meet boys soon enough.'

'Don't *you* think I should go to school like other kids?'

'School? I thought that was the place most kids wanted to quit.'

'Be serious for a moment. This is important!'

'Well, you know your mum's in charge of your education.'

'Dad! Take a look at yourself. Won't you *for once* stand up to Mum?'

'Now look here, Holly, I don't really have a say in –'

'Of course you do! You're my dad.'

'Yeah, but it's your mum who's paying for your education.'

I got to my feet. 'I don't believe I'm hearing this. What does it matter who's paying? I don't think you really care. Not enough to fight for me. You know what you are? You're a loser, Dad.' I could feel hot tears pricking in my eyes as I said it.

Dad stood up too and started stacking the DVDs.

'It's late, honey. You're tired. I'll call you a cab.'

'Yeah, I think you'd better,' I snapped.

I'm lying in bed feeling really guilty about what I said to Dad. I've hardly been back a day and I've shouted at the one person who has always been on my side. I called him 'a loser' and that was really horrid.

I start thinking over all the cool things Dad has done for me. Like the time he was going to take me on a trip to a safari park. We didn't actually get there, but that was because I got the mumps. Dad made me take a nap and when I woke up I found he'd turned the loft into our very own safari park. He'd torn pictures out of magazines of forest, and plains and mountains and stuck them all over the walls. And he'd brought in a load of plants and made a kind of jungle. Then he'd hidden Animal Crackers all over the apartment, so that I had to find them. He had penguins in the icebox and hippos in the bathtub and tigers roaming through the shagpile rug. There were monkeys hanging from all the light fittings – they kept falling on our heads for weeks after.

I guess 1 a.m. in the morning isn't that late to call someone up. Not Dad.

'Hi Dad, it's me.'

'Hi, Holly-Poppy.'

'I can't sleep.'

'No?'

'I can't sleep because I shouted at you.'

'Oh, I wouldn't have called it shouting – more like raising your voice maybe.'

'Thanks for getting in Animal Crackers.'

'Maybe . . . errm . . . I should let you choose the movies next time.'

'So you're not mad at me?'

'Honey, I'm never mad at anyone.'

'I'm sorry.'

'I know.'

9.00 a.m., The Wessex Hotel
Executive Conference Suite

I simply have not had time to do my homework. I try to explain to Mr Wallace that this is because I've been too busy 'sorting my life out'.

Mr Wallace's nose hair positively bristles at this. 'How am I expected to tutor you when I have to contend with this sort of attitude?' he grumbles.

We work on through the morning with Mr Wallace in a really bad mood and me in a worse one. I don't even get a lunch break. Mr Wallace has sandwiches sent down so that we can work through and catch up. He eats these with a really martyred expression on his face – normally he'd be tucking into three substantial courses in the Wessex Dining Room.

While he's not looking I send a text to Becky.

greetings from the wessex high security block
how was your date?

2.00 p.m. and beyond

The afternoon is no better. At four o'clock I get a text from Becky. It's just one word:

Blissful!

Hmm. Not much of an answer from a best friend. I think at the very least I deserve details. I text back.

has he x'd you yet?

This is important. Promise you won't tell a soul, but . . . although I've reached the age of nearly fourteen, I've never ever kissed a boy. I mean, not properly on the lips. You have to understand – my opportunities have been severely limited. A convent school since the age of eleven, and then living under total round-the-clock armed security with my mum. The opportunities for kissing boys have been thin on the ground – in fact, not on the ground at all . . . Becky, however, is at an advantage – she's in a mixed sex school. Is this fair?

Mr Wallace rudely interrupts this important train of thought. 'Is that a mobile phone I see you with, Holly?'

'Yes, Mr Wallace. It is.'

'Hand it over, please.'

'Pardon?'

'Mobile phones are not allowed in class in schools. I think we should respect the same rules, don't you?'

'No I don't, Mr Wallace.'

'I don't think we need to argue over this. It's a small enough matter.'

'It may be a small matter to you, Mr Wallace, but it's pretty important to me.' He confiscates my phone all the same.

I watch it disappear into the nasty dark recesses of his briefcase. There goes my lifeline to the outside world, my link to the only person who truly understands me – Becky. I glower at Mr Wallace as he sniffs self-righteously and snaps his briefcase shut.

For the rest of the afternoon I steam over the algebra exercise he's given me. In my present mood the symbols don't seem to mean anything. My mind is busy devising cunning plans to evict Mr Wallace from my life.

a) I could accuse him of sexual harassment. I glance over at Mr Wallace. He's busy scratching at a dried gravy stain on his tie. No one is going to believe that.

b) I could bribe Abdul to drive him out somewhere – like maybe Central Arizona – and abandon him. Knowing my luck he'd manage to hitch his way back.

c) I could suggest he's a terrorist threat and harbouring a weapon of mass destruction in his briefcase. I once spotted a lethal-looking pork pie festering in there.

Not surprisingly this train of thought doesn't do a lot for my concentration.

Sometime (but feels like for ever) later . . .

I'm watching over Mr Wallace's shoulder as he goes through my work making cross walrussy grunting noises, double-underlining things in red pen.

'I'm sorry, Holly. This isn't good enough. I'll have to keep you in after class.'

I growl at him that I'm being 'kept in' anyway – like for life.

'That's it!' he says in a nasty clipped tone. 'An hour's detention.'

'But this isn't a school, Mr Wallace! And I never had detention with my last tutor.' (If only!)

'Believe me, this is hard on me too,' he says with a self-righteous sniff. He opens his briefcase and takes out a copy of the *Times Educational Supplement*.

Even later . . .

I can hear him licking his fingers and flicking over pages and breathing through his nose hair while I bend over my books, which is SO-OO distracting. I bet he's got something far more exciting secreted inside that *TES*. I send him the evilest of evil hate-vibes.

It's OK for him. He's getting paid to be here. In fact, it now occurs to me, he's probably getting double pay for overtime!

I can feel a headache coming on. The walls of the conference room seem to be closing in on me. The air conditioning is hissing in my ears. And to top it all Mr Wallace has nodded off and he's SNORING!

'Mr Wallace!'

'Huh? What?' He wakes with a snort.

42

I get to my feet. 'I am not staying here a minute longer.'

'I think we should let your mother be the judge of that.'

'OK. Let's go and see her together.'

'Very well. If you insist.'

Mr Wallace and I go up in the elevator to Mum's suite.

Vix opens the door to us.

'We haven't scheduled a meeting, Holly . . .' she says.

I brush past her: 'We want to see Mum.'

'What is it?' A voice comes from the bedroom. Mum comes out dressed in her wrap. Mr Wallace goes bright red. You'd think he'd never seen a woman less than fully dressed before. (Actually, that's highly probable.)

'Is this important, Holly?'

'Mr Wallace says I've got to do detention and he's –'

Mum holds a hand up to silence me and looks at Mr Wallace. 'What are you detaining her for?'

We both answer in unison:

'Not doing a lot of really vital –'/'Not doing a load of really boring stuff.'

Mum makes it clear that she has far more important decisions than my education on her mind. Through the open bedroom door I can see she has a selection of outfits laid out on her bed and a choice of shoes.

'But do I or don't I have to do detention?'

'Oh, I don't know. Why don't you ring your father?'

We do that. Dad comes up with the suggestion that I go and do detention at his place. This seems to suit Mr Wallace, who goes off with his head held high.

9.00 p.m., Apt 12, 1794 South Mercer

Dad and I have had an ace detention. He's taught me six new chords on his keyboard and we've shared a family-size pepperoni pizza.

'So what's the problem with Mr Walrus?' asks Dad, when we're both feeling nice and mellow and full of pizza. (I've told him about the nose hair.)

I go into a long list of Mr Wallace's many faults and shortcomings.

'Bit long in the tooth, is he?' asks Dad.

I ignore this pathetic attempt to humour me.

'He's old *and he's grumpy*. And he's SO-OO negative. Do you know what he said to me? He said I'd never make a vet. At the rate I was going, I'd be lucky if I got a job in a poodle parlour clipping nails.'

A shadow of a smile crosses Dad's face. And this is SO NOT funny.

'AND he's confiscated my mobile. Can't you do something to get rid of him?'

'I guess I could call your mother and talk it over with her.'

'Thank you.'

Thursday 22nd May, 10.00 a.m.
The Wessex Hotel

Through Dad's kind intervention I've got my mobile back from Mr Wallace. Dad intelligently pointed out that me not having my mobile is a security risk. What would happen if we were attacked and Mr Wallace was bound and gagged and tied to a chair? (Oh, dream on!) So I'm in a much better mood, even though my mobile's meant to be turned off while in class.

We're doing French grammar and I manage to get right through from 'Je suis' to 'Ils/elles sont' without a single mistake.

'Good,' says Mr Wallace grudgingly.

So we move on to the future. Somewhere mid-future tense, I feel my mobile vibrating. A sly glance under the table shows I have a text from Becky. I take the teensiest peek at it.

It's only one word:

No

I sit there puzzling over this as we get to grips with the complexities of the past tense – or the 'passie composie' as Mr Wallace insists on calling it. He has the most terrible accent.

With skilful sleight of hand, I text Becky back:

No what?

The answer comes back before we get down to the imperfect.

x

That's when I remember my last question to her. Has Jamie kissed her yet?

No. He hasn't. So I'm not the last person on earth who hasn't been kissed. *Yet*. All I need to do is find one essential – like a boy. He'll have to be a pretty nice one though . . .

'Are you still with me, Holly?'

'Yes, Mr Wallace.'

'So what was it I just said?'

'Errm?'

'Hollywood? Have you been using your mobile again?'

'Just reading a vital text message. It was only one letter, Mr Wallace.'

I show him Becky's message.

Mr Wallace has insisted that even if it is a one-letter answer it obviously wasn't a one-letter question. So my mobile has been confiscated *again*.

OK, you asked for it. *Your days are numbered Mr Wallace.*

4.30 p.m., after classes

Mum is getting ready for a dinner date. Daffyd's doing her hair. Between bursts of blow-drying I manage to get her attention.

'Mum, I've talked to Dad about going to school . . .'

'Oh yeah? Daffyd, part it higher, OK?'

'Umm . . . He says it's up to you, so . . .'

(Rest of my argument is drowned by dryer.)

'Holly, I can't hear you . . .'

'Mum, I can't stand a day longer with Mr Wallace . . .'

'Daffyd, will you STOP for a moment.'

Daffyd switches off. Mum, hot and cross from the dryer, turns to face me.

'If you'll let me get a word in – I have been looking into schools, as a matter of fact,' she says. 'And I think I've found a solution.'

'Oh?'

'Go on, Daffyd.'

I watch as Daffyd finishes Mum's hair and she admires her reflection with a look of satisfaction. 'Yes', she continues, as Daffyd holds a mirror for her to check out her back view, 'there's this private place that's not far from here. Good security.'

'Brilliant! How did you hear about it?'

'Oh, this son of a friend goes there . . .' says Mum vaguely. 'That's fine, Daffyd. You can go.'

'Who? What's the school called? Do I know him?'

'Errm . . . yes, you've met . . .'

I search my mind for who it can be. Oh no! NO, please NO!

'Mum, it's not Shug? Tell me it's not.'

(Shug is my least favourite person in the Universe. He's the son of an ex of Mum's – Oliver Bream, this really arrogant English actor who thinks he's God. Which makes Shug Son-of-God. Both of them treat me like I'm some mistake Mum made in the past which she would've done better to get rid of.)

'I am NOT going to the same school as Shug!'

'I don't understand you, Holly. First we're arguing about you going to school and now we're fighting about you not going.'

'But there must be other schools in New York?'

'Not like this one. This is where all the stars' kids go. It's got maximum security and special classes. You know, some of those poor kids have missed loads.'

'If they're anything like Shug, they think they know it all already.'

'I don't know why you're so negative about him.'

'Even his stupid name makes me want to kind of . . . *regurgitate*.'

'I think it's rather cute. His real name's Siegfried. But he couldn't say Siegfried when he was little, so Shug kind of stuck.'

'I'm amazed he can manage Shug.'

'Anyway, there's no need to start making a scene because you won't be going there for a couple of months. Their spring semester's just ending.'

Mum is starting on her make-up now. She's leaning into the mirror applying lipliner.

'So . . . if I *was* at the school, I'd be going on vacation right now?'

'Yeah, I guess.'

'So why am I doing classes?'

'It's not holiday time yet in the UK.'

'But I'm not in the UK.'

'Well, I know, but –'

'Mum, if you're sending me to this new school I might as well start right now – on vacation.'

I watch Mum's reflection in the mirror as the logic of this gets through to her.

She stops putting lipstick on mid-lip and says, 'You've got

48

a point there. Why not? This means we could get rid of that Mr What's-his-name . . .'

'Mr Wallace. Mum, you mean you don't like him either?'

'It's not that I don't like him, babes. The thing is – he's never really gone with the decor, now has he?'

Friday 23rd May
VICTORY!

Mum has actually told Mr Wallace that we don't need him any more. I reckon she must have given him a massive pay-off though, because when he came to say goodbye, he didn't look the tiniest bit sad. In fact, he had this expression like a walrus that's just spotted a massive shoal of sardines approaching and all he has to do is keep his mouth open and they'll swim right in.

He told me he was going to treat himself to 'a little vaca-tion' in the Caribbean. I tried unsuccessfully to picture Mr Wallace laid out on a sunlounger on some exotic beach fringed by palm trees. I just couldn't think what he'd do with his briefcase. I had this awful vision of its sad, battered elephant-hide surface surrounded by cocktails with fruit and umbrellas and stuff in them, looking so out of place.

But anyway, he tried to be nice. He *did* give me my mobile back. He said he'd still mark my last three assignments and send them back, although this wasn't *strictly* in his contract. And he wished me luck and said if I ever wanted to get in touch in the future (!), I could use his mother's address in

Bognor Regis. For one dreadful moment I thought I was going to get a walrussy kiss goodbye. But then we shook hands instead. Phew!

Saturday 24th May, 9.00 a.m.
The Wessex Hotel

I wake up with that wonderful lazy feeling, realising that it's Saturday. And then I have to double the feeling because it's not only Saturday but *the beginning of the long vacation*! And then I triple it because it's not just the vacation, it's the end of classes *for ever* with Mr Wallace.

This leads me on to think about what I'm going to do with my vacation. All that time on my hands and nothing planned. I could travel with Mum, of course – she should be off on tour any day now. But think of all those hours hanging around backstage . . . Maybe I could get Dad to take me somewhere. Dumb idea – I can't even get Dad to take a walk. What I'd *really* like to do is go somewhere distant and exotic like . . . Tanzania, for instance. This conjures up a picture of Rupert in my mind . . .

I could well have lain in bed picturing Rupert for a good hour or more, but it occurred to me that I hadn't checked my email once since I'd been in New York and he might well have been desperate to contact me. So I leapt out of bed and opened my laptop and clicked on 'Mail' and up came loads and loads of spam which I had to erase to get to:

A rhino ate my homework

It was a message from Rupert. Oh, savour the moment! I didn't even want to open it – this moment should last forever. But of course I did.

Hi Holly!

How's life in the stratosphere? Does the Supernova still have you locked into her orbit? So much to tell you. Tanzania mind-blowing. Try to think of absolute and total opposite to the Royal Trocadero and you've got my current accommodation. It has floor (baked mud), walls (four), roof (partial), windows (unglazed), furniture (bedroll). I have made one important purchase since arrival. It currently serves as shower, stool, shopping basket and washing machine. I've christened it Basil – it can even be used as a bucket when I go to the convenient tap three hundred yards from my door. The 'schoolhouse' is currently in flat-pack form, i.e. branches, mudbrick and thatch, which seems to have been delivered without assembly instructions. Basically the job here is: first build school, then teach. But I do have students. They seem keen to learn – they've already started digging the foundations.

You may not get many e-s from me as in order to reach nearest 'internet café' – and I speak metaphorically – I have to rise at 4.00 a.m. and walk three miles thru waist-high scrub to intercept bus which takes two hours to reach nearest 'town' – the mecca of sophistication where I bought Basil.

Will try and send another e in ten days as I have to
come back here to meet fellow VSO worker. Juliette is
coming to teach infants soon as school's built.
Love and all that,
Rupert x

Juliette! Juliette? What do they think they're doing sending
a *female* volunteer to work with Rupert? I've a good mind to
get Mum to complain – I'm sure VSO must be one of the
charities she supports.

I study the email again. '*Love and all that, Rupert x*'. I concentrate for a blissful moment on the little '*x*'. I imagine '*x*'ing
Rupert – sigh! But unbidden, my mind starts sending unwanted
and totally out-of-line snapshots of this Juliette: waiflike and
blonde in a tight, white shirt, knotted at her perfect waist. Or
in *Out of Africa* khaki combats, her long russet curls wafting on
the hot Tanzanian wind. Or tall, brunette and raunchy in tight
denims. And I know for a fact that all these alternative Juliettes
are *dead set on snogging Rupert*. It's SO-OO unfair!

I have breakfast in my room, as I am too miserable to
descend to the dining room. All my holiday plans are in
ruins. What is the point in going to Tanzania now Juliette
will be there? In my mind I am desperately trying to compose
a suitable email in reply to Rupert's.

I try:

a) Noble–and–unselfish: I am so glad you have a female
VSO worker to share your lonely evenings under the
stars Ugghh!

52

b) Mature-and-far-seeing: Be careful NOT to get involved in a relationship just because you're marooned together miles from anywhere.

c) From-the-heart: Rupert you are my one and only true love I'll never love anyone else as long as I live. Wait for me!

None of these alternatives seems to have the totally cool and detached tone I'm searching for. But Rupert's not going to be checking his email for another eight days or so (when he goes to pick up *Juliette*), so I have eight whole days to think up the right response.

In the meantime I do what any girl in my place would do. I text my best friend:

Disaster!
Rupert has new female
USO volunteer
coming to live in his
shack.
advise please.
HBWX

A text comes back from Becky almost immediately:

poor you
try to
find a positive way

to deal with rejection
Bx

I stare at this answer in disbelief. How could any best friend be so callously cold-hearted? Just because she's got a date with Jamie. The text positively oozes self-satisfaction.

I text her back:

how?
HBW

Her text returns:

keep busy
Bx

Now this is a tall order in the Wessex Hotel, where even your robe is hung up for you if you happen to leave it on the side of the bath. I scan my suite for potential activities. In the end I take a nap. Well, I'm still jet lagged after all.

Sunday 25th May, 9.00 a.m.
Apt 12, 1794 South Mercer

I wake and have rather less of a euphoric feeling. Yes, sure I'm on holiday, but what precisely am I going to do with my time? I ring Mum. She's booked up recording all day. She suggests I spend the day with Dad.

So OK – I get Abdul to drive me over to Dad's. He's the parent who really cares for me. He's bound to think of some brilliant way to spend the day.

When I get to his place I have to ring for ages before anyone opens the door.

It's Dad. He's unshaven and his skin looks positively grey.

'Hi, Holly! What are you doing here?'

'Dad, you look dreadful.'

'Honey, I feel it. I'm going back to bed.'

He disappears into his room. I survey the place. It must've been some night last night. By the look of it, Fred has been making one of his movies. The apartment is like the scene of a chainsaw massacre. There are stray body parts from a load of shop window mannequins strewn around. Some of these have been roughly reassembled like some hideous evolutionary mistake. There are headless legless bodies with umpteen extra arms and armless leggy ones – goodness knows where the heads have gone. I track these down to the kitchen, where a load of black rubbish bags are leaking what looks like human hair. The janitor's going to get some shock when he throws out the trash.

The sink is piled high with dirty coffee cups and the air smells like an ashtray, so my 'positive way of dealing with rejection' takes the form of washing up, cleaning, and tidying loose body parts into black plastic bags.

At last I can hear water running in the shower. When Dad comes out of his room, I give him a lecture.

'Honestly, Dad – the way you lot live!'

'You sound like your mum.'

'In that case she's right. Just look at yourself.'

Dad looks at himself in the mirror and groans.

'Exactly.'

One by one the others wake up. They are in a similarly wasted state. Fred checks his body parts and insists I go through the trash with him. He claims I've mislaid a left leg.

Marlowe is nowhere to be seen but there is a constant stream of calls for him on Dad's phone. They're all girls and they all want Marlowe to call them back.

I suggest ordering up breakfast for everyone but this is greeted by a chorus of : 'No way!' I'm sent out for paracetamol and cola instead.

They sit for the rest of the day drinking cola and playing cards. The place is blue with smoke.

You know, sometimes adults can be SO-OO sad. I'm worried about Dad. No, correction, I am *seriously* worried about Dad. He never takes any exercise. He never goes out. He's turning into a fat, slobby version of his former self and I have to do something about it!

Monday 26th May, 9.00 a.m.
The Wessex Hotel, otherwise known as Prison

I call up Mum first thing and ask her what she's doing. She's recording all day again. I can hear from her voice that the last thing she wants is me tagging along.

'Why don't you go over to your dad's?' she suggests.

'I did that yesterday.'

'So?'

'Honestly, Mum. There are all these people there and they're smoking and playing cards.'

'You mean I'm still supporting those freeloaders?'

'I guess so.'

'What do all these people do precisely?'

'Nothing much.' I don't generally go into details. Mum's views on Dad's 'artist' friends don't bear repeating.

'They must do something.'

'Well, there's Fred who's a poet.'

'He writes stuff?'

'I guess.'

'And the others?'

'Well, Max makes films.'

'Umm . . . Good.'

'And there's Marlowe. He's meant to be a model. He's waiting for his agent to call.'

'Right,' said Mum. 'Leave it with me. In the meantime you better help Vix out.'

10.00 a.m.

When I announce I'm going to help Vix, she's less than enthusiastic. In fact she makes it pretty clear that having a thirteen-and-three-quarter-year-old helping her is the last thing she needs. She finds a game of patience on her computer and draws up a chair for me.

'If you've really nowhere else to go, sit, play, and don't speak. OK?'

'OK.'

I sit and play while Vix makes calls to umpteen travel companies who can't seem to provide the flights she wants. Eventually she slams down the phone and grabs her bag and says she's going down to the travel office in person.

My patience game refuses to come out for the third time. I look round for some other 'positive way to deal with rejection'.

Vix has got two piles of correspondence on her desk which she hasn't filed yet. I help out by filing all this correspondence alphabetically. I've got right through from A to W by the time she gets back.

She stomps through the door, flings her bag down and stares at the table.

'Holly? Where have all those papers gone?'

'I had a tidy-up. I filed them,' I say, waiting for praise.

She has one hand on her hip and she's looking at me with her head on one side. NOT good body language.

'You did *what*?'

'I filed them?'

'Oh my GOD!'

'Not a good idea?'

'Holly, do you realise – those piles – they were strictly in order of "do first". Now, I have no idea where the hell I am.'

Tuesday 27th May, 12.45 p.m.
The KWR Inc. Recording Studios

The big event of the day is having lunch with Mum at the recording studios. I turn up as arranged at 1 p.m. and find she isn't there. So I have sandwiches and Fanta in this little glass booth with the sound engineers.

2.00 p.m.
Mum breezes in and catches sight of me through the glass.

'Holly, what are you doing here?' she says through the mike.

'We were meant to be having lunch, remember?'

'Were we?'

'*Yes!*'

'Oh babes, sorry! I totally forgot. I'll make it up to you.'

'How?'

'Errm . . .' Mum exchanges 'Aren't kids a pain?' glances with the senior producer and he points meaningfully at the studio clock.

'I'll think of something,' she says hurriedly. 'You want to stay and watch?'

'I suppose so.'

I have the treat of watching Mum going over and over the same phrase like fifty times. Soon I'm feeling more frayed than the sound engineers.

By four I've had enough and I get Abdul to run me back to the Wessex.

4.30 p.m.

Abdul is taking a detour through the poor part of the city and I'm staring out of the window wondering how on earth I'm going to get through this summer. That's when a hoarding catches my eye. It has a picture of a really cute dog and cat on it.

PAWS 4 THOUGHT
Adopt a pet today.

It's an ad for an animal shelter. Underneath it gives a number to ring.

A dog! If I had a dog, I might be allowed to take it for walks – it would have to be a good big dog, mind. But something tells me the Wessex Hotel wouldn't take kindly to a dog. And Mum wouldn't be crazy about a dog in her new interior-designed apartment either. Maybe Dad would like a dog. Think of all that fresh air and exercise! It would do him so much good. Yes, most definitely, Dad *needs* a dog.

'Have you got a pen, Abdul?'

Abdul passes me over a biro and I note down the number.

5.00 p.m.

As soon as I got back to the Wessex I zoomed up to my suite to ring the animal shelter.

'Paws for Thought,' came the reply the other end. 'Miriam speaking. How can I help you?'

'Hi, Miriam,' I said. 'I want a dog.'

'Well hi, honey. You sound kind of young. Could you tell me your age? I'm afraid we don't do adoptions to minors.'

'Oh . . .' (Bummer!) Then I added: 'But it's not for me. It's for my dad.'

'Well, that's fine. But it's your dad I'll have to talk to.'

(Double bummer!)

'But it's meant to be a surprise.'

'Uh-uh. We don't do surprises here. That's how pets end up on the streets. You should see the rush we get post-Christmas.'

'That's terrible.'

'And every time they show *101 Dalmatians*, we get a whole load of Dalmatians in, a month or so after.'

'But Dalmatians are adorable.'

'True. But difficult to train. People go and buy them 'cos they're so cute, then they find out to their cost that a dog's not a toy. Now here, we have a one week cool-off. So if your dad's not happy with the dog, he can bring it back, end of the week.'

My mind was racing. How was I going to adopt a dog for Dad without his cooperation? And I knew for sure Dad wouldn't cooperate. I was going to have to rope in some other adult.

'Listen, Miriam, I need to have a chat with my dad, OK?'

'You do that, honey. We're open till seven.'

When I rang off I considered my 'rope-in' options. It didn't take long to decide on Abdul. He's the most easily bribable and blueberry jelly beans are way cheaper in the States. (Abdul is addicted to jelly beans, but only the blueberry ones.)

61

I went down to where the chauffeurs hung out in a little room with a TV in Lower Ground. Abdul was watching baseball but turned the sound down and half-concentrated while I explained my problem.

'So you want me to pretend to be your dad?' he said.

'Only to sign for the dog. After that we deliver it to Dad.'

'And what if your dad doesn't want this pooch?'

'It's OK. If you decide you don't want it, you can take the dog back at the end of the week. And it's in a really good cause.' I explained about Dad not going out.

Abdul grinned. 'OK, I suppose if that's the case you can count me in.'

Then I got Abdul to call up Miriam.

Miriam asked him some searching questions about whether he'd had a dog before and what sort of accommodation he had. Luckily, he had the phone on speaker and I was listening in, so before he could admit that he spent most of his life in a smoke-filled room below ground in a hotel, I'd fed him some more positive answers.

6.00 p.m., PAWS 4 THOUGHT animal shelter

Abdul and I have driven over in the limo. The shelter is in a really poor part of town and the minute Abdul parks, the car draws a crowd of kids who look set on carving their initials on it.

Miriam must've spotted us getting out of the car because when we go in she asks: 'You sure a pedigree breed wouldn't be more to your liking?'

62

'Oh no. We'd like to give a home to an animal in need,' I say.

'Right. Well, I've got the forms here. We better go through the formalities first, and then I'll get some dogs up on the screen for you to take a look.'

I was a bit disappointed by this. I'd expected to find this big shelter place with loads of pens with animals in, so that you could walk around and browse and maybe make eye and nose contact. I mean, this all seemed very one-sided. What if the dog didn't like you? To be fair, they ought to take our picture and let the dogs take a look too before they matched us up.

Miriam handed Abdul a form that looked like an exam. It had loads of multiple choice boxes to fill in. I'd primed him ahead, making him memorise all Dad's details like his age and address and the size of his loft.

Once our form was filled in, Miriam looked at it with an assessing eye. 'Hmm . . . eighth floor,' she commented.

'But there's an elevator – a really big one.'

'OK, let's get some candidates up on the screen.'

The minute I saw the dogs I wanted to adopt them all. They looked as if they'd been told to pose with really sad and pleading expressions. But the one who got me most was this really ginormous dog. He was described as a 'St Bernard/German Shepherd cross, male, age 3 yrs approx., friendly and docile'. He had this look in his eyes as if no one in the world would ever love him because he was SO BIG. He must have weighed in at at least 160 pounds. There were no two ways about it, this was the dog for me.

'That's the one,' I said, nudging Abdul.

'Oh yes, definitely,' agreed Abdul, raising an eyebrow at me.

'The St Bernard cross?' said Miriam. 'You sure? He's been a bit difficult to place. Been on our books for a very long time.'

'But he's beautiful. He's perfect,' I said.

'Do you realise how much it's going to cost per day to feed him?'

'That's not a problem,' I said and after a kick, Abdul nodded in agreement.

Miriam glanced meaningfully towards the limo. 'No, I guess not. But you may not like him spoiling the interior of your car.'

'That's true . . .' started Abdul.

'Oh, we'll put a rug down or something,' I said.

'OK, if you're really sure, you can have him on trial starting Thursday.'

'Can't we have him straight away?' I pleaded.

'No, soonest I can have the dog brought over is Thursday. He'll be here for five p.m.'

Wednesday 28th May
The Wessex Hotel

Nothing worth recording happened, except I've made a list of dog names. Current favourites are:

1) Gulliver
2) Methuselah
3) Genghis Khan
4) Caesar

I try to picture myself in the park shouting out, 'Genghis Khan!' Or 'Methuselah!', come to that.

New list:

1) Gulliver
2) Caesar

Thursday 29th May, 5.00 p.m.
PAWS 4 THOUGHT animal shelter

As soon as we opened the door there was this gigantic WOOOOF!

'That dog's certainly got a voice,' said Miriam. 'Come through and get acquainted. Brandy is out the back.'

'Brandy?' I asked.

'Brandy's the name he answers to. You can change it if you like, but he may not take much notice.'

'Hi, Brandy!' I said, bending down to greet him, but I didn't have to bend very far because this was one mountain of dog. I gave him my hand to sniff and he got to his feet wagging his tail.

'Sure you still want him?' said Miriam, looking at Abdul.

'Yeah, I guess,' said Abdul, backing away slightly as Brandy started to get friendly. In fact Brandy, sensing that

Abdul was the saviour who was going to release him from an uncertain future, was up on his back legs with his paws on Abdul's shoulders, licking his face.

'See, he likes you,' said Miriam.

Abdul was doing his best to look as if he was enjoying these doggy caresses, but was saying, 'Down, boy!' in a very firm manner.

'That's right. You've gotta show him who's boss. I can see you're going to get along just fine. Now, if you'll sign here . . .'

Abdul sent one last warning glance at me but I handed him a pen.

'Come on, *Dad*, sign. We don't want to keep the lady waiting, do we?'

A few minutes later we were back in the car. All three of us. I was in the front with Abdul, and Brandy was taking up the entire back seat.

'Holly, I sure hope you know what you're doing,' said Abdul.

'Of course I do.'

'You don't think it would be better to take the dog back right now?'

'No way!'

'But your dad's not going to want a dog this big.'

'Dad loves animals. And he's got loads of space. Come on, Abdul, let's get going. Miriam's watching.'

Abdul turned on the ignition. Brandy leaned over and licked the back of his neck.

66

'And Abdul, try to look as if you're enjoying that, please.'

6.00 p.m., Apt 12, 1794 South Mercer

We had a little trouble getting Brandy out of the limo. He evidently liked travelling in cars and Abdul had to enlist the help of a guy who was passing before the two of them could push him out.

'You want to take him back now?' asked Abdul.

'No. It's just a matter of training, that's all.'

'Look, I don't want to be involved in this. From now on you're on your own, Holly. You take that dog up to show your dad and I'll wait in the car. I bet my life on it that you'll be back down, complete with dog, within minutes.'

So it was just Brandy and me in the elevator. Brandy sat obediently on the floor and nuzzled my hand.

'Now, this could be your big break,' I told him. 'Don't louse up. No leaping up. No face-washing. OK?'

I went ahead to Dad's door. When he opened it, I said: 'Hi, Dad. Surprise! Guess what I've got for you!'

'Aha! Let me think . . .'

'WOOOOF!' said Brandy.

'Oh my God, it's a dog!'

'Isn't he beautiful!' I said, pulling Brandy forward by the collar.

'Well yeah, but where's he come from?'

'He's from an animal shelter. Dad, he really needs a home.'

'But he's so big!'

'I know. That's why no one wants him. He's been on the shelter's books like for ever.' (I decided to lay it on a bit.) 'I mean, if no one gives him a home, *anything* could happen.'

At that point Brandy showed what a brilliantly intelligent dog he was. He put his head on one side and looked up into Dad's eyes with this terribly stricken expression. I could swear he was almost forcing the tears out.

'But Holly-Poppy, I don't want a dog . . .'

'But Dad, you did say if you've got it, share it. And you're sharing with all these people already. And *they're* not under sentence of death if you push them out . . .'

Brandy let out this heart-rending whine right on cue.

'Hey boy,' said Dad, holding out a hand. Brandy inched forward and gave it a delicate, servile lick.

'I've only got him on trial. If you really don't want him, I can take him back at the end of the week,' I said.

Dad stood there staring at the dog, obviously trying to make his mind up.

'And just think,' I added. 'It will give me a bit of freedom too. Mum can't have anything against me going out in the street if I've got Brandy with me.'

'That his name?'

'Umm.'

'Hi, Brandy,' said Dad.

But Brandy wasn't listening. He'd already walked past Dad, and was surveying the loft as if he owned the place.

'Uh-huh,' I said as I climbed back in.

Abdul looked up from his newspaper. 'Where's the dog?'

'With Dad. I told you he'd have him.'

'Holly,' said Abdul, shaking his head, 'sometimes you amaze me.'

'Thank you.'

'You sure do take after your mum.'

'Do I?'

'Yeah. You've got her powers of persuasion. Don't you ever take "no" for an answer?'

Friday 30th May, 9.00 a.m.
Apt 12, 1794 South Mercer

I go over first thing to check on Brandy. Marlowe opens the door to me dressed in a bath towel, which means I get the treat of seeing his perfect bronzed chest and medallion. He is just such a poseur.

'Have you come for the dog?' he asks.

'He could probably do with a walk,' I reply. 'Has Dad been out with him yet?'

'Took him to the corner of Mercer and Spring Street.'

'Where is he right now?'

'Come and see,' he says. He tiptoes to Dad's door and pushes it open a crack.

Splayed out on the bed, right in the centre, sleeping like a baby . . . is Brandy. Dad is asleep too, with one arm thrown over the dog. (Now this is the guy who didn't want a dog, remember?)

'Dad, are you going to get up and take this dog out?' I demand.

Dad opens one eye. 'What's the time?'

'It's nearly ten.'

'Uuuurrghh!' says Dad, and turns over.

'We had a bit of a night of it last night,' says Marlowe.

'I s'pose I better walk him on my own.'

On hearing the word 'walk' Brandy leaps off the bed and nearly knocks me flat.

Later: heading very fast towards the East Village

Brandy walks me rather than me walking Brandy. Within minutes we're out of SoHo and the shops have switched from cool and stylish to alternative and wacky. This is the East Village.

Now the East Village is a dog-friendly kind of place. It has loads of trash bags with nice doggy smells round them, and it's not overrun with pedestrians so a dog can take up most of the sidewalk without being shouted at. But Brandy doesn't seem inclined to pause. He's straining on the leash like a dog with a mission. And he's dragging me behind him through streets that would have Mum reacting like an overcharged rape alarm.

Shops are whipping by like a commercial break on fast forward: Live Food-Tarot Reading-Psychic Planning -Total Body-Karma-Nails-Vintage-hippy-tie-dyed-Afro-dayglo-sequinnedstuddedslashed – at the speed we're going any potential molester would be lucky to catch me.

Brandy comes to an abrupt halt in a place called Tompkins Square. He's stopped by a gumball machine. He stands there panting and staring at me expectantly.

Something tells me that in Life-Before-Dog-Shelter Brandy has been here, because this is no ordinary gumball machine. This one sells 'Hashed Liver Flavor Dog Treats'.

'OK boy, you win.'

I feed five quarters into the machine and out comes the dog treat in its little plastic bubble.

I stand getting my breath back while Brandy chews contentedly on his dog treat. Automatically, I check my mobile.

I have a text message.

It's from Becky:

B+J = X!!!!!

I puzzle over this odd equation. Is Becky losing it? Overwork, perhaps? But then its full meaning dawns on me with all its shattering implications. OK, that's it. It's now official – I'm a freak. Becky has been kissed. I gaze around the square as I take this in. Suddenly everyone in Tompkins Square Park is a person who has been kissed, even that big fat lady who's feeding the pigeons over there. I am the only person who hasn't. I'm a sad, lonely thirteen-and-three-quarter-year-old who has never been kissed. As far as I can see ahead, I may well go through my entire life un-kissed.

Saturday 31st May, 7.00 a.m.
The Wessex Hotel

I wake up realising that I've been dreaming I'm at this new school and that Shug is one of the teachers and I've walked up to the blackboard and taken the chalk from him. He's staring at the blackboard because I've just written out this equation – about a hundred symbols long – which has solved the whole mystery of time, motion and the age of the universe, with the kind of neat solution that's absolutely clear in your brain when you're dreaming but total rubbish when you wake up. My answer is simplicity itself. It all equals x. But Shug is staring at it and kind of sneering, which gives me an uncomfortable feeling that maybe I've loused up.

I lie in bed trying to work out what the dream means. *Shug! Ugghh!* His very name makes me feel like I'm going to break out in something terminal. And that dad of his – that beastly cold fish Oliver Bream who oh-so-very-nearly became my stepdad! But Mum ever-so-wisely stood him up at the airport when they were going to fly to Vegas for the ceremony.

And then I have an even more uncomfortable feeling. 'The son of a friend goes there' – how did Mum know where Shug went to school? She must be back on speaking terms with Oliver Bream. Or even *seeing* him.

8.00 a.m.

I was intending to have a quiet private breakfast. I've actually spotted a pack of Lucky Charms buried among the little individual cereal packs in the dining room and I'm homing in on it, intent on a deliciously unhealthy feast well out of Mum's sight lines, when Vix comes storming into the restaurant. She's carrying her organiser and has her mobile on headset. She's looking frayed.

'What's up?'

'Your mother's meant to be on location. I've got the director on the line going spare and she's not in her room. Have you any idea where she is?'

'No. I've been with Dad. I didn't even speak to her yesterday. Did you try her mob—'

(Silly question. Mum always has her mobile turned off when she's not working.)

'Can you think of anyone?' demanded Vix. '*Anyone* she might be seeing?'

'No, but . . . hang on, maybe . . .' I'm getting this horrible feeling in the pit of my stomach. Who were those lunches with? My suspicions are all pointing to one person.

'What? Tell me! He's bawling me out as if it's my fault.'

'Is Oliver in town by any chance?'

'Oliver Bream? Last thing I heard he was in Cannes – at the film festival.'

'I reckon she's been seeing him.'

'But they broke up.'

'Something tells me they're back on.'

'Right,' said Vix. 'There's one way to find out.'

She stabbed at her mobile. 'Sid, that mate of yours – Oliver's driver. Call him up. We've got to know if Oliver's in New York. And if so, where he's staying.'

'. . . . .'

73

'I know you're all sworn to secrecy. But this is like life and death . . .'

'. . . . .'

'OK, if Kandhi's with him, you sort it out. If she's not on the corner of Murray and North End Avenue *like ten minutes ago*, I'm out of a job.'

'Right, Holly. I've got to go.'

'Can I come with you?'

'Haven't you got anything better to do?'

'No.'

Vix and I took a cab to the corner of Murray and North End. The street had been cordoned off with red-and-white tape. There were several police cars and a fire engine standing by. Parked along the curb was a bank of those massive location trailers that film companies use, their tangled web of cables snaking out across the street. I'd already spotted Daffyd waiting on the steps of one marked 'Wardrobe', anxiously smoking a cigarette.

Vix went up to the security guy who was manning the cordon.

'Has Kandhi shown up yet?'

'No, ma'am. Looks like things are getting pretty tense in there.'

Once inside the cordon, you could feel tension in the air like static before a storm. They'd done up this old disused cinema to look like a tacky nightclub. It was plastered with flyers featuring 'Kandhi and the Popsicles'. (Sad but true – that was the name of Mum's first backing group.) A couple of guys were stretching a big white reflector over the entrance, and the cheap glitzy stars around the doorway kept flashing on and off. I could see a body double who was standing in for Mum, poised in the foyer as they took camera readings off her.

A guy with big headphones stormed over to Vix.

'So where is she?' he demanded.

'Hang on,' said Vix, cupping her hand over her ear as she listened to her mobile. Her face cleared: 'It's OK, she'll be here in five.'

The guy, who I later found out was the director – and awesomely famous – went over to a fellow with a megaphone and a voice rang out:

'Right, everybody. Back to starter positions. Looks like we might even get something in the can this morning.'

'OK, Popsicles, stand by. We're going for another take.'

Three blondes dressed in glittery pink minidresses and huge platform boots clambered down from one of the trailers.

'Did Mum's backers actually look like that?' I whispered to Vix.

'Unfortunately, yes,' said Vix. 'This was her retro phase.'

'Silence, everybody!'

A bank of lights flashed into life and a boy with a clapper-board leapt in front of the camera and slapped the clapper shut.

The Popsicles started tottering on their platform soles towards the entrance of the 'club'.

There was a tense silence as a camera inched forward, tracking them.

Just then a scarlet Maserati screeched up, went straight through the cordon tape, slammed into a bank of trash bins sending them crashing to the ground, and lurched to a halt.

Mum climbed out.

'Cut!' went the voice on the megaphone.

The director strode across the set.

'Where the hell have you been?' he demanded.

Mum stood her ground.

'Am I late or something?'

'Late? You were due on the set *two hours ago*!'

'Well, I'm here now,' said Mum, and started to head towards the trailer where Daffyd and June were standing waiting.

'Now, you listen to me,' said the director. 'You may be Kandhi the star. You may even be Kandhi the Supernova. But on this set you are one of the actors, and like all the others you are under my direction, and if you don't toe the line, one of us is going to be out of this film.'

Mum turned and eyed him levelly. 'Well, it certainly won't be me,' she said.

It was at that point that another figure climbed out of the car. As he rose to his full height, my worst fears were confirmed. Large as life and just as creepy, there stood Oliver Bream! My mind went into a flat spin. Mum must have spent the night with him. Oh. My. God. So it was true – they were back on.

'Errm, excuse me . . .' he was saying in that ultra-posh English voice of his, 'I think this could be my fault . . .'

The director turned and stared at him threateningly. There was absolute and total silence on the set.

'You see, the thing is, right now, Kandhi might have had other things on her mind. Because . . .'

There was a pause in which you could have heard a *cotton ball* drop.

'This morning I asked her to marry me and she agreed to be my wife.'

There was a kind of sigh like a deep communal 'Aaaah' from everyone. Two of the Continuity Team embraced. I saw a camera man drying his eyes.

Mum turned shyly and walked back to Oliver and put up her face to his, and he leant down and kissed her.

At that, the whole set exploded into applause.

The director threw up his hands and shook his head, but even he was smiling. 'OK, I know when I'm upstaged. Come on you folks, break it up. And let's get this movie moving.'

All right, so it was a touching scene. But back to *me* and *my reaction*. Oliver had released his hold on Mum and she was heading towards the wardrobe trailer. And I was running towards it too . . .

I clambered up the steps behind her: 'Mum! You can't mean it. After all that's happened. You're not going to marry *Oliver* of all people!'

Daffyd slammed the door shut and Mum fell into the seat June held ready for her.

'No, Holly,' she said with a sigh. 'I'm not.'

Daffyd and June set to work on Mum like it was a resuscitation job in *ER*.

'But Oliver just said –'

'Oliver said that to get me out of a scrape. Marvin is the most brilliant director. If Marvin walks out, we've had it.'

'But you turned round and kissed him like –'

'Acting, babes. We're both actors in case you'd forgotten.'

'But why *were* you so late?'

'Because we overslept, which was *all Oliver's fault*. So we were having this *almighty* row! When he came out with all that stuff about proposing, you could have knocked me down with a . . . a . . . whatever.'

'Oh, I see . . . So he hasn't proposed?'

'Not unless I missed it in all the shouting. Now, can you leave me in peace to get dressed? Where's my wig, Daffyd?'

I climbed slowly down from the trailer, going over this in my mind. Phew! What a relief! She wasn't going to marry Oliver. But everyone now thought she was. How were they going to get out of this one? Nightmare!

'Hi, *Sis*!' a voice hissed from the far side of the trailer.

I froze. It wasn't! Yes, it was. It was SHUG. He moved in and trapped me in the narrow bit between two trailers.

'Where did you spring from?' I said. 'Crept out from under some stone, maybe?'

'Charming! I was in the back of the car as a matter of fact. Glad I didn't miss that moving little scene.'

'Well, don't get your hopes up. That's just what it was – a scene. *Acting*. Mum wouldn't want to marry your dad if he was the last man on earth.'

'Hopes? To have an ex-*Popsicle* for a stepmum? Oh purr-leese!'

78

'Well, you were there. What was going on in the car?'

'Your mum was doing the hysterical bit, blaming Dad for lousing up her movie.'

'But it was only one tiny sequence.'

'Not if Marvin Helpman walks out on her and directs the film Dad's casting.'

'That's what the row was about?'

'Among other things.'

'You mean, Mum thought your dad made her late on purpose?'

'She didn't put it *quite* so calmly, but yes, I guess.'

'But I still don't get this. Why *were* they late?'

Shug looked at me sideways and then came out with a slow grin. 'Maybe someone cancelled Dad's wake-up call. Maybe someone thought they wouldn't want to be disturbed seeing as they'd just got back together again . . .'

I stood staring at him in amazement. 'You *sabotaged* their wake-up call? You caused this row on purpose?'

'Well, neither of us think they're suited, do we?'

'No, but that was way out of line.'

'Oh come on, don't start giving me that self-righteous stuff!'

'Let me pass,' I said. 'I want to see what's going on on the set.'

Shug was standing in the way. I had to squeeze really close to get past. He was tall for his age and I couldn't help noticing that, for sixteen, he was pretty well-built. Despite myself, I found I was blushing as my body brushed up against his.

Shug noticed. In fact, he was lapping it up. 'Hey, you're growing up, Holly. And in all the right places . . .'

'Get out the way before I kick you!' I said.

'Go on, say pretty purr-leese nicely then . . .'

'Oh, shut up!' I said and squeezed past him all the same.

I glanced back and saw him sizing up my back view. The *cheek* of it! I composed my face into a suitably cross expression and glared back at him.

On the set things had moved on somewhat. Mum was out of the trailer and making strides towards the 'club', followed by her three Popsicles. It was weird seeing Mum in that oh-so-obvious wig and those totally over-the-top false eyelashes. An actor who was meant to be playing her first manager was waiting for her at the entrance. They were shooting a scene in which they have this blazing row and she fires him. Actually, it made me realise how far Mum had come. She didn't talk about the past much, but it must have been like this. Tacky clubs. Weeks on the road. She likes to give the impression that she took the easy route to fame, but no way.

Sunday 1st June, 10.30 a.m.
The Wessex Hotel

It's Sunday. Traditional day for a good long laze in bed. And it's the holidays too which should make it doubly delicious. Except that I haven't got that much to do – well, nothing actually. Which makes me feel rather sorry for myself. So I should be able to indulge in a nice satisfying wave of self-pity. But can I get any peace? No such luck. I'm cruelly woken by the phone by my bed.

'Hi, Holly! Where are you? Didn't see you at breakfast.' It's Vix.

'I *was* having a lie-in.'

'Well, you'd better stop lying in and get your butt down here because you're wanted downstairs.'

'What for?'

'Your mum wants a family picture.'

'Family? Is Dad here?'

'Not with Pete, dumb-brain. Your *new* family.'

My heart turns over with a thump. What new family? Oh my God!

Down in the Lobby, the place looked like a war zone. Frantic staff were trying to keep some kind of order as a heaving crowd of journalists waving press cards tried to force its way – like toothpaste through a very narrow tube – through the entrance doors.

I spotted Vix at the far side beckoning me over and I squeezed my way through to her. She eyed my jeans and crop top dismissively. 'What have you got on? Oh, it'll have to do.'

Then she hauled me behind her through a side entrance into a suite that had been set up for a press conference. The press were being held back. I could hear the muffled roar of their voices coming through the double doors.

Mum and Oliver were already there, seated on a couch in front of a kind of antique tapestry screen thingy flanked by banks of flowers. And then out from behind the screen came . . . oh great! It's *Shug*.

'Hollywood, babes, we've been waiting for you,' said Mum, holding open her arms.

'Hi, Mum,' I said, giving her kisses on both cheeks.

'Hi, Oliver.' It seemed I was expected to kiss him too. I gave him only the teensiest peck on one cheek.

I glanced at Shug. He leant forward and tapped his cheek too, so I stuck my tongue out at him.

'God, this is a farce!' said Oliver, looking thunderous.

'And whose fault is that?' snapped Mum.

'OK! It seemed like a good idea at the time. I hadn't envisaged the press reacting like this.'

'Yeah, Dad, *and so many of them*,' said Shug, grinning evilly at Mum. 'I wonder who let on?'

'There were hundreds of people at that shoot – it could have been any one of them,' returned Mum. Then she smoothed her skirt and added: 'Anyway, it doesn't take a genius to know that anything *I* do is going to get noticed.'

'Yeah,' said Shug. 'It must be tough being *worshipped* like you are, Kandhi.'

Mum shot him a hurt look. And Oliver actually said: 'Cut it out, Shug. Kandhi's got enough on her plate as it is.'

Vix was standing at the doors listening in to her headset. She started signalling violently to Mum.

'Maybe we should let them in,' said Mum.

'Yes. Let's get this whole charade over with as fast as possible,' said Oliver.

'Yes, why not?' said Mum in a clipped tone that perfectly matched his. 'Open the doors, Vix.'

As the doors were flung open, the photographers stormed in like a river in full flood bursting a dam. They were jockeying for a place in the front and they'd started taking pictures way before I'd composed my face into anything like a smile.

'Hey, closer in there! Get your arm round the little lady.'

'Oliver – give her a kiss.'

'You kids at the back – close up, won't you?'

Shug moved a half-step towards me and I moved a half-step away.

He grinned at me. I glared at him.

'Come on,' said Shug between clenched teeth. 'We're meant to be like brother and sister, aren't we?'

'Ever heard of sibling rivalry?' I shot back.

'Nice one! We're in good hissing form today, aren't we, *pussycat*?'

'Don't you *pussycat* me . . .'

'Will you two belt up!' said Oliver over his shoulder. 'There's a guy with a sound-boom over there – he could be picking up every word.'

So Shug contented himself with moving up really close. I could actually feel the warmth of his body through his sweatshirt. And then he put his foot on mine and started very gently to increase the pressure until . . .

'*OUCH!*'

'What's going on?' snapped Mum, getting to her feet.

83

'Shug's standing on my foot.'

'Oh sorry,' said Shug. 'I didn't realise they reached out so far.'

I stared at him with hot tears starting in my eyes. I know I've got big feet, and I hate them. But I didn't need him to point them out to *the whole world*.

'Look, Shug, for God's sake,' said Oliver, standing up as well.

'Great. You're all on your feet. Now can we close in for a big happy family hug?' called out a voice.

We all turned at the same moment. Cameras flashed like strobe lightning.

And that was the shot that appeared in all the papers: Oliver frowning, Mum pouting, Shug glaring, me practically bawling.

Some happy family!

Oliver and Shug left as soon as the press had gone. I went up in the elevator with Mum and Vix.

'Thank God that's over,' said Mum.

'But Mum, what's going to happen?' I said. 'I mean, you're going to have to go through with the wedding and everything now . . .'

Mum looked at me witheringly. 'Don't be so silly, Hollywood. We can easily break off the engagement. Let's face it, we've done it before.'

'Mum, how can you treat marriage like some . . . some . . .'

'. . . totally outmoded form of feminine repression?' suggested Vix.

'But it's not! It's totally romantic. Don't either of you believe in *love* any longer?'

Mum and Vix exchanged 'Isn't she sweet?' glances. (Don't you just *hate* it when they do that?)

'Oh to be thirteen again!' said Mum.

'Or maybe sixteen,' agreed Vix.

I left them on the sixth floor and stomped off to my suite.

Monday 2nd June, 7.30 a.m. (Thoughts in the bathtub)

I cannot believe the callousness of adults. Treating love and marriage as if they're just *nothing*! I mean, I know how I feel about Rupert. His very name makes my heart turn over with a strange wobbly thump. Just thinking about him makes the lights in the room grow brighter, the colours stronger and the ground take on a kind of bouncy surface like it's made of that foam-rubber stuff they make mattresses out of.

The fact that Rupert is totally unaware of my devotion makes it so much more poignant.

At that moment the thought of 'Juliette' enters my mind and the light in the room dims, the colours go a kind of murky grey and the floor settles into that hard, flat carpeted surface we are all familiar with.

I send evil hate vibes towards 'Juliette' and wish her an eternity of bad hair days, a rabid VPL, and a severe case of that nasty ring of flab that always seems to creep its way to the top of your low-cut jeans, no matter how slim you are.

Then I feel really guilty. I shouldn't be so mean to her. After all, she is doing her bit for Voluntary Service Overseas – which means she's giving up precious months of her youth to tend to the underprivileged of the world. The fact that she is only doing this in order to snog the first vulnerable male VSO volunteer she comes across counts against her, however. I add 'chronic verrucas' to my anti-Juliette list.

Then I lie there for a good while working on the first draft of my email to Rupert:

'Hi . . .'

'Hi, Rupert . . .'

'Hi there!'

Oh, indecision! I put off writing the email till later.

Later: Apt 12, 1794 South Mercer

I went over to Dad's to make sure he was walking Brandy.

He wasn't. He'd roped Marlowe into doing it.

When I hit the roof Marlowe was unrepentant.

'You have no idea how many girls you meet when you're out with this old fellow,' he said, patting Brandy's head. 'I'm telling you, he gives a whole new meaning to "pulling power".'

'This dog is not intended to help you chat up girls. This dog is for exercise. And it's Dad who's meant to be walking him.'

'Well, I don't have to walk him every day,' said Dad.

'Yes, Dad. That's the whole point of having the dog.'

'Well, I've been busy . . .'

He was still in his bathrobe and I could see he hadn't shaved.

86

'Dad, don't give me that. Come on, you've got to get out and get some exercise.'

'OK, OK, I'll get dressed. You wait here, right? You're coming too, Holly.'

'Certainly I'm coming too. I'm going to see this for myself.'

It took some time for Dad to get dressed. First he had to find some comfortable sneakers. Then I was sent out to test the temperature so he could decide between sweaters. I got back to find him with the TV on, checking the weather forecast. It was sunshine and showers so he went to find his baseball cap and sunglasses and his mac and an umbrella. When I eventually got him down to street level, I was sent back for a muffler because he thought he could detect a breeze getting up.

'Dad, how long is it *precisely* since you took a walk?'

Dad looked thoughtful.

'You know, honey, I don't rightly remember.'

By this time, Brandy was practically throttling himself with his leash. He was clearly keen to get Dad acquainted with the gumball machine. He set off at a cracking pace with Dad and me trailing behind.

Sunshine had got the better of showers and by the time we reached Tompkins Square we were all pretty hot. Brandy was frothing at the mouth – he looked as if he was about to choke on his dog treat.

'We ought to get some water for him,' I pointed out.

'I could do with a beer,' said Dad.

87

We went over to a café that was right by the park and sat in the window in the sun. It was a cute little place full of retro tin advertising signs and character teapots and they were playing jazz over the speaker system.

'Nice place . . .' said Dad, loosening his muffler a little.

The guy who was serving us brought a big bowl of water for Brandy. I couldn't help noticing that he kept looking at Dad in an odd sort of way. I guess he didn't get many customers dressed in a mac and sunglasses and a muffler in June. But as he slipped the cheque under Dad's saucer, he said, 'Pardon me asking, but aren't you Pete Winterman?'

Dad eyed him slowly up and down. 'What if I am?'

'Yeah, you are. I know you are. I've got all the Icemen albums,' said the guy, his voice kind of cracked with excitement.

Dad sat up straighter on his chair. 'You have?'

'Oh boy, I don't believe this! Pete Winterman! Look, you wouldn't sign one of my albums for me, would you?'

'Well, I don't as a rule . . .' said Dad.

The guy had already gone off into the back room. The speaker system stopped abruptly mid-phrase and then on came one of Dad's songs. One of the oldies.

'Dad, listen . . .' I said.

'Yeah, well. That was . . . yeah. That was kind of OK,' said Dad.

The guy came back with the album sleeve in his hand. You could see it was scuffed where he'd taken the record in and out from years of use.

On the front was a picture of Dad with long curly hair and a moustache, wearing a skinny leather jacket. The guy handed Dad a pen and Dad scrawled his signature across one corner. Then the guy stood looking at it as if it was like the best thing he'd ever seen.

I was staring over his shoulder, searching through the band.

'Where's Mum?' I asked without thinking.

'This was before I met your mother,' said Dad.

For one awful moment I thought I'd blown it and that the café owner was going to go off at a tangent and he'd start asking about Mum, the way people always did. But this guy didn't seem interested in Mum. He said: 'Do you mind if I join you?' and drew up a chair. 'The name's Al. I've just taken over this place. So what are you doing these days, Pete?'

'Well, you know, a bit of this and that.'

'It's just that . . . well, I know it's not much, but we're planning to give these nights when we play music. We've got a big space down underneath. Brilliant acoustics. Now, if you could see your way . . . Maybe play a number . . . Or even if you just dropped by. Well, I know it would draw a crowd.'

'Why don't you, Dad?' I urged.

'I'll think about it,' said Dad. 'Now we ought to be on our way,' and he reached for the bill.

But Al took it. 'Oh no, this is on me. It's been a pleasure. And you won't forget, any time you can spare a moment of your time . . . I know how busy you must be . . . Just call . . .'

He handed Dad a card. Dad looked at it briefly then put it in his pocket.

I wake to find my 'post' has been slipped under my door. It's a little blue envelope with a proper stamp stuck on, addressed in scratchy fountain pen. A letter! Such a rarity can be from one person only – Gi-Gi, my great-gran who doesn't trust any of these new-fangled inventions such as fax or email, although I've tried to explain them time and time again. And she won't make international calls because that's a wicked extravagance, although Mum pays her phone bill.

As I slit open the envelope I think I can smell the faintest whiff of Gi-Gi's rose talcum powder. Inside are two folded pages covered in her looped and curlicued writing – both sides. I then engage in the tricky problem of deciphering this ancient code.

After fifteen minutes, I've gleaned that Gi-Gi has made fifteen pounds of (I think) quince jam. She's won sixty pence at bridge, and Mr Robinson (from Number 57)'s leg is much better – he may even be walking without a stick soon.

Having made my way through this riveting news, I am concerned to find that my rabbit Thumper is happy and *eating well*. Knowing Gi-Gi (who spoils him rotten), this means he's Michelin Rabbit by now, blown up to such a size he has a leg on each corner.

I consider writing back to Gi-Gi. I need to update her with the latest news. This is tricky. Currently Mum is Not Properly Engaged to Oliver Bream, but by the time a letter reaches her the non-engagement will probably be a non-event. I decide to shelve the letter to Gi-Gi until things have sorted themselves out.

Over breakfast (I have located that mini-box of Lucky Charms and poured myself a big bowlful) I try to decide what to do with my day.

I am just about to take my first delicious mouthful of cereal (I've sorted all the pink heart-shaped ones on to my spoon) when Mum wafts into the dining room.

'Babes, there you are! I've been looking for you everywhere . . .'

I shove the incriminating bowl of Lucky Charms on to the next table and say: 'Hi, Mum!'

'Haven't you finished your breakfast yet?'

'No . . . I mean, yes. Why?'

'Good, because, guess what? Anthony's called up to say the apartment – *our home*, Hollywood – is *finished*.'

'Oooh . . .' I say, as I see a waiter deftly scooping up my untouched bowl of Lucky Charms and taking it away.

'Well, you could sound a bit more excited about it.'

'But I am.'

'Good. So what are we waiting for? Let's go round there right now.'

'The site' has changed somewhat since our last visit. The billowing corridors of canvas have been whisked away to reveal a lobby lined with shiny white marble, flanked by an endless line of vases of arum lilies. We enter the cylindrical elevator, which has now had its wraps off and is all brushed steel and glass. Mum punches in the code for the forty-fifth floor.

'Close your eyes,' she says as we are whisked upwards.

I open them to find the apartment doors opening on to acres of white. The floor is now a sheer expanse of burnished metal. There's a column of transparent shelving with rows of white books on it. There are four white leather sofas forming a square with a clear glass table in the middle. And on the centre of that is a clear glass vase filled with nothing but water. On the walls are four identical white paintings. At least I think they're paintings. They're in frames, which is a bit of a giveaway, but they could well be part of the soundproofing.

Mum follows my gaze. 'Aren't they brilliant? I had to bid against the Saatchi Gallery for them. They really took me to the cleaners.'

'Are you sure you didn't just get them to go with the decor?' I asked.

'They're Minimalist, babes. You'll understand this sort of thing when you're older. It was a movement. Big in the Seventies.'

'But that one's even got a mark on it.' I point out a tiny smudge in the far right corner.

Mum looks at the smudge lovingly. 'I had to pay double for that one. That is the artist's original thumbprint. He's dead now, of course, so this is a one-off.'

I turn to the door of my suite with dread. If Anthony has worked his 'Winter Wonderland' magic in there, I am going to make a scene.

'Go on, take a look,' says Mum.

Tentatively, I push the door open. I can hear jungle noises. I push it further.

'Wow, Anthony – you are a genius!

Anthony has transformed my room into a tropical jungle. He's filled it with beautiful fringed palms which are waving in the breeze created by a rattan fan. Because of the mirror walls, this forest seems to go on forever. I part the palms and discover my bed. It has been hung from the ceiling on ropes like a hammock and has floaty mosquito nets enclosing it. A load of antique leather cabin trunks are dotted around to take my belongings. There's even one with shelves and hanging space inside like a wardrobe.

I push open the bathroom door. The entire far wall has been replaced by a huge ceiling-to-floor tank of tropical fish, so when you take a shower or a bath it's as if the fish are swimming alongside you. There are angel fish with long fluttering wings and a shoal of little electric blue fish. There are soft-winged black rays and a little flotilla of bright yellow ones . . .

I come out of the bathroom to find Mum watching me from the doorway.

'Well?' she says.

I'm so knocked out, I'm totally speechless.

'You don't like it?' she asks.

'Mum, it's wonderful! It's the most beautiful room I've ever seen. It's unbelievable. Thank you.'

I go and hug her.

Mum hugs me back. 'Well, at last I've got something right.'

'What's that meant to mean?'

'Oh come on, Holly. You don't have to pretend we always see eye to eye.'

I pause, not quite sure how to react. I'm not accustomed to Mum being like this.

'Well no, I guess not,' I say tentatively.

'And we don't get nearly enough time together. But that's going to change.'

'It is?'

'Of course it is, now we've got our own home.'

I'm so used to fighting with Mum, I don't know what to say when she's being really nice.

'Come and sit down, Hollywood,' she says, leading me across to one of the big white sofas. I perch uncomfortably on the shiny white leather. She leans towards me, asking confidingly, 'Tell me honestly. Wouldn't you really like to be a proper family again?'

For one insane moment I think she's talking about me and her and Dad. But her next sentence puts me right on that one. 'How would you feel if I actually did marry Oliver?'

So that's what this is all about. She's trying to get round me. She wants me to give the seal of approval to her *big romance*.

'Do we have to talk about this now?' I reply grumpily.

'It's as good a time as any.'

'You know I don't like him.'

'Well, maybe in time you could get to like him. He's always very nice about you.'

'Oliver's *nice* about everyone. It doesn't mean anything. He's just being his oh-so-British self. And what about that son of his – *Shug*!'

'I'd be marrying Oliver, not Shug.'

'But Shug is always hanging around him like some sort of – ugghh! – fungus.'

'Holly, honestly!'

'And I thought Oliver had made it perfectly clear that he doesn't want to marry you anyway – that this "silly engagement idea", as he called it, was just temporary, to help you out.'

'I know,' says Mum, and she sniffs and fumbles in her pocket for a hanky. 'But we can't get un-engaged just like that. I don't want to be made to look ridiculous.'

I feel like pointing out that their current romance looks pretty ridiculous anyway, when I notice a tear running down Mum's face.

'Mu-um? You're not crying, are you?'

'No.' But she blows her nose hard.

I can't stand it when Mum cries. I'm so used to her being strong and self-willed, when she breaks down I kind of go to jelly.

'Mum? Surely you're not still keen on Oliver? You can't be. He's so . . . so . . .'

'What? (Sniff.)'

'Well, pig-headed . . . and arrogant . . . You can't be in love with a man like that.'

Mum bites her lip: 'I didn't think I was when he was being so nice to me. But now he's being horrid and insists we've got to call the whole thing off . . .' This came out with a sort of shuddering sob. 'I can't get him out of my mind!'

'Oh Mum, *honestly* . . .'

'I know it's silly. I know we're always fighting. But Holly . . . Oliver's the only man who really stands up to me. And you know,' she pulls herself together with an effort, 'I really respect that.'

6.00 p.m., The Wessex Hotel: Some pretty profound thoughts in the bathtub

Looking at Mum and Oliver objectively, their romance seems to go something like this:

1) If you admit you're keen on someone, you get dumped.
2) Once dumped you immediately fall violently in love with the dumper.
3) So you do everything in your power to get un-dumped.
4) Once undumped, you can enjoy the ultimate satisfaction of dumping the dumper.

Even with my current level of experience I can see that this was no recipe for success.

Wednesday 4th June, 11.00 a.m.
The Plaza Residenza

I've spent the morning packing, unpacking and rearranging all my stuff in *my new home*!

It's just Mum and me in the apartment – the rest of her entourage have a staff floor lower down. This means that Thierry can pop up and make our meals and Daffyd and June can zoom up for their 'hair and beauty' act, and Abdul and Sid can guard our bodies, but they don't have to be 'under our feet', as Mum puts it. Although they are of course, literally, living down there.

I've been right round my room taking pictures on my cell phone for Gi-Gi and Thumper. I know Thumper will really rate the decor – although he might express his approval by eating it, so it's probably a good thing he's not here 'cos these palms look as if they cost a fortune.

Anthony's thought of everything. He's even had a CD player built into an old gramophone – the kind you see on those old memorabilia cards which have a dog listening to a kind of loudhailer. There's a flat-screen TV too, disguised behind one of the wall panels. And most important of all, there's a study nook for my laptop with broadband so the instant I get an email from Rupert it will come up as Mail.

Hang on, I'd better check it right now just in case . . .

Oh. My. God! There is!

Waiter, there's an iguana in my soup!

I open it.

Hi, Holly!
How's things?
I'm back in the city to pick up Juliette.

As a 'Welcome' gesture I took her to sample
local specialities in Blimii's smartest eatery.
(I'd booked the VIP table nearest the tent flap.)
The dish of the day was of the clawed and scaled
variety.
It tasted a bit like chicken (why do they always say that?)
But Juliette, after eating said chicken (I thought it might
seem condescending to translate the menu for her), has
had a severe humour failure and is not talking to me.
Things could be tricky back at the 'school'.
How do you say in sign language: 'Don't panic, but I
think there's a scorpion climbing into your sandal'?
Thought you might have got in touch.
But no 'e'.
Love and all that,
Rupert x

x! (Sigh!) And he and Juliette are 'not talking'. Hmm, doesn't
sound as if it was love at first sight. And yet on the other hand
he took her out for a meal . . .

I try to compose an 'e' back to him.

Hi Rupert . . .
Hi there! . . .
Rupert!

I try to picture Rupert reading my email in some romanti-
cally ramshackle Third World café. And then someone else

materialises beside him. It's *Juliette*. Her long, shiny, blonde hair/russet curls/dark locks (delete as appropriate) brush against him as he reads my 'e'. How can I possibly write to Rupert when there is this total lack of privacy? Instead, I get Abdul to drive me over to Dad's to check on Brandy.

2.00 p.m., Apt 12, 1794 South Mercer

Fred lets me in. The others are sitting around playing cards. Dad is nowhere to be seen.

'Where's Dad? Is he out with Br—'

'Not exactly.'

Fred leads me to the kitchen, where a sad figure is slumped over a bowl with a towel over its head.

'What's up?'

There's a snuffle from under the towel, followed by Dad's voice sounding all rough and grainy, saying: 'I guess I must've caught a chill, going out all of a sudden like that.'

'But Dad, it wasn't even cold!'

Dad's face, hot and red from inhaling, emerges from under the towel. A heavy waft of eucalyptus fills the air.

'Yeah, but what about the microbes? There are germs out there.'

'Oh come on, Dad! Lighten up. You've only got a cold.'

'Yeah, but think what it could lead to,' says Dad.

'Look at what he sent out for from the pharmacy,' says Fred.

There's a stack of packs on the table: cold cure, cough linctus, nose drops, decongestant, ibuprofen and the eucalyptus.

'I reckon if he's taken that lot he must feel terrible,' I say.

'I'll be OK,' says Dad. 'As long as I keep nice and warm inside.'

'It's nice and warm outside, Dad.'

'Oh yeah, but I don't want to risk it.'

'OK, I guess I'll walk Brandy for you. Just this time.'

'WOOF!' says Brandy, bounding out from under the table.

When Brandy and I arrived at Tompkins Square we found Al standing outside his café enjoying the sunshine. I wandered over to talk to him.

'Hi, Holly! How you going? You want a Coke on the house?'

He went inside and brought me a Coke and a big bowl of water for Brandy.

'How's your dad? Not with you today.'

'Not too good. He's got a cold.'

'What's he been doing lately? I've been looking out for his stuff, but –'

'Ever since Mum got famous he seems to have stopped writing music. In fact, he seems to have stopped doing anything. He hardly leaves the loft. I was hoping having a dog would help.'

'That's too bad,' said Al. He leant down and rubbed Brandy's head. Brandy gave him a sloppy dog lick.

'Well, remember what I said. Any time he wants to drop by, he'll get a big welcome here.'

It's 5th June already. The precious days of my summer vacation are seeping away and I haven't even had a holiday yet. Before I know it, it will be autumn semester and I'll be at that new school Mum's found. And so will (ugghh!) *Shug*! I'm not even looking forward to school now. I'll be coming face to face with him all the time – in the corridors, at the lockers, at meals . . . Grrr!

To make things worse I can hear sounds of discord coming from Mum's side of the apartment. I'm tempted to stay where I am until these die down. Discord is hard to take first thing in the morning. But I'm ravenous and I need to get through the salon and into our ultra-hi-tech kitchen and see if I can figure out how to get some breakfast.

I haul on my white towelling robe and hope that this will act as camouflage as I creep through the salon.

I slide open my door. Mum has her back to me and is absorbed in going through what looks like a pile of garbage on the floor while bawling out Vix.

Vix is standing with her organiser, trying to take notes fast enough to keep up with Mum's comments.

I reach the kitchen without being intercepted and start searching for food. There's nothing that looks like food. No bright inviting packs – only a range of designer containers with anonymous substances inside. The white expanses of wall have nothing resembling a food cupboard either . . . or a fridge . . . or a hob or a kettle. I spot something that may or may not be a sink. It's an inverted cone of pale green bottle glass with no visible means of obtaining water.

I peek out of the door again.

'And what does he expect me to do with this?' demands Mum furiously, holding up what looks like a chain-mail vest.

I dodge back in again.

I hadn't noticed a remote control lurking on the worktop. I start pressing buttons and – hey presto – doors in the walls open. Inside, there's every culinary gadget that has ever been dreamed up. There's even a machine for rolling the seaweed round sushi. The fact that this kitchen will never be used to actually cook food, since Mum is still on her 'only raw foods' diet, seems a bit of a waste to me. However, once I locate the fridge I find a small bowl of fresh fruit salad inside and some plain organic yogurt.

I venture back into the salon with it.

'It's no good,' Mum is saying to Vix. 'I can't wear any of this.'

'What's the problem?' I ask.

Vix gives a weary sigh. 'We're shooting the very last link sequence. And we still have problems.'

'It's my punk phase. I'm meant to be in vintage clothing and look what they've sent.' Mum points towards the pile of garbage.

'Looks pretty vintage to me.'

'OK, so when you're seventeen you can wear a bin-liner and a safety pin through your nose and get away with it. When I want vintage, I want it flattering.'

'I could tell them to go buy another lot,' suggests Vix.

'No time,' says Mum. 'I'm due on set at two sharp this afternoon.'

'Why don't you buy it yourself?' I ask Mum.

'Where am I going to find vintage clothing in New York?'

'In the East Village. I've seen loads of places when I've been out walking Dad's –' (Oops!)

'The East Village? You've been *out walking* in the East Village?'

'Mum, hold on. I wasn't alone. I was with this dog. Dad's dog.'

'Holly, in my book, walking in the city – even with a dog – is still *alone*.'

'But you haven't seen the dog. He's huge. If anyone came near me, he'd eat them as a between-meal snack. And anyway, Dad thinks it's OK.'

'I don't believe this. Your father is totally irresponsible.'

'But it's not a bad idea of Holly's,' interrupts Vix. 'Choosing the stuff yourself. You've got nothing else on this morning.'

11.00 a.m., the East Village

We've managed to get Mum dressed down enough to go incognito. She made a big fuss about what to wear. She didn't seem to realise that no one would believe it was her sifting through a load of second-hand clothes in the East Village.

The vintage clothing shops are just opening when Abdul drives Mum and me along Fourth Avenue. It's taken a while to get there because there's some sort of demonstration or march going on up Broadway.

'So where are these places?' demands Mum.

I point out one of the stores I've spotted with Brandy.

'Can't take the car up there. It's one-way going the wrong way,' says Abdul.

'OK, so we'll get out and walk. Curses! Where's my mobile?' says Mum.

'It's OK. I've got mine.'

'Now, Abdul, hand me my card . . .'

'Mum, these kind of stores – they don't always take cards.'

'They don't? What kind of places are they?'

Abdul leans over and takes a bundle of dollars from his pocket. Mum never carries a chequebook or cash. As she puts it, she has 'people' to look after stuff like that.

'I've got nowhere to carry cash,' says Mum.

'I'll take it.' I fold the dollar bills and button them safely into the pocket of my jeans jacket.

So Abdul is instructed to drive round and hang on for us up the other end of the one-way street.

'May be a long way round,' he says. 'And it looks like rain. Sure it wouldn't be better for me to wait here?'

'Abdul, don't make things difficult. Do as I say, OK?' says Mum.

'When we're through, I'll call you,' I add.

With that he drove away and Mum and I set off down the street and soon came across a place that looked as if it had the right vintage image – at least it was scruffy enough. It took a moment or two to convince Mum that this was a retail outlet. She ventured in as if crawling down a pit searching for the lost ark.

We didn't find anything Mum deigned 'fit to try' in that first shop. So we moved on further down the street and found a place that only seemed to do weird porno clothing.

'This is hopeless,' said Mum. 'I should've got Wardrobe to design me something.'

'Don't give in, we've hardly started looking yet,' I said. I was enjoying this outing. Some of the clothes were really, errm, 'groovy'.

I set off at a determined pace down a side street. Mum followed, grumbling all the way. Her shoes rubbed and her hair was getting wet. It had started raining.

'You better call up Abdul,' she said. 'I'll make do with the stuff we've got already.'

'No way! I know I've seen a really good place somewhere round here.'

We had to double back through several streets before we came across the store I remembered. There was a model in the window wearing a stretchy sequinned miniskirt that I'd noted at the time.

'How about that?' I suggested.

'Hmm . . . maybe,' said Mum.

Inside this store she seemed to gain interest. She gathered an armful of psychedelic flimsy top things.

'Where are the changing rooms?' she hissed at me.

I pointed to a rather rank-looking curtained-off area.

'I'll try something too, to keep you company,' I said.

I'd found a really cool remodelled leather jacket and some flared trousers that looked about my size.

We were crammed in the changing room with two other girls and Mum kept rolling her eyes at me as if to say this just wasn't on. But she started trying on the clothes all the same. I did my best to ignore her and stripped off to try the flares. Actually, when I got them on I realised why they'd been dumped. They had the really curious effect of giving you 'clown thighs'. I reached for the jacket. This was better. I jostled against the others, trying to get a glimpse of my back view. Mum was fussing like a scalded cat, stuck halfway in and halfway out of a stretchy spandex minidress. I hauled the dress off Mum and suggested she try getting into it feet first. Actually, the jacket didn't look that good on me. Regretfully I took it off.

Peering out of the curtain, I wondered whether to venture out for something else to try. I spotted a girl wearing a nice cropped jeans jacket walking out of the store. Just like *my* jeans jacket . . .

I swung round and searched frantically over the floor. Hang on . . . that *was* my jeans jacket!

'Mum, I think that girl just walked out in my jacket!'

'Well, don't fuss, Holly. Jackets like that are two a penny. I'll buy you another. Now, what do you think of this skirt?'

'No – but Mum, you don't understand. That jacket had my mobile in the pocket and all the mon—'

'OK, so we get another mobile . . . I think it's a bit saggy, don't you?'

I was hauling my clothes on.

'Wait here,' I said to Mum, and dashed out of the shop. Once outside there was no sign of the girl or my jeans

106

jacket. I searched down the street but it was no use. She'd disappeared into thin air.

I got back to find Mum fully dressed. She had a little pile of vintage clothes set to one side.

'Well, it wasn't such a bad idea after all. I reckon the sequinned miniskirt, the Lycra boob tube and the Shetland hand-knit and we've got the Look.'

I followed Mum as she strode up to the guy behind the till.

'OK,' said Mum. 'We'll take this lot.'

'But Mum . . .'

The guy made a great fuss about writing down all the items in an exercise book. He chewed on his pencil as he added them up.

'That'll be seven dollars,' he said at last.

'*Seven dollars?*' said Mum incredulously.

'Well, I could knock off a dollar, maybe. But ma'am, this is for charity.'

'No, but seven dollars . . .' said Mum. I think she was trying to work out if he'd missed a couple of noughts or something.

'Mum,' I whispered, pulling on her sleeve, 'we don't actually have seven dollars. My jacket . . . remember?'

'Oh . . .' said Mum as she caught my drift. 'Right. Do you do credit?'

'Oh no, ma-am, I'm sorry, but –'

'But you don't seem to understand. I *need* this stuff.'

'That's what they all say.'

'You mean, you won't let me take this – this *trash* just for the sake of seven measly dollars?' said Mum.

'Now look here, missy. You listen to me. If you don't like the merchandise, there's no need to to be offensive . . .'

'*Missy? Offensive? Do you know who I am?*' said Mum.

'Oh sure, yeah. You're one of the Rockefellers. We have them in every day,' said the guy.

Mum bundled up the clothes in her arms and was making for the door. I ran after her.

'Mum, don't –'

But it was too late. The guy came out from behind the till, grabbed at the bundle of clothes, and they had a little tussle. The guy won.

'Now just leave quietly, OK? And I won't have to call the cops,' he said.

I don't think I've ever seen Mum so furious. She was storming down the street. It had started to rain really hard too and she was getting soaked.

'Where's Abdul? Where the hell is Abdul? Call him up, Holly!'

'Mum, my mobile! Don't you remember? It was in the pocket of my jack–'

'Oh my God!' said Mum, turning to face me. 'You mean we're stranded. In the East Village!'

'Well, no. I mean, maybe we can find a public call box and –'

Mum started striding again. 'A call box? What do they look like?'

'There's one!'

I leapt at the call box. I knew you could make a call collect if you didn't have money, but the call box phone sounded ominously dead and when I looked down I could see why. Someone had ripped the cord out of its socket.

'We'll take a cab,' said Mum. 'We can pay at the other end.'

So we stood on the curb, hailing every yellow cab we saw. But empty cabs tend to be thin on the ground when it's raining, and it was raining hard.

In fact, a puddle had built up in the gutter. When we'd been doused in water for the third time, I turned to Mum.

'I guess we could take the subway,' I said.

'*Subway?*' said Mum, as if I'd suggested wading our way back home through the sewers.

'But we don't have any money for tickets,' I added lamely. 'Perhaps we'd better start walking.'

'We can't walk all the way to The Plaza!'

'I know. I've got it! We'll go to Dad's. It's not far. We can call Abdul from there.'

'Dad's?'

'Yes, it's only a few blocks.'

'Oh, I really don't think I can just turn up . . .'

At this point a kind of tidal wave swept through the puddle and muddy water slopped into Mum's shoes.

'Ugghh! Yuck!' she said. 'OK, whatever. Frankly Holly, I'm past caring.'

We arrived at Dad's front door dripping. Mum was running her fingers through her hair, moaning about how awful she looked.

'It's OK, Mum. You look really good with your hair all slicked back like that.'

'Do I?' She gave me a stiff smile.

Dad opened the door. He still had a red nose but it looked like he'd got over the worst of his cold. 'Why, hi, Holly! What happened to you? And . . . oh! Hi, Candice!'

'Don't call me Candice,' said Mum. 'You know I hate it. The name's Kandhi.' She walked past Dad as if he didn't exist.

'Well, you'll always be Candice to me,' said Dad, following her as she squelched into the loft.

I explained about Abdul and the one-way street and how the girl had walked out of the shop with my jacket and my mobile.

'You folks look like you could do with a shower and a hot towel,' said Dad.

'Thanks,' said Mum. She cast an assessing gaze around the loft. 'Well, nothing's changed much here.'

'WOOF!' said Brandy, ambling over and providing a welcome diversion. He sniffed at Mum enquiringly.

'Except this guy,' said Dad. 'Meet my new life-partner, Brandy.'

'Isn't he lovely, Mum?'

'Is this the dog you've been walking?' she asked me.

I nodded.

'I see what you mean.'

I let Mum take the first shower while I called up Abdul. He said he was gridlocked on Fifth Avenue and might be some time.

Mum came out wrapped in Dad's big bathrobe with her hair done up in a towelling turban.

'Don't look at me,' she said to Dad. 'I look a sight.'

'Brings back old memories,' said Dad kind of wistfully.

'Forget the memories,' said Mum. 'You got a hairdryer?'

While Dad searched for a hairdryer, Marlowe let himself in.

'Wow!' he said. 'It's raining cats, dogs and hippos out there.'

He shook the rain off his jacket and turned and saw us.

'Hi, Holly! And *who's* this girlfriend you got with you?'

'She's not my girlfriend. She's my mum.'

Marlowe paused where he was and just stared.

'Oh, wow! The famous Kandhi! How do you do?' he said, staring at Mum as if he'd seen a vision or something.

I expected Mum to be all dismissive, the way she was with fans who got too close. Just the icy smile and her standard cool 'Hello, and it's really nice to meet you too'. But she was staring back at Marlowe. The two of them stood for a moment as if glued to the spot. And then Marlowe took a stride forward as if to shake her by the hand. But he didn't shake her hand, he held her hand in his like it was an ultra-precious object and stared into her eyes,

Hang on! Mum was blushing! And Mum never blushes. Maybe it was the way she was dressed. I could see Mum was kind of uncomfortable but pleased at the same time.

'Yeah, well. I'd be doing a lot better if I had dry hair and my own clothes,' said Mum kind of coyly, retrieving her hand.

'No, on the contrary. You look great like that. It reminds me ... It reminds me of, yeah, that Holly Golightly bit on the fire escape – Moon River.' He kind-of breathed the words 'Moon River' as if it was the most romantic thing ever.

'No . . .' said Mum. 'Don't be silly.'

I stared at her. I'd never seen Mum so soft and girly. What was going on here?

'No, truly. All you need is a guitar,' breathed Marlowe again. He didn't need to talk any louder seeing as how close he was standing to Mum.

Dad arrived back with the hairdryer.

'Hey, Pete! How did you let this little lady escape your grasp?' asked Marlowe.

Dad frowned. 'I guess you could say she just went her own way.'

I took my shower after that. Dad came knocking on the bathroom door with some clothes he'd brought for me and Mum to borrow. A few moments later I came out dressed in someone's tracksuit to find Mum and Marlowe in the kitchen drinking coffee, deep in conversation.

'Yeah, well, I did the couture shows in Milan and Paris this year, but it's all gone kind of quiet. My agent's on to it,' he was saying.

'Well, maybe I could introduce you to some people,' Mum said.

'Look, I hope you don't mind me saying this,' Marlowe interrupted. He dropped his voice bashfully. 'But, you know, this is kind of like a dream for me, actually talking to you in person.'

I felt really bad for Dad. Here was Marlowe blatantly chatting Mum up, right in front of him.

But true to form Dad didn't react. All he did was comment despondently to me, 'Get a load of that technique! Never met a woman who could resist it.'

'Oh, but it won't work on Mum.'

'Wanna bet? Marlowe could chat up the Queen of England, if she happened to drop by.'

'But Mum wouldn't be interested. Not in Marlowe.'

Later

On the way back to the hotel we dropped by the vintage store where Mum had chosen the clothes. I went in to fetch them. The guy was still pretty hostile, but he was a lot less hostile when I handed him the bundle of notes Mum had got off Abdul for his charity. In fact, he came out with me to shake Mum by the hand and presented her personally with the battered plastic bag full of clothes.

'Any time you want to come in, just call me up. I sure don't know why I didn't recognise you,' he said.

'Well, maybe I wasn't looking my best,' said Mum, grabbing the bag. 'Now put your foot down, Abdul, or we'll be late.'

So that was OK. Mum had her vintage outfit and she was off on location. I had the afternoon free. It had even stopped raining.

I got Abdul to drive me back to the apartment so that I could get into some of my own dry clothes. And I asked Thierry if he could rustle me up some lunch. I had just finished blow-drying my hair when Thierry came knocking on my door.

'Hi! What is it?'

'There's someone to see you. A young man. Good-looking,' he said. 'I took the liberty of laying a table for two.'

A young man! Good-looking! My brain immediately did fuzzy whizzy things and came up with Rupert. He'd flown all the way from Tanzania because I hadn't emailed him back! He'd been worried about me – so worried he'd caught the first plane out of . . . whatever-the-place-is-called and come hotfoot as soon as his plane landed at JFK.

I checked my reflection with my heart thumping in my chest and applied a double coat of lipgloss.

Flinging open my door, I had my lips at the ready only to find, standing in the middle of the salon – oh what a let-down – *SHUG*!

'What are you doing here?' I demanded rudely.

'Oh, hello. You're looking nice,' said Shug, staring pointedly at my least impressive measurement (which is *gradually* becoming more impressive). 'Is that a Wonderbra you're wearing or is that all you?'

'Wouldn't you like to know?

'So how are you today?'

'OK until I saw you. Now I feel kind of queasy.'

'Oh, that's a pity, because I've just been invited for lunch,' said Shug.

'Lunch?' I demanded, staring hard at Thierry. He did one of his totally OTT French shrugs.

'See, he's laid a place for me.'

'Do you think you can handle a knife and fork?'

Thierry was standing by, looking totally amazed at this exchange.

'I thought, seeing as thees is your friend . . .' he said.

'Some friend!'

'Oh now, come on, we're practically *related*,' said Shug.

I was hungry. Very hungry.

'Well, I guess we might as well eat. Your portion would only go in the garbage anyway, so it would come to the same thing.'

'Charming!' said Shug, following me to the table which Thierry had set with a cloth and flowers, and where a big dish of shredded vegetables stood waiting.

'Isn't this nice,' commented Shug, pulling out a chair for me.

I sat down, holding well on to the chair. For all I knew he was about to pull it out from under me.

'Is it?'

'Look,' said Shug. 'You could make an effort, seeing as we're going to the same school in the fall.'

'Don't remind me.'

'Afraid you won't be able to keep up?'

'Afraid I may not get on with *the other students*.'

'You know something, Hollywood Bliss? *You* have an attitude problem.'

'Attitude problem? Me?'

'Yeah. Or maybe you just take after your mum.'

'Or maybe you take after your dad? You spend enough time tagging round after him.'

'I'm in New York as it happens, for stuff of my own.'

'Oh yeah? What?'

'Publicity.'

'What are you so famous for, apart from bad behaviour?'

'My debut album.'

I was so surprised I swallowed a lump of shredded carrot and choked on it.

Shug got up and patted me on the back a lot harder than was absolutely necessary.

'Enough!' I gasped as I tried to get my breath back. I'd heard about Shug's 'brilliant music career' but thought it was empty boasting.

So I said, in as cutting a tone as I could muster, 'I must rush out and buy a copy.'

'It's not out yet. Next week. But you know what? I'll give you one for free.'

'Oh, thanks. Is that why you came round? Have you got a signed copy in your pocket right now?'

'No. I've got something else as a matter of fact.'

He drew out of his pocket a page torn from a celebrity magazine. 'I want you to make absolutely sure your mum sees this. You know how she hates to miss out on anything concerning her.'

It was a picture of Oliver with some minor starlet wrapped around him. 'SWEETER THAN KANDHI?' ran the headline.

Oh my God! Mum was going to be *so* not happy about this!

Underneath there was a load of editorial about how Oliver was going out with this new girl and had broken off his engagement to Kandhi.

'But that's not true!' I burst out. '*Your dad* hasn't broken off the engagement.'

'As I recall, it wasn't ever "on", anyway. It was only my dad trying to help your mum out.'

'Well, he's not helping her out right now, is he? Who is this girl? Has he known her long? Or is she simply someone he hired for the shot?'

'I don't know why this is upsetting you so,' said Shug, looking at me calculatingly.

'It isn't upsetting me.'

'Oh yes it is.'

'It is not!'

'Hang on a minute . . . It couldn't be that Kandhi actually *cares* for my dad, could it?'

'No, of course not.'

'Just think . . .' continued Shug. 'She sings about love. She moans and grunts and sighs like some lovesick heifer. But of course the supernova couldn't actually *be in love* – that would be far too human.'

Thierry swept in at that point.

'You want main course?' he asked. He was carrying a melon scooped out and filled with smoked salmon in gloopy stuff. For a moment I was tempted. How I'd love to see all that gloopy slime running down Shug! But I wasn't going to sink that far.

'No, my guest's leaving now. He's had enough,' I said. I got to my feet. 'Well, that's it. You've eaten. You can go now.'

'What, no dessert?' said Shug.

'Don't you think you're sweet enough already?'

Shug got up too. 'Well, I'll leave you the page anyway. You will make sure your mum sees it, won't you?'

I slammed the door after him. UGGHH!

7.30 p.m.

There was no need to show Mum the picture. The story of Oliver-plus-starlet had spread like wildfire. It was plastered on billboards next to every newsvendor in New York.

I was hovering in my room when Mum scorched into the apartment. I could see her through the gap in the doorway. She'd come straight from the set, still in costume, which didn't do a lot for her credibility. She came raging through the salon, looking like a feral cat which had sneaked in through some plush pad's catflap.

'Who does he think he is?' she was snarling.

Vix was running after her. 'It was probably just to save face, you know. He didn't want people to think *you* were dumping *him*.'

'Save face! Who *is* this *nobody* he's with?'

'Well, she's not exactly a nobody. She's just made this film and it nearly got the Palme d'Or at the Cannes Film Fest–'

'I don't care what it got! Oliver has no right to humiliate me like this!' She stormed into her bedroom and flung herself down on the bed.

I peeked round her door, trying to think of something comforting to say. I tried, 'Hi, Mum! You're better off without him. You know what I've always said about Oliver . . .'

'Yes, Hollywood,' Mum said between clenched teeth. 'I do know. And I am now going to take a bath and I do not want to be disturbed by *anyone*. Hand me my mobile, Vix.'

'Good idea,' said Vix. 'Get an early night.'

Mum disappeared into her bathroom and locked the door behind her.

Vix slumped down on one of the sofas. 'Oh boy!' she said. 'Quel nightmare!'

'Do you think Oliver's really going out with this new girl?' I asked. 'He can't have known her long.'

'They must've met when he was in Cannes at the festival a few weeks back,' said Vix.

'Typical of him. Arrogant bastard! Dumping Mum like this.'

'We better try and think up something pretty damn quick to tell the press.'

I took refuge in my room, thinking hard. Mum and Oliver. Oliver and Mum. It was like watching a sitcom stuck on Fast Forward. Every time you took a breath they were into a new confrontation. Which was odd really when you came to think of it. I mean, Mum and Oliver should know more about love than anyone. How many Kandhi lyrics can you think of that *aren't* about love? And Oliver Bream is currently the screen's greatest lover. Whole cinemas full of people are reduced to jelly by the way he can say, 'The thing is, I think I might be in love with you.'

And yet the two of them simply can't get it together.

I make Mum's breakfast and put it on a tray. After a good night's sleep, hopefully, she'll be feeling better.

I creep to her door and knock gently. There's no answer. I venture in. Mum's out for the count with her eye mask on and her earplugs in, and her clothes and shoes strewn all over the place.

Something tells me she must've gone out last night in spite of what she said. Dotted round the room are various items that suggest she's been on the town. A bunch of red roses – wilting. A bottle of champagne – empty. And a load of helium balloons slowly deflating.

I creep out again. She's going to be *wrecked* when she wakes up.

11.00 a.m.

Mum emerges from her room fully dressed and made up. I'm engulfed in a waft of 'K' perfume, from inside which her voice is saying, 'Kiss me goodbye, babes, and wish me luck.'

'Why? Where are you going?'

It seems Mum's leaving for Vegas today for the next leg of her Heatwave tour. The way things stand, she's decided to leave early.

'But what about me? Can I come to Vegas?'

'No, Hollywood. Not this time.'

'But that's not fair! You bring me halfway around the world because you want me to be with you, then the minute we get a home together, you make off. You can't simply dump me here and leave.'

'You've got to understand. At a time like this, I really feel I want to be alone,' says Mum with a tragic expression. The fact that she's taking Vix and Daffyd and June and Sid and Thierry with her doesn't seem to matter.

'So what's going to happen to me? I can't stay here by myself.'

'I'm leaving you Abdul so you'll have transport. You can go and stay with your father,' says Mum.

'But it's so crowded – there are all those friends of his lazing around the place.'

Vix comes in behind Mum, carrying a load of files.

'I don't think so,' she says, dumping the files with the pile of luggage. 'Not any more.'

'What do you mean?'

'Looks like some of them just made it,' she says. She and Mum exchange knowing looks.

12.00 noon

This is meant to by *my* holiday, but it's Mum who's jetting off for Vegas, where I know for a fact that it's brilliantly hot because I checked the weather forecast. Whereas I'm being driven over to Dad's in the pouring rain and I've been having a big moan to Abdul about it and he isn't even trying to sound sympathetic.

He's taking a diversion through the East Village. Because of the rain the traffic is dreadful as usual. We're crawling along when suddenly I spot – oh no, I don't believe this!

There's a professional dog-walker. One of those ladies who has about ten or so dogs on leashes. And this lady is heading out of Tompkins Square Park at one hell of a rate because right in front, straining at his leash, is Brandy. He's making for the gumball machine and dragging the lady and the nine or so other dogs behind him.

'Stop right here!' I say to Abdul and leap out.

Brandy catches sight of me and totally forgets 'hashed-liver-flavor-dog-treats'. He hauls the professional dog-walking lady and the nine other dogs towards me instead. He covers my face with doggy kisses.

'You know this dog?' asks the lady, panting.

'Yep, he's my dad's dog, Brandy.'

'He sure has a mind of his own.'

'Has he had his walk?'

'We've been twice round the park.'

'OK, I'm going to my dad's right now. I'll take him.'

The dog-walking lady doesn't need any more reassurance that I'm the bone fide daughter of this dog's owner. She seems only too relieved to hand him over.

Brandy climbs haughtily into the limo while the other dogs look on, and spreads himself out on the back seat.

When Brandy and I arrived at the loft, it was Dad who opened the door.

'Oh . . . hi, Holly! Great to have you coming to stay,' he said. 'Oh, you've got the dog . . .' He looked really guilty.

'Dad! How could you hire a dog-walker?'

122

'Well, what with the rain and the microbes . . .'

'Dad, it was only a cold.'

'Besides, I've been busy,' he said.

'Busy?'

Dad put an arm round my shoulders and walked me into his music room. There was a load of score scattered around the place, all marked up in Dad's wild black notation.

'You've been writing music?'

He nodded. He had that old, crinkly smile on his face that I remembered from way back.

'That's brilliant, Dad!' I said, hugging him.

He grinned. 'Well, yeah, I guess. I had to find a pretty damn good excuse to get out of walking that dog.'

'By the way, where is everyone?'

'That's the odd thing. Seems like some lucky star's been shining overhead. Max got this call from a guy in LA. He's out there writing lyrics right now. And Fred's been optioned for a feature-length art movie.'

'Cool! What about Marlowe?'

'When I looked in on him this morning, I found he'd gone too. I guess his agent must've called at last.'

'So it's just us here?'

'Looks like it.'

'Brilliant!'

Saturday 7th June, 10.00 a.m.
Apt 12, 1794 South Mercer

I wake up to find Dad is still asleep. As usual there is absolutely nothing to eat in the loft, so I call up the deli.

I order a list of totally healthy organic foods that I know Dad should eat. Then I ring them again and ask if they could include a box of Lucky Charms and a bottle of Strawberry Kool-Aid.

10.30 a.m.

I take Brandy for a walk and get back to find Dad's in his music room.

So I settle down to email Rupert. I have to plug my laptop into Dad's phone line. He hasn't even got broadband – the loft is positively prehistoric.

Once plugged in I'm faced with the same old problem.

'Hi, Rupert . . .'

'Hi there . . .'

'Rupert . . .'

10.32 a.m.

The deli delivery arrives and Dad wanders through with the crunchy bag of groceries.

He leans over my shoulder. 'What you doing, Holly-Poppy?'

Do I get a chance to concentrate? No way.

'Just sending an email.'

'Who to?'

'If you must know, my old tutor.'

'What? Mr Walrus?'

'No, the one before that. Rupert.'

'Rupert!' says Dad. 'Now hang on. Didn't your mother have to fire that guy for something?'

'We were only having a hamburger together. She totally over-reacted.'

'That young man is far too old for you, Holly.'

'I'm only sending him an email. He sent one to me.'

'So you've been corresponding?'

'No. Yes. Dad, don't get heavy. He's in Tanzania!'

This seems to reassure Dad.

'OK. I guess if he's out of the country that's all right.'

'Thank you.'

Dad has totally broken my concentration. This is SO-OO not fair. I give up again. The minute I log off, the phone rings.

It's someone for Marlowe.

'He's not in,' Dad calls from the kitchen. 'If it's his agent, take down the details.'

It isn't his agent, and whoever it is doesn't want to leave his name.

I can hear Dad taking the groceries out of the bag. Is that the sound of a box of Lucky Charms? Then there is a kind of shriek.

'*Oh my God!*'

I rush to the kitchen door, thinking maybe he's found a tarantula in with the bananas or something. If so, I'll have to save it before it gets stamped on.

But no, he's staring at the front page of the *New York Times*.

There's a picture of Mum and Marlowe coming out of some New York night spot with the headline SHOCK SWITCH – KANDHI TO WED.

'I thought she was meant to be engaged to Oliver Bream,' says Dad.

'Errm . . . kind of NOT,' I say. 'At least, not really . . .'

But she couldn't possibly dream of marrying *Marlowe*, could she?'

At that point the apartment phone rings again.

Dad goes to answer it. I hear him say, 'OK, I'll tell him.' He puts the receiver down and the phone instantly rings again.

'Marlowe? No, who wants him? Who? No, I don't know where he is.'

The next time the phone rings Dad simply picks it up and shouts 'He's not here!' and slams it down.

'Oh my God!' says Dad. 'I thought I'd escaped from all this.'

Sunday 8th June, 10.00 a.m.
Apt 12, 1794 South Mercer

There have been press photographers camped outside our front door since dawn, trying to catch a glimpse of Marlowe. Our assurances that he is NOT in the apartment, and that we don't know his whereabouts, are not heeded.

Dad is SO-OO not happy with the situation. He says it's 'an invasion of his privacy'. *And* a few things way stronger. And he's been really grumpy with me. In some way it all seems to be my fault – which I suppose it is in a sense. Mum would never have met Marlowe if I hadn't brought her to the apartment.

Dad refuses to go out any more. In fact, currently no one's leaving the apartment except for Brandy. The press have even found their way round the back to the fire-escape exit. We are literally prisoners. All my good work has come to nothing. The dog-walker has been re-hired. Even Brandy is looking depressed. He is back to the humiliation of being walked with nine other dogs, and they're all pedigree so no doubt make bitchy remarks about him – at least the females probably do.

In the middle of all this I find I have a call on my brand new mobile. Hardly anyone's got my new number yet, so it can only be Mum. It's from the Vegas Plaza.

'Hollywood, babes! Are you all right?'

'Mum! Have you any idea what you've done?'

'Me?'

'Yes! We're holed up like hostages in the apartment. And it's all because of you and Marlowe.'

'But Marlowe's here with me . . .'

'In Vegas?'

'Of course we're trying to keep the whole thing secret, but . . . You want to speak with Hollywood, darling?'

Marlowe comes on the line.

'Hi, Hollywood! Have there been any calls for me?'

'Calls? There have been nothing *but* calls for you!'

'Yep, looks as if my career might be taking off again,' he says in that happy-go-lucky brainless tone of his.

'Could you put me back to Mum, please?'

Mum comes back on the line.

'Mum!' I hiss. 'Can I speak to you without Marlowe listening in?'

'Well, I guess so . . .'

There are sounds at the other end like Mum shutting herself in the bathroom.

'Well?'

'What's going on?'

'What do you mean what's going on?'

'What about you and *Oliver*?'

'Oliver?' says Mum. She lets out a sigh and switches to her *deeply pained* voice. 'After the way he hurt me? But that all seems ages ago now.'

'Mum! It was *two days* ago.'

'Hollywood, sometimes I don't understand you. You go on and on about not liking Oliver. Then, when I dump him, all of a sudden he's flavour of the week.'

(Once again Mum has rewritten history. Now she's the one who's dumped Oliver.)

'But Mum, you can't go out with *Marlowe*.'

'Why ever not?'

'Because . . .' I try to think of the right way to put this. Like take his hat off and you won't find a brain underneath. Like if you laid all his girlfriends end to end they'd stretch right the way down Broadway. Like he's only using you,

Mum, to salvage his career. But right now, I know Mum doesn't want to hear any of this, so I say: 'I don't think he's right for you, that's all.'

'Well, he seems right for me right now. Marlowe's what I need after the way I've suffered. You do realise I have a concert tonight? I have to feel good about myself. I can't go out on stage unless I do. Aren't you going to wish me luck?'

I give up. I can't fight Mum and her professional ego all at once, so I reply, 'Good luck, Mum.'

'Thank you, babes. Now you take care, OK?'

'You take care too, Mum.'

I click my mobile shut.

6.00 p.m.

There's an insistent buzzing on the intercom. It's been going on all day. We don't dare disconnect it because we need to have food delivered.

Dad's sitting in a heap watching TV, which has been on non-stop. Brandy's asleep on Dad's bed.

This has gone on long enough.

I walk to the door.

'Where are you going, Holly?' asks Dad half-heartedly.

'I'm going to sort this whole thing out once and for all.'

I take the elevator down to the ground. As I open the front door I'm blinded by camera flashes.

'Stop!' I say, holding up a hand. 'If anyone wants to know the whereabouts of Marlowe Feisher, he is in Las Vegas, staying at the Vegas Plaza Hotel. Thank you. Goodbye.'

There are a few shouts of, 'How's Kandhi? Has she told you her plans?'

But basically the press disappear from sight like water sliding down a plughole.

All of a sudden – GLOOP – they're gone.

Monday 9th June, 10.00 a.m. Apt 12, 1794 South Mercer

All is peace in the apartment. Dad's working in his music room. I quietly take Brandy off for his walk because Dad seems truly involved in his music and I don't want him to break off.

It's a sunny day and we've been round the park once and are on our second lap, when someone comes up behind me and grabs me! I totally freak out because, for a lightning flash, I think Mum's right about all those murderers and molesters and kidnappers.

Brandy's growling fit to bust as I hear a voice in my ear saying, 'Hi!'

It's a voice I know *only too well*.

'Shug! Let me go. What are you doing here?'

'I was just passing in a cab and who should I see, walking her dog in the park, but Hollywood Bliss Winterman! So being a good stepbrother, I thought I'd stop by and say hi.'

'Well, doesn't look like you're gonna be a stepbrother now, does it?' I start walking at some pace. 'Come on, Brandy.'

Shug keeps up with us. 'Not if your mother plays around with other guys when she's meant to be engaged.'

'Your dad started it by going out with that Vanessa girl.'

'Uh-uh! That Vanessa girl pre-dated the engagement.'

I stop and stare at him: 'What do you mean?'

'That Vanessa picture was a publicity shot. From the film festival, three weeks back.'

'That's not what the papers said . . .'

'Maybe, but that's what it was.'

'You mean, your dad *isn't* going out with that girl?'

'Correct.'

'So how did the press get hold of the idea they were?'

Shug bends down and starts fiddling with the laces of his trainers.

'I guess someone must've told them,' he says.

'You . . . It was *you*, wasn't it?'

'Well, it seemed like a good idea at the time.'

'Hang on. Why are you telling me this?'

'OK, I'll come clean. My dad's in a kind of state. Someone let on about who leaked that story. In fact, he's totally mad at me. So's Vanessa. They say I've got to put the whole thing right.'

'Why doesn't your dad simply call Mum up?'

'He tried. She wouldn't listen to him.'

'You mean, your dad's in a state because Mum's going out with someone else?'

'Improbable as it seems, yes . . .'

My mind is racing. This means Oliver must really care for Mum. But Mum's switched to Marlowe now. What a mess!

131

'And now you're expecting me to sort this out for you?'

Shug looks at me like a whipped dog. 'Not expecting, exactly . . . But look, Holly, couldn't you just call your mum and tell her it was a mistake? I mean, the press get these things wrong all the time . . .'

Why should I? Why should I help Shug? I stretch myself up to my full height. The power! I want Shug to beg, to plead, to go down on his knees and grovel. It's SO-OO good to see him suffer!

So I say, walking somewhat faster, 'No way! This is your problem. You caused it, you solve it.'

'Great!' says Shug, practically running to keep up with me. 'Thanks a lot. I'll know where to come next time I want a favour.'

'I don't see you doing *me* any favours.'

We've stopped at the kerb. An empty cab is just rounding the bend, so I hail it.

I hold the cab door open for Shug.

'Nice of you to drop by. Have a good day,' I say.

'Oh, get a life!' he snaps as he slides into the cab, slamming the door behind him.

Afterwards

I reckoned I'd earned a Coke or something to celebrate this encounter, so I went over to where Al was winding down the awning over the café.

'It's going to be a hot one,' he said. 'You want an iced tea? Lemonade?'

'A Coke would be nice.'

'How's your dad?' he asked when he came back with a couple of chilled bottles. He sat down at a table with me.

'He's good. Very good. He's writing music again.'

'You don't say! Do you think he might start recording?'

'Not unless some recording company comes and knocks his door down. Dad's not exactly pushy.'

'But if people knew he was writing again . . .'

'No one seems interested in Dad any longer. Mum's the one everyone raves about.'

'That's too bad,' said Al. 'Still, if he's willing to do a gig here any time . . . You know the offer stands.'

Tuesday 10th June, 10.00 a.m.
Apt 12, 1794 South Mercer

As predicted, Mum's Vegas concert was a massive success. Dad and I watched it on TV. The cameras kept on swinging back to focus on Marlowe, described as Mum's 'new companion', who was sitting, complete with his ten-gallon hat, in the VIP seats.

The people behind him must've been pretty peeved that they'd forked out all that money for seats when they only got a view of a hat. But I guess they had the compensation of getting their faces on TV whenever he lurched to one side.

The show ended with this stunt where Mum appears to fly down from the ceiling and across the auditorium perched on a trapeze. Of course it's done by a body double who is a real trapeze artiste, but nobody knows that – including Marlowe, by the look of it. At any rate, he did a very convincing act of looking shaken out of his wits.

Wednesday 11th June, 10.00 a.m.
Apt 12, 1794 South Mercer

I was just composing a congratulations email for Mum when the loft phone rang. Dad answered it.

'It's someone for you, Holly.'

'Is that Holly B. Winterman?'

'Speaking.'

'Hi! Great to get you. I'm calling from *Teen Hits*. It's a cable programme. You must have seen it?'

I had. Actually, I seldom missed it. They have this live show every Saturday where they interview up-and-coming people in the charts. There's an interviewer called Gerry Maine, who's quite young and cute and baby-faced, who I had a crush on for ages when I was a kid.

Programmes like this were always trying to get hold of Mum, but I knew there was no way. Mum only does really big-time shows like Oprah's. And she never does live shows in case she louses up.

So I said, 'I guess you want to interview my mum. I'm afraid you'll have to talk to her publicist.'

'No, it was you we wanted to talk to.'

'Me?'

'We're doing a feature on what it's like having a star for a parent.'

I was about to say 'No' (unlike my mum, I have a real phobia about performing – even the school carol concert totally freaked me out), when a thought struck me. This would be an opportunity to put in a good word for Dad. I mean, all the record companies watched the programme. That's how they picked up new talent. Dad was more like old talent for sure, but you never knew. It would give me a chance to mention his name – to say he was writing music again.

Without really thinking, I heard myself saying: 'Well, maybe. When would you want me to do it?'

'This coming Saturday, if you're free.'

'I'll have to ask my mum.' (She'll probably say no.)

'You do that. Then can you get straight back to me?'

The girl left her number. I rang Mum right away.

'Hollywood! Were you watching last night? Marlowe said it was really awesome.'

'Of course.' With great restraint I ignored the reference to Marlowe and said, 'You were great, Mum.'

'I didn't feel I was as good as at Wembley . . .'

'Oh yes you were. Better if anything.'

'Hmm . . . well,' she purred. 'It was nice of you to call to say so, babes.'

'Mum, would it be OK if I went on *Teen Hits*? They just rang me.'

'They rang *you*?'

'Mm-hmm. They're doing a programme about what it's like to have a parent who's a star.'

Mum sounded reassured. 'Oh I see, so they'll be asking you about *me*?'

'Mmm . . . I guess.'

'Well, as long as you keep to my music. I'll get Vix to e you over the latest press briefing.'

My heart sank. 'So you think it's OK?'

'You're always going to be in the limelight, babes. You've got to start some time.'

Thursday 12th June, 9.00 a.m. Apt 12, 1794 South Mercer (forty-nine hours to go)

Why, oh why, did I agree to go on *Teen Hits*? I swear I haven't slept a wink since I said I'd do it. And I haven't eaten either. Every time I look at food, my stomach does this big churn-and-turn thing.

But I've got to overcome this because it's my one big chance to put in a plug for Dad. I keep telling myself to think of something else. I can manage 'other thoughts' for about two minutes and then my mind slips back and *remembers*, and it hits me with renewed force that I am going to be on television, live, in front of thousands or even *millions* of people in only forty-nine hours' time . . .

Hang on, what's the time?

No, *forty-eight* . . . Oh my God, another hour gone by! This very thought has sent shock waves through those tiny hairs that go right down my back.

I lie in bed trying to have nice thoughts. Any thoughts, in fact, that don't include TV or Teens or Hits or Gerry Maine.

Friday 13th June, 10.00 a.m.
Apt 12, 1794 South Mercer (only twenty-four hours to go)

Last night I actually dreamt my way through the interview.

In my dream I was really confident. I dreamt myself saying:

'Of course, I'm not just Kandhi's daughter. Pete Winterman is my father . . .'

In the annoying way dreams have, instead of saying, 'You don't say! What's Pete up to these days?' Gerry said, 'Who?'

'Pete Winterman of The Icemen. You must've heard of him.'

Gerry sadly shook his head.

'But he's brilliant! He was the one who wrote all Kandhi's early hits.'

This was received with a sigh of total non-comprehension. 'Who is this guy?' Gerry was asking.

I got to my feet. I stood up on the set, shouting at the audience, 'Please, someone . . . *someone* must have heard of Pete Winterman!'

But they were all booing and throwing stuff.

I woke in a cold sweat.

11.00 a.m. (twenty-three hours to go)

Dad has caught me biting my nails, and I haven't done that in months.

'What's up, Holly?'

'Nothing.'

'You're not nervous about this TV thing, are you?'

'Oh no. It'll only be like a five-minute interview,' I say, wondering if I'm going to vomit at the very mention of it.

'I could call them and say you've changed your mind.'

Now I know what those saints felt like – the ones they told us about at school – when they were waiting to be burned at the stake or disembowelled or hanged upside down or whatever, and they were given the chance to recant. But I wasn't going to go back on my word any more than they did.

'No, Dad. It's OK. I said I'll do it, so I will.'

Saturday 14th June, 7.00 a.m.
Apt 12, 1794 South Mercer (three hours to go)

I'm lying in bed, frantically memorising the crib sheet Vix has sent me with all the press information about Mum. At the bottom, double-underscored is a warning NOT to talk about Mum's private life *under any circumstances*. Good advice. I can't figure out Mum's private life for myself.

8.00 a.m. (two hours to go)

My nerves have taken on another humiliating physical symptom. I've been to the bathroom so many times, Dad has asked if I need medication. I daren't leave the apartment so for once Dad is forced to walk Brandy.

10.00 p.m. Teen Hits studios

Abdul is accompanying my body (what's left of it) into the studios of Teen Time Motion International Inc. I'm so empty, my stomach is positively flapping against my backbone. I know what's going to happen. I'm going to walk on to the set and pass out in a heap on the floor from sheer starvation.

Abdul is given a coffee and seated in Reception. I'm told I'm going to have a quick chat with Gerry before the audience arrives, but first I'm taken down to Make-up to get my face fixed for the cameras.

'See you after,' says Abdul, giving me an encouraging wink.

I think this unlikely. There is no way I am going to survive this ordeal.

Downstairs, I'm so nervous that I stumble through the make-up studio door and lurch into the room as if jet-propelled. There's already another person sitting at the mirrors having his make-up done.

'Oops!' he says.

Oh my God! It's *Shug*! Shug of all people! The last person in the world I expect to see. No, correction, the last person in the world I *want* to see.

'What on earth are you doing here?' I ask. The total amazement of finding Shug in the room actually stops me feeling nervous for a moment.

'Promoting my new single perhaps? You must've heard it.'

His tone is as arrogant as ever. I give him a mock smile. 'Must've missed it,' I say. 'But maybe it'll be on again.'

'Oh, very funny! It's been on a lot, for your information.'

'So what number is it? In the charts?'

(I know for a fact Mum's Heatwave numbers are occupying almost all the Top Ten.)

'*Charts?*' he says condescendingly. 'I don't think we're talking the same kind of music, do you?'

'You mean popular or *unknown*?'

'So what are *you* doing here?' he retorts.

'Same reason as you, I guess. Aren't we being interviewed about our oh-so-famous parents?'

I sat down in the chair the make-up lady was offering. She went to work on my face. Pinned to the chair, I was forced to confront Shug's reflection. God, he looked pathetic! He'd gelled his hair till it stood up in spikes like a stegosaurus.

He contented himself with making silly faces at me in the mirror.

Once made up, we were shown into the studio and introduced to Gerry. He was a lot smaller than he looked on screen, but had the same friendly baby face.

He'd prepared a load of questions to ask us. Most of mine were about Mum, and I'd got the answers off pat because I had literally learned Vix's crib sheet by heart. I'd have to find a way to slip in a few references to Dad when we were doing the programme for real. Shug was visibly impatient all through my questions, obviously dying for Gerry to get on to him, so . . . I . . . took . . . my . . . time . . .

Shug was doing his bit (and showing off like mad) when all of a sudden the studio got tense. Gerry said they were about to bring the audience in. We were sent to 'take five' in the room next door. Someone would come and get us when the time came.

In the room next door (literally minutes to go)

We were given a coffee and told to relax. Coffee was a *big* mistake. On an empty stomach the caffeine kicked in and my nervousness made a big comeback. I was now positively shaking.

Shug sat slumped on a chair fiddling with a biro, clicking the nib in and out.

This was really getting to me.

'Can you stop doing that!' I snapped.

'Nervous?'

'No way. Are you?'

'Nervous about a stupid five-minute interview? Give me a break!'

But I could tell he was, by the way he kept jerking his foot.

We waited for what seemed like for ever. My mouth had gone dry and I felt sicker than ever. And then a girl wearing a headset came to get us.

'You're on in twenty seconds,' she said.

She was listening intently to an earpiece. Then she opened the door and ushered us through.

I am now having a total out-of-body experience. I see myself as if from far, far above, walking on to the set.

Our entrance is covered by Gerry, who's getting the audience to give us a big hand.

'A big welcome to Hollywood Bliss Winterman!'

The body I'm out of sits down and does a wobbly smile.

'And Shug Bream . . .'

Shug slumps into his leather seat and glares at the camera.

'So, Holly. Tell us. What's it's like being the daughter of the world's biggest superstar?' asks Gerry. Before I can answer, he turns to the audience and says, 'News just in – sales of Kandhi's *Heatwave* album have just topped a million! Which means another platinum disc is winging its way to her . . .'

There's a burst of applause at this.

Shug slumps even further. Gerry turns back to me.

'So is the superstar a super mum, Holly?'

'Well, to me she's just my mum,' I hear myself saying.

Out of the corner of my eye I can see Shug off-camera making 'I-want-to-vomit' signs. This gets a titter from the audience.

'But there's my dad, of course. Now I'm in the States I spend a lot of time with him . . .'

'Oh, Pete Winterman?' says Gerry. (Nice one). 'What's he doing these days?

'He's started writing music again.' (Shug's now drumming his fingers.)

I persevere. 'His new stuff's really brilliant.'

'I spend a lot of time with *my* Dad too,' interrupts Shug doing a silly imitation of my voice. The audience laughs uncertainly. I glare at Shug. Gerry's totally losing it. I can see

142

his eyes glazing over as he listens to something that seems to be buzzing in his earphone.

'Interesting,' says Gerry, turning back to me. I can see he's ad-libbing now. 'Wasn't it Pete who wrote Kandhi's early hits?'

'Mm-hmm. "Sweet Dreams" and "Kandidly Yours" and "Sweet-Talkin" –'

Shug interrupts again. 'Of course my music is really different from Kandhi's . . .'

Gerry has trouble keeping his screen smile fixed on me. I wonder if the audience will notice if I pinch Shug *hard*? He's just within reach.

'Not just trashy popular –'

'Yes, now Shug,' says Gerry, cutting in and stopping him mid-sentence, 'You've recently recorded a single. Let's take a look at Contrôle Technique's new release, 'Grab-Machine'.

With that the music slams in and Shug's video comes up on the big screen.

While the cameras are off us, Gerry whispers frantically: 'Look, you two, can you stop this?'

I sat fuming through Shug's single. I was so furious I'd even forgotten to be nervous. It was pretty pathetic. I mean, he wasn't even singing. He was kind of grunting the words. Self-pitying stuff about a guy who feels like the whole world is against him. He was in this massive machine like you see in cheap sideshows where you pay five quarters and this big clamp comes down and picks up a ball and takes it out.

When the last chords faded out, Gerry concentrated on Shug for a while. Shug did some typical aggressive showing off about how he didn't give a damn about charts and popularity. The rowdier guys in the studio were egging him on, clapping and whistling. I reckoned he must've had loads of his mates in the audience.

Then Gerry turned back to me . . .

'So, Holly, what do you think of the news about the *Heatwave* album?'

'It's really great, but I still love Mum's old stuff. The stuff Dad wrote.'

'What she's trying to say is that good ol' Kandhi's gone downhill since she split with – ' interrupted Shug.

'Well, that's all we've got time for, I'm afraid,' cut in Gerry, and the music drowned out the last words of Shug's sentence.

As Gerry went into his wind-up, we were led off the set.

'Has anyone ever told you it's rude to interrupt?' I asked Shug as cuttingly as possible.

'Were you intending to hog the whole interview, or did you just do it on impulse?' demanded Shug.

'What about that stuff you were doing with the audience?'

'Oh yeah? And what was all that stuff about your dad?'

Gerry came off set at that moment and stormed into the room.

'Jeez! You guys gave me a bad time. What's up with you two?'

Shug just slumped on a chair. 'You ask her.'

'Oh great! Ask me! I was the one who was giving the hard time, was I?'

144

'Takes two to make an argument,' said Shug.

'You should know – you're the expert.'

'Cut it out. Enough!' said Gerry. 'Holly, I don't know what to say to you. And Shug, this is a warning. If you want to get blacklisted by the media, you're going the right way about it.'

Sunday 15th June, 7.00 a.m.
Apt 12, 1794 South Mercer

I'm in BIG trouble with Mum. She's seen the interview and she's gone ballistic. She was furious at Shug and none too pleased with me either – bringing up all this stuff about Dad when she wanted me to rave about her.

'I expect, at the very least, that my family will stand by me,' was how she finished tearfully. Then she put down the receiver.

I stared at the phone indignantly. That was rich coming from Mum! Her family standing by her? Wasn't she the one who was always walking out? She walked out on Dad, didn't she? She walked out on anyone she judged wasn't quite up to her standard: agents, friends, managers, publicists, husbands. Not to mention me.

It gets worse. Not only am I in trouble with Mum, I'm in trouble with Dad. He'd seen the interview and has gone catatonic!

It seems the music he's writing now is pure stuff – deep and serious. He's trying to live down all that early stuff he did with Mum. Oh, how could I have got it SO-OO wrong?

I don't think I'll ever be happy again as long as I live.

It gets worse. Next morning I find Dad is on the kitchen floor, trying to tempt Brandy to eat. He has a spoonful of dog food and he's offering it to him, saying: 'Yum-Yum!'

'What's going on?' I demand.

'The old boy's acting up.'

'Acting up? How?'

'Well he's kind of off his food. Gone really picky. Thought maybe it was the food. I changed the brand, but he won't eat this new stuff either.'

Brandy? Off his food? Picky? Normally the second you put his food down, it's gone.

'Come on, boy! This is good stuff. Look, I'm eating it myself,' says Dad, pretending to shove some in his mouth.

'Dad, this dog is really sick. We've got to get him to a vet.'

'You think?' says Dad, panic in his voice. (This is the guy who didn't want a dog, remember?)

I calm Dad down and take things into my own hands. I call up Directory for a list of local vets.

11.00 a.m., Mr Herman Matlock's Veterinary Clinic

I got Abdul to drive me and Brandy to the clinic. Dad didn't want to come. He said he still wasn't quite over his cold. I reckoned the way he was panicking we were better off without him.

Mr Herman Matlock's Clinic is way down in the poor end of SoHo. But the waiting room has a nice reassuring disinfectant smell and there are pictures of happy, healthy animals on the walls. (There are also pictures of nasty parasites and diseases and things, but I ignore these.) I leave Abdul reading a leaflet on Pet Psychology and follow Mr Matlock in his clean white doctor's overall into his consulting room.

Mr Matlock oozes reassurance too. He strokes Brandy's head. 'Now, what's up with this little fella?' he asks.

I explain about him not eating and he asks proper vet questions about how long for, etc. Mr Matlock's already got Brandy on his back and is feeling his stomach with expert hands.

'All seems OK down here.'

He takes his temperature, which is normal.

Then he puts a lamp on his head and looks down Brandy's throat.

'Uh-huh,' he says knowingly.

He's found something. In my imagination it's some horrible growth. I steel myself for the tragic news.

Mr Matlock isn't saying anything. He's scrabbling round in a drawer full of instruments. He takes out a long pair of forceps, saying, 'Now you, young lady, do you think you could hold his head still for me?'

This is an epic moment. I am assisting at my very first veterinary intervention. I clamp my arms round Brandy's head and say calming things to him.

'Got it!' says Mr Matlock.

He holds up the forceps. Clamped in them is a tiny semi-circular sliver of transparent plastic.

'Now what on earth could that be?' he asks.

I shrug. Whatever it is is a total mystery.

'I'll give him a shot of antibiotics. His throat is pretty inflamed, but he should be fine in a day or so.'

Mr Matlock is washing his hands. 'Incidentally,' he says, 'I liked the way you held that dog. You've got a way with animals.'

I glow with pride. Suddenly I can picture myself – something like on the front of that vintage *Sound of Music* album. Only it's not Julie Andrews but me with a string of happy healthy animals alongside striding across the hillside.

'Actually,' I admit, 'I want to be a vet.'

'You don't say!' says Mr Matlock, leaning up against the edge of his operating table. 'Now, why in the world would you want a job like this?'

'Well, I want to do something kind of different and more worthwhile than my mum.'

'And what does she do?'

'She's a singer.'

'Winterman . . .' says Mr Matlock thoughtfully. 'Pete Winterman . . . You're not –' his voice kind of cracks – 'you're not *Kandhi's* daughter?'

I nod. 'Yep, she's my mum.'

'Oh boy!' says Mr Matlock. 'Wait till I tell my kids I've had Kandhi's daughter in my clinic!' And then he glances back at me. I guess he can tell from my expression that I'm SO NOT impressed by this.

'But you, you want to be a vet – which is very commendable. Young woman, do you realise how hard it is to become a vet?'

'Oh, I'm willing to work hard.'

'Did you know that it's as hard or even harder than being a doctor? Because you've got all these species to learn about. Like cold-blooded creatures and invertebrates and birds as well as mammals.'

'Yeah, I know that.'

'And that it takes six years to qualify.'

'That's what everyone keeps telling me. They're doing their best to put me off.'

'Don't let them,' says Mr Matlock. 'Stick to your guns.'

'Thanks. I was aiming to do that.'

'Well, any time you want to drop by for advice, or when you want work experience, remember me. OK?'

I am flushed with pride. I'm going to be a vet! I float back to Dad's, fantasising about the brilliant veterinary clinic I'm going to have. It's going to have a waiting room where calming music is played and there are videos for animals to watch while they're waiting to be treated. In fact, a choice of videos on a paw-pad like you get in Club Class. Perhaps greyhound racing for dogs and things like figure skating and snooker for cats . . .

12.00 noon

Dad has admitted guilt.

'But I didn't think he'd eat the packaging!' he said.

Apparently he let Brandy get his teeth into his Gumball Treat *while still wrapped in its plastic bubble*.

Looking on the positive side, however, Dad is so relieved that Brandy's OK that he has totally forgiven me over the *Teen Hits* interview.

Hang on – there goes my mobile.

It's a text:

> **I think jamie's 2-timing with emma**
> **(3rd violin)**
> **what did I do wrong?**
> **Bx**

Uh-huh! So even Becky has love-life problems. She's not immune. Remembering her hard-hearted texts about Rupert, I restrain my sympathy and text her back:

> **j. s not only boy in world**
> **think laterally**
> **there's always the woodwind section**
> **HBWx**

After that we spend a long texting session back and forth. Becky is coming out with dumb stuff like:

> **do you think**
> **I should write him a note?**
> **Bx**

> **no way!**
> **HBWx**

or buy him a present maybe?
Bx

purrleese!
HBWx

I know I'll never ever like
another boy
Bx

believe me
you will
HBWx

no I won't
Bx

Eventually I resort to diversionary tactics and try:

Hey!
maybe I can get
mum to donate to
your strad fund
i'll add you to her
list of charities
HBWx

Becky saves every penny she has, because one day she thinks she'll be able to make a down payment on a Stradivarius.

151

That's like the most famous kind of violin ever made and, although they're really old, apparently they sound way better than any violin made today. But Becky doesn't get that much pocket money and she's always borrowing from the Strad fund. So the Strad is like an impossible dream, which is going to stay way up at the top of her Ultimate Wish List – like forever.

I get a text back:

Cool!

Huh! Diversion worked.

Tuesday 17th June, 11.45 a.m.
The Plaza Residenza

Mum is due back today at two thirty, so Abdul's brought me and all my gear over and I've moved back into our apartment. I spend the morning doing a big virtue thing to placate her (kind of the equivalent of vacuuming and tidying if you're a normal daughter).

Except there wasn't any vacuuming to do, seeing as Mum has this team that comes in daily and goes through the apartment searching for dirt like a forensic team on a murder hunt. They literally work magic, leaving everything undisturbed bar the dust. I left a paperback on the floor as a test. It was put back just where it was, except that it was closed and it had a book mark inside which said:

ANGELS
from
'Next 2 Godliness'
have passed through this way.
Thank you.
Have a nice day.

But back to my virtue thing. I took out the Gold Card that Mum says I can use for emergencies. Well, this is an emergency, isn't it? Mum will be back in *under three hours*! I called up Takashimaya on Fifth Avenue and had three hundred white gardenias sent up. I was kind of tempted to order other colours to cheer the place up some, but I knew this would SO NOT please her. Then I got on to Dean and Deluca and had them fill the fridge with her favourite foods: oysters, wild asparagus and raspberries. I didn't trust them on caviar, so I sent out to Petrossian for that. Then I spent the rest of the morning spray-misting my palms and feeding my tropical fish – a jungle-themed suite is pretty labour-intensive.

2.30 p.m. precisely

I am on my balcony. Down below the street is pretty crowded. TV teams have been out in force since dawn with their cameras fixed on the entrance. They've had to move the horses and carriages and stuff further down the street.

2.33 p.m.

I can hear what sounds like a parade coming up Fifth Avenue. A stream of limos draws up with a convoy of paparazzi in hot pursuit.

I watch from above as the tiny figure of Mum climbs out of the first limo and walks up the red carpet into the Plaza Building. And then, as if on rewind, she goes back and does it again. Not until a third rewind are the press happy. Mum enters the building and disappears from sight.

A minute later she's up on our floor and in through the apartment doors.

'Hollywood, babes!' I'm enfolded in waves of 'K'.

'Hi, Mum!'

'Oh babes! Was I horrid to you on the phone?'

'A bit . . .'

'I'll make it up to you, I promise.'

I hear the elevator clunk to a stop and the apartment doors open again.

'Look what I've bought you . . .' says Mum.

Standing in the elevator, swaying beneath a tottering pyramid of gift-wrapped boxes, is Marlowe.

'Oh! Hi, *Marlowe*!'

'Hi, Holly! Where shall I put these?'

'They're all for Hollywood, so you can put them in her suite,' says Mum.

'All for me?'

Marlowe follows Mum. I follow the gifts.

'It was Marlowe's idea. I just hope you haven't changed size.'

There are five big expensive-looking boxes. I guess this is kind of the equivalent of your mum's new boyfriend giving you candy to get on the right side of you.

'Well, aren't you going to open them?' asks Marlowe.

I open the first box and inside there's a really beautiful pair of soft leather riding boots.

'Wow! Thanks, Mum and, errm, Marlowe . . .'

I try them on. They fit. My feet seem to have stopped growing at last.

Inside the next box there's a pair of suede chaps like cowboys wear. A third reveals a pair of riding jodhpurs and then a fine suede shirt. And in the last box there's a ten-gallon hat. A complete cowboy outfit made for me. The only thing they haven't packed is the horse.

'Oh Mum, you shouldn't . . .' I say, giving her a hug.

'It's just a little something to go with the gift I bought Marlowe,' says Mum.

'Oh? What was that?'

'A ranch,' says Marlowe with a wide grin.

I give Mum a hard stare. Mum avoids my gaze.

'Won't that be nice for you, Hollywood? You know how you love animals. Now you can learn to ride . . .'

I am about to reply to this when I notice some sort of commotion coming from the salon.

The doors of the apartment have been left open because people have been coming in and out, delivering Mum's fifteen perfectly matched Louis Vuitton suitcases, her hatboxes, her shoeboxes and the specially designed Louis Vuitton zip-up bag with the single down pillow inside which she takes everywhere.

155

But back to the commotion . . .

A voice is raised. A male voice in the salon is demanding: 'Where the hell is she?'

I can hear Vix trying to make out Mum's left the apartment. Clumping footsteps cross the salon. I hear Mum's bedroom door being opened and then slammed again . . .

Mum doesn't seem fazed. She walks over calmly and leans out of my bedroom door.

'Is someone looking for me?'

'What do you damn well think you're playing at, Kandhi?'

I creep up behind Mum. It's Oliver. But this is not the cold-fish oh-so-English Oliver Bream we're familiar with. His face is scarlet and his hair is all over the place.

'Hello, Oliver,' says Mum levelly. 'How nice of you to drop by. Is your girlfriend with you?'

'*Where is he?*' storms Oliver, ignoring the reference to the girlfriend.

'Who?'

'*You know who!*'

Marlowe meanwhile is behaving in a very un-cowboy-like fashion. He's not exactly poised for a shoot-out. No, he's actually slipped into my bathroom and locked himself in.

'He's in here somewhere! I know he is!' rages Oliver, striding into my suite. He starts thrashing through the palms. 'Come out, you bastard!' he's saying. 'I know you're in there.'

Mum has wandered off into the salon, not getting involved. In fact, she has this totally serene and gratified look on her face. And suddenly I realise that this is what she's planned all along. She's loving it. She's relishing it. She's got Oliver exactly where she wants him.

Oliver has peeped in my clothes trunk, checked my balcony, and now he's homed in on my bathroom door.

'Come out you . . . you . . . *coward*!' he shouts at the door.

There's no answer from inside.

'You can't stay locked in there for ever,' continues Oliver.

(But he could for a pretty long time. After all, he's got plenty of water. And he could eat all the tropical fish.)

'OK,' says Oliver. 'Take your time. I'm in no hurry. I'm outside the door and I am *not leaving* . . .'

Mum walks slowly back into the room with her arms folded. She leans against the wall and looks Oliver straight in the face.

'Don't you think', she asks. 'That you are being just the teensiest bit childish?'

'*Childish*?' returns Oliver.

'Yes,' says Mum. 'After all, you started this.'

'No I didn't.'

'Yes you did. By going out with that Vanessa *Nobody* girl.'

'Excuse me. I was not "going out", as you so coyly put it, with Vanessa. I was simply helping her with her publicity.'

' "Helping her with her publicity" didn't have to include having her wrapped around your body for the whole of the world's press to see. Not when you were meant to be engaged to ME.'

'But we weren't engaged.'

'I know we weren't *properly*, but everyone thought we were, so it came to the same thing.'

'No. You don't get it! *We were NOT not-properly-engaged when that shot was taken.*'

'What?' Mum demands. (A sentence with so many negatives in it is totally beyond her.)

Oliver looks as if he's going to self-combust.

'Can't you get it through your dumb head?'

'Don't you talk to me like that, Oliver Bream!'

Now this could go on for ever. Clearly the time had come for me to intervene.

'*STOP! Both of you,*' I shouted. Miraculously, they did. 'Mum, listen. That shot was taken at the Cannes Film Festival. I had the truth from Shug. It was taken two weeks before you got "not-properly-engaged" to Oliver.'

'Was it?' demanded Mum.

'Yes,' said Oliver. 'It was.'

'So you're not going out with that Vanessa girl?'

'I haven't set eyes on her since Cannes.'

Tears welled up in Mum's eyes. 'So does this mean we're . . . still . . . not-properly-engaged?' she said haltingly. Her lower lip was wobbling. She bit it.

'It looks like it,' said Oliver. He took a step towards her. All the anger had gone out of his voice.

'Oh . . .' said Mum.

'Look, Kandhi . . .' said Oliver gently.

'Yes, Oliver?' Mum was looking up into his face.

'Errm, the thing is, I think I might be . . .' This could well have led to the most romantic moment in the history of the universe had the door of the bathroom not shot open at that point and Marlowe emerged brandishing a loofah.

'Right. Back off, *you!*' he said threateningly to Oliver, as he slid round the inner wall of my suite, making for the door. Having located said door, he literally fell through into the salon. Oliver didn't even bother to follow.

'. . . in love with you . . .' finished Oliver, taking another step towards Mum.

'Oh Oliver!' sighed Mum, taking a step towards him.

I went out to check that Marlowe hadn't landed on the floor or broken a leg or something, but he'd actually fled. The apartment was empty.

I went to close the front door after him.

And then on second thoughts I went out through it. Right now I reckoned Mum and Oliver could do with some quality time together.

Later

Abdul drove me to Dad's. The way things stood it seemed tactful to stay there the night.

By the time I arrived, Marlowe had called in, grabbed his stuff and taken a cab to JFK Airport. He was on his way to the ranch Mum had so kindly given him.

Wednesday 18th June, 9.00 a.m.
The Plaza Residenza

When I got back the following morning, I found Mum on the phone.

159

She held up one hand to me, indicating not to interrupt.

'Yes, Armando, it's vital. *Why* can't you fly out till tomorrow?'

'. . . . .'

'What's wrong with a private jet?'

'. . . . .'

'Of course, Armando – just put it on the cheque.'

She put the phone down.

'Honestly, people can be *so* penny-pinching.'

'Why do you need Armando so urgently?'

'To design the *dress*, Hollywood. Sometimes I don't think you're quite with it.'

She got up and made for her bedroom. I followed her.

'Dress? What dress?' I said.

She turned and looked at me with one eyebrow raised.

'You mean, *wedding* dress?' I continued. 'Isn't this all happening a bit fast?'

'Why wait? Oliver and I know we're right for each other. We're planning the wedding next month. In LA – so as we can be sure of the weather. And it will fit in nicely as I've got to be there anyway for my premiere.'

Mum had seated herself at her mirror and had started rubbing white base coat into her face.

'Are you sure you know what you're doing, Mum?'

'Marrying Oliver? Of course I do. Who else could I possibly marry?'

'Well, last week everyone seemed to think you were marrying Marlowe.'

'*Marlowe?*' Mum was fussing around looking for eyeliner.

160

'I thought you were really keen on him.'

'Don't be ridiculous, Holly. He's only a model, and not a very successful one at that.'

'Mum, honestly, you should be ashamed of yourself. I think you were simply using Marlowe to make Oliver jealous.'

'Sometimes men need a little something to bring out the red blood in them,' said Mum, leaning into the mirror and lining one eye thickly with black. 'Let's just say Marlowe was in the right place at the right time.'

'But it wasn't fair to simply pick him up, then drop him like that.'

'Fair?' said Mum, turning on me with one eye lined and the other not. 'He got a ranch out of it, didn't he?'

'Mum, *really*!'

'Oh well,' said Mum, turning back to the mirror. 'I don't think Marlowe truly cared for me. It was just my fame that attracted him. It's hard, you know, Hollywood, being me.' (!) 'At least I know with Oliver it's *me* he really cares about. You see, Oliver's so famous he could have any girl.'

I couldn't argue with that.

'So you will be our bridesmaid, won't you?'

'I suppose so ... As long as *Shug* isn't going to be pageboy.'

'I can't exactly see Shug in knee breeches now, can you? But of course he's got to be there.'

'Ugghh!'

'You two are going to have to try to get along.'

'Great!'

'Now, Hollywood, don't be difficult.'

'I'm not being difficult. But Mum, you must realise it's Shug who's been making trouble between you two all along.'

'Hollywood, you must understand. That poor boy's mixed up. And it's no wonder. He's never had a proper mother –'

'She had a lucky escape.'

Mum looked me in the eyes, sincerity oozing from every pore. 'Yes, Hollywood, I am going to be a mother to him and I hope you'll do your bit and be a sister.'

'A sister!'

I remembered the way Shug looked me up and down. The suggestive comments he always made. I dissolved into giggles.

'I don't know what you find so funny. Now, I'm meeting Oliver for dinner. He's got to fly off to Italy tonight – they start shooting his new movie tomorrow.'

Thursday 19th June
The Plaza Residenza

Vix is in Mum's office trying to write a press release to communicate to the media that despite all the reports that have been flying back and forth:

a) Mum's Not-Proper-Engagement is NOT OFF.
b) It's now a Proper-Engagement and it's ON.

Vix is in a really bad mood. Not only is this a very difficult press release, but she herself doesn't believe in marriage. It offends her feminist principles. Every time anyone mentions a word like 'ring' or 'dress' or 'cake' she positively bristles.

Mid-morning I get a text from Becky:

> william - 3rd violin
> is so cool! we're sharing
> a score in orchestra
> practice
> Bx

Hmm. How can people be SO-OO fickle? But I text her back:

> go for it
> seems like
> you've got a lot in common
> HBWx

Later

I find Mum busy in the salon with Mr Bateman, her lawyer, drawing up a pre-nuptial agreement (pre-nup for short). Which is basically a way of saying 'paws off' to any potential husband who wants to get his hands on her money.

When I go to the kitchen for breakfast I find Thierry busy riffling through his cookery books working out if he can provide a buffet for a thousand people totally out of fresh raw food. I quietly help myself to a bowl of fruit salad and yogurt and take it back into the salon.

Mum is lying on her couch flicking through a magazine while Mr Bateman reads a list out to her. She's looking really bored, although I guess this is pretty important.

Mr Bateman wants to make sure that should this marriage not last, Mum will still be in possession of:

Item 1) Her penthouse in the Plaza Residenza

Item 2) Her Greek island

Item 3) Her palazzo in Venice

Item 4) Her beach house in Belize

Item 5) Her castle in Scotland

Item 6) Her yacht in Monte Carlo

Item 7) Her stable of race horses

Item 8) Her two Picassos, her one Matisse and her Damien Hirst

Item 9) Her Kandhi Store designer label, including Kandhi Klub Klassics

Item 10) 'K', her own perfume, including all spin-offs – right down to scented drawer liners

Item 11) 'K.W. Inc.', her record label

Item 12) 'In the Kan', her film production company

Item 13) 'UnKanny', her organic food company

Item 14) 'Kan-Kan Klubs', her string of nightclubs throughout the world

Item 15) 'Chateau Kandhi', her vineyard in California

Item 16) The royalties from her biography 'Kandidly Yours'

Item 17) The profits from her movie 'Supernova'

Item 18) The royalties from her children's book

'Kandy's Kingdom' and all Kandy dolls and their accessories, including the new 'Kandhi limo drive-in kar wash'

Item 19) ME . . .

'But Cyril,' Mum interrupts . . .

Mr Bateman pretends he hasn't heard her. He drones on: '. . . all items using the word Kandhi or the symbol "K" as it relates to Kandhi the person or property or used as a logo or brand name . . .' He pauses to draw breath.

'Cyril, this marriage is going to last. It truly is true love this time,' Mum insists.

Mr Bateman is SO NOT impressed by this. He's small and bald and I reckon he'd need a legal definition of the words 'true love' before he'd allow them into his vocabulary.

'You said that last time,' he says in a flat tone.

'No, but Cyril, I've never felt like this about anyone . . .'

'You said that too,' he adds in the same flat tone, and continues: '. . . any item purporting to have come from the Kandhi empire unsolicited will be in breach of –'

'Oh for God's sake, show me where to sign,' says Mum. 'I've got to be measured for the dress in twenty minutes.'

She gets up from the couch and catches sight of me.

'Hollywood, babes! Come and say hello to Mr Bateman.

'Hello, Holly. Wow, you've grown!'

'Thank you, Mr Bateman.' (He gets to his feet. He now reaches up to somewhere near my chest.)

'You just hang on there while I sign this stuff, then we can talk,' says Mum.

Mr Bateman is shuffling through sheaves of paper and has passed Mum his fountain pen. Each time Mum signs, he runs a big leather-bound blotter over the signature. I wonder if he realises the value of that blotting paper. True, her signature is round the wrong way, but it would still fetch a fortune on eBay.

When Mr Bateman leaves, Mum says, 'Well, at least that's all settled.' She wanders into the bedroom to find the right height heels to be measured in.

I follow. 'Isn't Oliver going to mind, Mum? I mean, isn't marriage meant to be about sharing "all your worldly goods"?'

'True. But unfortunately, Hollywood, so is divorce,' says Mum. 'Cyril is one of those people who likes to err on the safe side. You can't blame him – it's in his blood, he's a lawyer. Now where are those Manolos? I've got to be at Armando's by twelve.'

'Can I come with you?'

'Of course, you're expected, babes. Who else could design your bridesmaid's outfit?'

12.30 p.m., Armando Me₃₃o – First Floor Private Clients' Suite, Fifth Avenue

The showroom is lined with blow-ups from Armando's latest couture show. There's not a sign of any bridal wear. We're clearly more at the drawing board stage.

Armando's looking a little frayed from his overnight flight, but he's fussing round Mum like she's the first bride ever.

'White!' he's saying. 'It's an idea, yes, maybe . . .'

'You don't think white?' demands Mum.

'We-ell,' says Armando, obviously searching for the tactful way to put this, 'white is very much First Wedding, don't you think? And this is your . . .'

'Second,'

'Third,' Vix corrects her.

'Well, you don't have to count Fernandez. That only lasted a week. Never trust a polo player,' says Mum.

'Hmm,' says Armando. 'Of course, there's always off-white, or pearl or cream or beige . . .'

'Beige!' says Mum. 'That's like sackcloth! This is a wedding, Armando, not a pagan ritual.'

'That's debatable . . .' mutters Vix under her breath.

Mum's heard this. Suddenly she's on the defensive.

'Vix! Do you have to be like . . . like the *witch* at the *christening*?'

'I don't know what you're talking about,' replies Vix.

'You are not going to spoil my day. Why don't you take yourself down to Tiffany and discuss rings? I want matching designs. They've got my size, I'll have Oliver's sent over.'

'Right,' says Vix, taking up her organiser. 'I'm off to Tiffany . . .' she drops her voice as she passes me and adds, 'for the shackles.'

Once Vix has left, Armando summons up a swatch book. This has seventy different versions of off-white. He opens it at the pure raw silk section. These silks are handwoven from the thread of silkworms fed on specially selected mulberry buds. Mum flicks through the swatches to keep him happy. I can see she's set her heart on white.

They have a little argument and then settle on 'pearl'. It's white with just the merest hint of pinky-cream in it.

'And for zee bridesmaid?' says Armando, suddenly remembering to use his foreign accent.

'Anything *but* pink,' I say quickly. (I once had a v.v. bad experience wearing pink in Paris.)

'But pink is perfect to go with zee pearl,' says Armando. 'And for a beautiful young girl . . .'

He's not going to get round me by flattery.

'Anything but pink,' I insist.

Armando sighs and suggests I have the pearl too.

'Won't we look too alike?' asks Mum.

'Ah, but wiz a different cut . . .' says Armando. 'Marguerite, will you bring in zee book of modèles?'

Marguerite, the minute antique lady Armando takes everywhere with him, staggers in with a white leather-bound book.

Reverently Armando places it in front of Mum. Mum starts going through it. I lean over her shoulder. The dresses are shown as sketches. They are all *yummy*. But Mum is going through them at speed with little grunts and sighs.

'Mum, that one's gorgeous!' I stop her at a particularly heavenly design.

'It's no good, Armando, you'll have to design me an original.'

They start discussing it. Mum wants it low-cut but demure, short to show off her legs, and with a big train to trail behind for maximum effect. Armando is doing sketches

168

as she speaks. At length, they agree on a drawing. It's a strapless, backless dress with a tight, short skirt which kind of dips down behind and fans out into an endless peacock's tail.

After Mum's dress, mine is easy. Mum says that it mustn't have a low neck because bridesmaids need to be demure. And it shouldn't be short because I'll be standing behind her and she doesn't want everyone ogling my legs. In the end they settle on a high-waisted dress that goes up to my neck and down to the ground. My arms are judged innocent enough be shown. And it's going to be in the palest palest shell pink.

'See? Holly is zee shell to go wiz zee pearl,' says Armando. Which just about sums the whole thing up. *Great!*

1.30 p.m., in the limo going back to the Plaza Residenza

I sit staring out of the window at the crowds thronging the streets of the city. Hundreds of them, thousands of them, millions of them – all with homes and lives that are so nice and homey and normal. Most of the them will be taking a commuter train home tonight, to an ordinary home in an ordinary street. My American dream home is one of these. It's a white clapboard house in a street lined with trees. Not a large house, but big enough for me to have a room up under the eaves where I can look out on my dad doing ordinary things like mowing the grass and my mum . . . errm, yes, here she comes carrying a basket of freshly picked fruit. Soon the house will be filled with the rich heady smell of home-baked blueberry muffins . . .

'You OK, babes?' Mum interrupts my train of thought.

'Umm, fine. Why?'

'You look kind of . . . pensive.'

'I was just thinking . . .'

'Umm? What about?'

'Oh, nothing really. Just what it would be like to be one of those people out there – I mean, like, an ordinary person.'

Mum peers out of the tinted window. 'Yes, I know, poor things . . . but they can't all be famous.'

'No, Mum, you don't understand. I'd like to be normal. Just an ordinary person for once.'

'You are an odd child. All those people would give their right . . . whatever-it-is to have what we've got.'

'I know, but Mum, now you're going to marry Oliver, we're going to be more famous than ever. I mean, like we'll have all his fans too.'

'Mmm. Just think what it will do for my career.'

'Mum, you never think of anything but your career. You never do anything but work. When did you last have a vacation?'

'Vacation?'

'You know, those things that other people take? They pack all their stuff up and go places. *Interesting* places.'

'There's no need to take on that tone Holly.'

'No, but Mum listen, I don't have school for another ten whole weeks and there's ages to go before the wedding . . .'

Mum looks at me thoughtfully. 'You know, Holly, you may be right. As a matter of fact I was thinking of taking time off before this marriage. I've told Vix to cancel all my engagements.'

'Really?'

'I was planning to go some place and detox. Oliver's got to stay over in Italy shooting that *Centurion* thing of his, so I'll be all on my own.'

'So we could spend some time together. We could get out of the city. Go somewhere where nobody knows who we are!'

'Hmm . . . maybe we could do that log cabin thing. Walk in the forest, bathe in the lakes, feel the fresh wind on our faces . . .' muses Mum.

'Exactly!'

Thursday 19th June
In a four-by-four en route for Pookhamsee,
way out in the Appalachian Mountains

Mum's driving. She looks tiny behind the wheel of our four-by-four. She's dressed for the part, though, in a checked shirt, blue jeans and cowboy boots, and she has her hair scraped up into a ponytail. I'm wearing my cowboy gear that she brought back from Vegas.

Mum's singing. Not the kind of stuff she sings on records, but silly campside stuff like 'She's a comin' round the mountain'. I'm doing the 'when she comes . . . when she comes . . .' bit and we're both in giggles because I keep coming in late and flat.

She'd wanted to book us into this luxury log-cabin resort – each suite had its own infinity pool and personal 24-hour butler – but I put my foot down. If we were going to have a true log-cabin experience, we needed an authentic log cabin. So a friend of Dad's has lent us a place way out away from it all. It's so authentic we'll have to pump our own water and it doesn't even have a telephone. But it's surrounded by umpteen square miles of virgin forest and it's on the edge of a lake we can bathe in. I'm hoping we may get a sighting of bears but I haven't mentioned this to Mum yet – she's not exactly into wildlife.

We're not taking any of the entourage with us. Not even Thierry. We are actually going to self-cater. Which shouldn't be too difficult, seeing as Mum will only eat raw food.

We're also going without bodyguards. Sid and Abdul have been given time off as this is a strictly girls-only vacation – except for Brandy, who's laid out on the back seat. We've borrowed him from Dad as stand-in security.

Even Daffyd and June are getting a holiday. Daffyd has flown back to Bangor where, at last, he'll have time to marry Bronwyn – although it may have to be a Register Office as it's such short notice. I'm wondering if she'll manage to cram the twelve bridesmaids into the office with them.

7.00 p.m.

We left before dawn and we've driven all day, but it still doesn't look like we'll get to the cabin before nightfall. At seven in the evening we are climbing steadily up a road that snakes its way through a dense forest of pine trees. I'm map-reading – a rather queasy business on this winding road.

'Keep an eye out for a turning that says Chug-a-hoopee Ridge,' I tell Mum.

'Right or left?'

'Errm . . . right.'

We go another thirty miles and we're still climbing. Although it's summer the air outside is getting cold and a mist is rising. There's a sheer drop on my side which I haven't told Mum about because I know she'd freak out. I just pray we don't meet anything coming the other way. This becomes more and more unlikely as darkness falls. Only a madman would drive down this road at night.

'We should be there by now,' says Mum.

'I know. I wonder if we've missed it.'

'It's near a town called Salinec and we haven't seen a town in ages.'

'But Salinec was way back,' I point out.

'Was it?'

'Yes, Mum, it was.'

We have to go another ten miles before Mum finds a place wide enough to turn round.

It takes three more hours of searching before we eventually nose the car into a forest clearing and find our 'truly authentic backwoods log cabin' illuminated in the car's headlights.

Mum is exhausted and I have a headache.

'Is this it?' demands Mum.

'It must be. We've tried all the roads and there's no other building.'

Mum climbs out of the car and stretches. I follow her. Brandy yawns and looks reluctant to descend. I just hope we don't have to push him out.

Well, the cabin certainly is authentic. Some of the gutter is hanging loose and there's a deep drift of leaves going up the steps. It doesn't look as if the place has been visited in years.

I try to distract Mum from the cabin by pointing out how brilliant the stars are and how silent it is.

There's a scurrying sound from above which sounds ominously rat-like.

'What was that?' says Mum clutching me.

'Probably a pine marten,' I say.

'What's a pine marten?'

'A cute little furry thing. You'll love them.'

'Vermin! I think we ought to go back right now.'

'Mum, we can't go down that mountain. It's too dangerous at night.' I now tell her about the sheer drop that was on my side. She freaks out.

'I'll sleep in the car then,' she says.

'Don't be so silly, it's fine. Now the key is meant to be hanging in the woodshed. Where's the woodshed?'

'That whole *thing* looks like a woodshed to me,' says Mum.

The woodshed is a kind of lean-to on one side of the cabin. It has a pump fixed to the outer wall and there's a door with a heart cut in it from which comes the unmistakable smell of a chemical lavatory.

We hadn't thought of bringing a torch. I fumble through a skein of spider webs before I locate the key.

'Got it!'

'Thank God for that! At least I can have a shower,' says Mum.

I force my way through the drift of leaves. The key turns with difficulty in the rusted lock and we stumble in.

'I can't find the light switch,' says Mum, feeling her way along the wall. I hadn't thought to mention the lack of electricity. There's a kerosene lamp on the table and a box of matches. I light a match and lift the glass and after a splutter the lamp leaps into life. By its illumination we find we're in a rough wood room, bare except for a bench, a table and a broken chair.

'Is this your father's idea of a joke?' demands Mum.

'No, honestly, I think Dad would love it here. The guy who owns it really likes to "get away from it all".'

'Might've been a better idea if he'd brought some of it with him,' commented Mum. 'So where's the bathroom?'

I open a door at the back which leads to a pantry with a stone sink in it.

'It must be upstairs.'

There's a ladder that leads to a kind of platform which seems to be the bedroom. At least there are two mattresses on the floor.

'It's not up here either,' I report.

'But it must be,' says Mum. 'Mustn't it?' she adds as the terrible truth sinks in. There is no bathroom.

'I think there's a loo outside,' I say.

'But where's the shower?'

'Dad said there's a lake.'

'Ugghh! Ugghh! Ugghh!' says Mum, sitting herself down on the stairs. 'I do NOT believe this.'

12.00 midnight

I got some water from the pump so at least we could have a wash. We have both washed. We have eaten what was left of the lunch from the coolbox and we are laid out on the mattresses, which are dry and clean and have sheets and blankets.

We've even sampled the 'facilities' and Mum is still recovering from her encounter with the spider webs. The spiders round here must be gargantuan – you could knit argyle sweaters with their webs.

Brandy has been tempted out of the car by a bowl of dog food and is now lying between our two mattresses, exuding a welcome kind of doggy heat.

'We're leaving soon as it's light,' is the last thing Mum says before she swallows a couple of sleeping pills and falls asleep.

Friday 20th June, 7.30 a.m.
Paradise!

I wake and lie listening to the sounds outside: birdsong, the wind in the trees, the occasional scuffle of pine martens(?) in the roof. These are all lost on Mum, who is dead to the world with her eye mask on and her earplugs in.

Our 'bedroom' has two tiny windows that go down to floor level. These are closed by little wooden shutters that I can reach from my mattress. I lever them open and find I'm looking straight out on the most breathtaking view.

A rocky path leads down between the pines to a lake shrouded in early morning mist. There's a jetty with a wooden canoe moored to it. The sun is already warm on my face and the air smells deliciously of fresh pine and herbs.

I leave Mum sleeping, throw on my clothes and take Brandy for a run. Once outside he goes plunging ahead of me down the path towards the lake. I lose sight of him as he lumbers round a corner and then hear a gigantic SPLASH!

Oh my God, he's fallen in the lake! Dad will never forgive me if he drowns. I am trying to remember the instructions for resuscitation and wondering whether the same applies to dogs when I round the bend and see Brandy swimming strongly out into the lake. He's after a floating branch and having secured it, he turns and swims back with a great doggy grin on his face. He climbs out and shakes himself, sending a rainbow shower of water over me, then lies on his back with his legs in the air rolling on the beach. It seems we have reached dog heaven.

There's a great flat rock that overhangs the water. It's already warm from the sun. Brandy and I stretch out on it and stare down into the water. The lake is so clear we can see fish swimming through a waving forest of weed far below. I turn over on my back and stare up into a sky that is a clear forget-me-not blue. Not a cloud to be seen. The sun is rising and it's getting hotter by the minute. It's going to be a perfect day.

The perfection is disturbed by the sound of footsteps. Mum appears, stumbling unevenly on platfom espadrilles. She's holding her hand to her head. 'Oh my God it's bright out here! Have you seen my sunglasses?'

'They're in the car, I think.'

'I could kill for a shower.'

'There's always the lake. Brandy's already been in.'

'Is that meant to be a recommendation?'

'It's cold. But it's lovely and clear.'

Mum came and joined us on the rock and stared down into the water.

'But there's plants and things *living* in there!'

'I know, but they're way down. We can swim over them.'

'What if there are crabs or octopuses or something in those weeds?'

'You don't get crabs or octopuses in lakes. Only fish.'

'They might bite.'

'Mum, fish don't bite people. They're too busy swimming away.'

Mum bends down and fills her hands with water and dips her face in.

'Oh, that's better,' she says. Then she walks to the edge of the rock and stares out over the lake with her arms crossed.

'It's so quiet here,' she says. 'I can't remember when I've heard quiet like this. It's kind of eerie.'

'No cars, no phones, no people hassling us,' I add.

'I think there's an island out there,' says Mum, screwing up her eyes.

'We could go in the canoe and have a picnic.'

'But we haven't any food left,' says Mum dreamily. 'We'd have to buy some.'

'Mum? I thought we were leaving?'

Mum turned and gave me a smile. 'Maybe we could stay just one day.'

'Oh thank you!'

'I guess they must have a supermarket somewhere round here.'

'OK, I'll make a list,' I say.

'I do hope they have fresh blueberries. I don't like to go a day without. They're anti-carcinogenic.'

11.30 a.m., Pookhamsee General Store

We have to drive thirty miles before we find a town. At the entrance I note signs directing us to two drive-thru fast-food restaurants.

My tummy rumbles despondently as the first one hoves into sight. Naturally, we're not drivin' thru, we're drivin' past. I catch tantalising glimpses of people happily dipping into packs of hot french fries and squidgy burgers and yummy, thick milk shakes . . .

'Mu-um?'

But Mum has a set expression on her face. We are NOT going to 'ruin' our 'authentic log cabin experience' by consuming processed foods.

Instead, after searching through countless sad little streets of single-storey dwellings, we come across Pookhamsee General Store.

The woman behind the counter is wearing size twenty Levi's and an outsize T-shirt with 'The Simpsons' printed on it. She looks as if she spends most of her life happily drivin' thru and tuckin' in. She eyes Mum and me with the wary look of someone not used to 'furriners' in her store.

'And what can I do for you today?' she asks, leaning on the counter chewing gum.

'Oh hi!' says Mum, brandishing our list. 'We've got all the stuff we need written down. It's mostly fruit and vegetables.' She hands the list over.

The woman reads down it, sucking her breath past her gum. She turns slowly and casts a knowing glance along her shelves.

I've been having a look round. I haven't seen much in the way of fresh fruit or veg – apart from a couple of grapefruit dimpled with age and some blackened bananas. But I guess she keeps the fresh stuff out back in a chiller cabinet or something.

'Veg-e-tables,' says the woman, spelling out the syllables as if this is some strange new word. 'Well, I can do beans . . .' She reaches down a can of baked beans and slams it on the counter.

'No, you don't understand,' says Mum. 'It's fresh vegetables I want, not cooked in tomatoey ketchuppy stuff.'

'*Fresh* beans?' says the woman, as if we're asking for caviar or something. (That's further down the list.)

'Everything fresh. I'm on this diet, you see . . .'

This is not exactly tactful in the circumstances. The woman eyes Mum's body up and down, vainly searching for a stray bit of surplus flesh.

'And what kind of diet would that be?' she asks suspiciously.

'Well, as diets go, it's really simple,' says Mum, launching into her 'Diet according to Saint Kandhi' sermon. (If Mum

180

thinks she has a convert on her hands, she is SO-OO wrong.) 'You just keep to raw foods, you see . . .'

The woman shifts her gum over to the other side of her mouth.

'Raw?' she asks uncomprehendingly.

'Raw . . . fresh . . . food . . .' says Mum, as if she's trying to communicate with someone hard of hearing. She's fast losing her cool.

I am starting to squirm with embarrassment.

'Mum,' I pull at her sleeve. 'I don't think they stock fresh food apart from . . .' I point out the fruit.

'What *is* that fruit?' demands Mum.

'Why, that's grapefruit, ma-am.'

'Is it?' (I don't think Mum's recently seen grapefruit that isn't all cut round and perfectly segmented by Thierry.) 'I'll take them,' says Mum. 'And you must at least have some salad or something.'

The lady calls out the back: 'Hal!'

'Yeah?'

'Lady here wants some salad.'

'Yeah?'

'Hal!'

'What is it, Ma?'

'You get out here and take the lady round to Barney's patch – she wants salad.'

There's a sound of creaking bedsprings and Hal comes out. He's as gaunt and spare as his ma is large. He eyes my mum thoughtfully.

'Well, howdy!' he says.

'Salad,' says Mum, still in her 'I'm-trying-to-communicate-with-deaf-imbeciles' tone of voice. 'And anything else you might have that doesn't have additives or preservatives or anything else toxic in it.'

'You'll be meaning organic?' says Hal, who's starting to get her drift.

'Exactly.'

'Well, ma-am, you don't get more organic than Barney's patch.' He's leading us round the back of the shop.

Mum and I follow. Out at the back, between the rusting hulk of a Cadillac and a pile of tyres, there's a patch of soil with some vegetables growing in it. There's an old boy sitting on an oil drum under a tree. He's pointed out to us as Barney. He looks like he dates back to a time when if you needed food, you grew it.

Mum stares at the patch with a creased brow. This is nature in the raw, attached to the soil – nothing like the stuff you get on assorted salad platters.

Hal takes out a pocket knife and opens it. As a mark of respect to Mum he wipes it on his jeans, then bends down and chops off a lettuce. He passes it to Mum.

'That's as fresh as you'll get round here,' he says.

'And how about some of that parsley . . .' says Mum, indicating towards some fluffy leaves wiffling in the breeze.

'That ain't parsley, that's carrots,' calls out Barney.

'How clever of you. We'll have some of those too. What else have you got?'

'I got beets . . .' says Barney.

'No, Mum . . . we don't need . . .' (Beetroot!)

'Fine. Good. We'll take some of those too.'

Back in the shop Mum also buys some salad oil and vinegar and tinned dog food for Brandy.

While we were out the back the woman has warmed to Mum's raw food idea and has started to think laterally. She's found some packs of nuts and sunflower seeds, and Mum adds a great big tub of yogurt and a couple of litres of milk. I'm wondering if I can sneak in some Lucky Charms or potato chips or Snickers while she isn't looking, but I'm feeling faint with hunger by now and in no fit state to be devious.

Back at the cabin we stagger into the kitchen with our produce. I think Mum's hungry too. She's gone rather quiet.

I'm sent to pump water while Mum dismembers the lettuce.

As I'm filling the bucket there's a muffled scream from the house. I find Mum with a knife in her hand, backing off from the salad.

'What's wrong?'

'There's like squirmy things in it.'

I look. There are three eelworms and a minuscule slug.

'Why don't I do the lettuce and you do the grapefruit?' I suggest. 'You know, segment it, like Thierry does.'

'OK, if you're sure you know what you're doing.'

I repatriate the eelworms and the slug to the great outdoors and wash the lettuce.

Mum, meanwhile, is standing over the chopping board looking confused.

'There's something wrong with this grapefruit,' she says.

'It's probably just old.'

'No, it's all different inside. It doesn't have those little triangles like it's meant to.'

I peer over her shoulder and identify the cause of the problem. Instead of cutting the grapefruit round its equator, Mum's taken a North/South axis and encountered the segments sideways on.

2.00 p.m., on the island

We'd rowed out to the island with our 'meal', complete with fishing rods and swimming costumes.

The salad wasn't bad. I put lots of nuts and sunflower seeds in it. The carrots were sweet but kind of gritty. I think maybe we should've peeled them. To my relief, I was let off the beetroot – even Mum couldn't chomp her way through that raw.

Once we'd finished eating we stretched out on the beach sunbathing.

'Honestly, Mum,' I said as I rubbed suntan lotion into her back. 'What did you and Dad do for food before you got famous?'

'Eggs,' said Mum after a moment's hesitation. 'We lived on eggs. There was this poultry farm near the trailer park. They sold the eggs that were odd shapes off cheap. I could do eggs every which way. Never been able to touch them since.'

'Was that before I was born?'

'Yeah. I was only a kid myself. Sixteen when I met your dad.'

'You were only three years older than me.'

'Uh-huh. Wasn't very bright of me, was it?'

'Who cares – if you really loved him.'

184

Mum stretched out with a sigh.

'I worshipped him. I thought he was a god. The greatest genius that ever lived.'

'So what changed?'

Mum turned over and stared up into the sky. 'I grew up, I guess. I found out he was only an ordinary human being like everyone else. And I couldn't take the disappointment.'

'But he *was* a genius, wasn't he?'

'He was holding me back,' said Mum with a frown. 'I could see the way forward. I was going to dig my way out of that mobile home if it killed me. You've no idea what it was like. People rowing next door sounding like they were in the trailer, you screaming, no money – you don't want to know about it.'

She turned on to her front and closed her eyes.

I did want to know about it, but I could tell that Mum didn't want to talk any longer. She fell asleep after that.

I contented myself with playing with Brandy, throwing sticks for him as far as I could into the lake.

After half an hour or so Mum must've woken up. She came over to me fiddling with her mobile.

'What's happened? I can't seem to make it work,' she said.

I looked over her shoulder. 'You're not getting a signal, that's why. It must be because of the mountains.'

Mum looked at me with big horrified eyes. 'You mean we're out of contact?'

'Mum, what do you think people did before they had phones?'

'But what if someone's trying to get hold of me? To make a decision or something?'

'Vix can deal with it. You're supposed to be on vacation. Whatever it is can wait.'

She stared at me. 'You know something? You're right.'

'No phones, no people, no decisions. Think about it.'

A slow grin spread over her face. 'Jeez, you're right!'

'You up for a swim?' I asked.

'Well, I guess since there isn't a gym, I'd better do something . . .'

'OK, last one in the water is a –'

I didn't have time to finish the sentence as Mum was already plunging in ahead of me.

Ten minutes later Mum, Brandy and I were swimming way out in the lake. After the first shock of the plunge in, the water was heavenly. I have to say this for her – all those workouts Mum does keep her pretty fit. She easily outpaced Brandy and me. When we reached her she was floating on her back staring up into the sky.

'Heaven!' she said with a sigh.

'Mmm, it is, isn't it?'

'Maybe we should stay another night.'

We spent the rest of the afternoon fishing from the shore. Now you'd think fishing would be against my principles, but I revised my principles as the day wore on due to hunger. By evening my principles had subtly switched from 'no killing innocent animals' to 'no killing innocent animals unless to eat in times of real need'.

Just as we were about to give up and paddle back, Mum's fishing line went taut.

'Oh my God! I've caught something!' she squealed. 'What do I do now?'

I hadn't seen her this excited since she got her first platinum disc.

We could see the fish thrashing around. It was a big one. Back and forth it went, dragging the line with it. We both stood on the beach feeling helpless. I'd always thought of fishing as a nice peaceful outdoor activity. The reality of actually having to haul out a live fish and kill it was something else.

This dilemma was solved by Brandy, who swam out and brought the fish back in his jaws. He dropped it at my feet. It was dead. And it was a salmon.

Mum came and joined me. 'Do you think if we sliced it thin, we could make sushi?' she asked.

'Don't you have to smoke salmon for sushi?'

Mum shrugged. 'I guess we could build a fire.'

8.00 p.m.

We've paddled back from the island with Brandy and the salmon. Mum and I are now well and truly hungry. Lunch seems like hours back. Grapefruit and salad, even with lots of nuts and seeds in it, doesn't keep you going for long.

We have collected a great big pile of brushwood and I've managed to hang the salmon above it by the ingenious use of a piece of bent metal. Brandy is watching all this with curiosity. It's OK for him, he's had a big bowl of dog food. When I opened the can it gave off the most delicious smell of rich beef stew. I nearly ate a spoonful. So you can see how hungry I was.

'I reckon we could light the fire now,' I say to Mum.

'How long do you think it will take to smoke?'

'Probably depends on the weight. It's a pretty big fish.'

'Oh my God! Guts!' Mum exclaims with a sudden uncharacteristic bit of foresight.

'What do you mean, guts?'

'It's got guts in it. I remember now from when I was a kid. You have to ask the fishmonger to take them out,' says Mum.

I stare at the fish. Hazy memories of my convent Biology lessons tell me she's right – *nothing can live without guts*.

8.30 p.m.

As an aspiring vet, I can now claim to have had my first experience of surgery. The salmon came off worse – marginally. Mum went and sheltered in the cabin while I attacked it with a knife.

The fish was full of horrible, slimy, slithery stuff which smelt disgusting. Even Brandy backed off a bit. But with tremendous strength of character I have performed the operation, buried the guts, and the salmon is now back suspended above the fire ready for smoking.

'Can I come out now?' asks Mum.

'All clear.'

It is a brilliant fire. The brushwood is really dry and the flames are soon licking up round the fish. We can hear it fizzling and crackling.

'It's smoking nicely,' comments Mum.

I say nothing but go and get plates and knives and forks and what is left of the salad.

After about twenty minutes the fish is done. I take it down and carve it. It has beautiful pinky white flesh and not too many bones. I don't let on to Mum that the fish isn't smoked but cooked because I know she won't eat it.

When we finish our meal I give what is left of the fish to Brandy.

Then I go out and join Mum. She is down by the lake lying on her back on the rock, staring up into the sky. The first bright star of the night, Venus, is just appearing above us.

'I guess we don't really have to leave first thing in the morning . . .' she says dreamily.

'You mean we can stay for one more day?'

'Why not?'

So that's what we did. Each day we extended our stay by another day. Mum even managed to persuade Hal to haul himself off his bed at regular intervals and drive out with supplies. He'd kind of cottoned on to Mum's diet thing and from somewhere he conjured up things unheard of in Pookhamsee – like parma ham and smoke-cured beef and sun-dried tomatoes.

He was helpful too. I was carrying out the trash when he said, 'I'll take that for you if you like and dump it in town.'

Monday 23rd June, 11.30 a.m.
Paradise Lost

Mum and I are sunbathing on our favourite beach on the island. The water is lapping against the rocks . . . birds are singing . . . I've never seen Mum so relaxed and happy.

189

'What's that noise?' asks Mum sleepily.

I listen. 'Sounds like a car.'

'More than one.'

'Probably forest workers or something.'

'Sounds like they've stopped at the cabin.

They have. I can hear footsteps crunching down the path. There are figures moving on the jetty and some of them are pointing in our direction.

'Oh my God!' says Mum, covering herself up.

I sit up too. 'What's going on?'

There's the sound of automatic cameras going off in the distance.

'It's the press,' says Mum. 'How on earth did they know where to find us?'

2.30 p.m.

Mum and I are in the four-by-four heading along the winding road down the mountain. Mum has her dark glasses on and is spitting fire.

'Never, never let anyone get their hands on our garbage!' Mum is saying.

'But how was I to know? I thought he was just being kind.'

'Every single scrap of trash has to be incinerated under supervision. And that's *after* the paperwork has been through the shredder. Fans have been known to spend months collaging together as little as a cheque stub.'

'But we can't be sure it was Hal.'

As we pass Pookhamsee General Store, Hal is leaning up against the doorway looking dead pleased with himself.

Beside him is a big hand-painted sign. In wonky letters
it says:

POOKHAMSEE GENERAL STORE
Suppliers to the stars
KANDHI SHOPS HERE

Mum settles her dark glasses more firmly on her nose and
drives past, ignoring his frantic waving.

Tuesday 24th June
The Plaza Residenza

Once back home I check my mobile. I find I have a text from
Becky.

> **Greetings from an ancient**
> **civilisation. Remember England?**
> **I'm up for Young Musician of the Year**
> **again.**
> **But don't stand a chance on my**
> **current violin.**
> **anything happened about the donation?**
> **luv**
> **Becky x**

I'd better go check whether Mum's donated to her charity
list lately.

I locate Vix in Mum's office.

'Yeah, she's pretty up to date,' she says. 'She's given to all the major disaster funds, art foundations, research organisations, the blind, the dumb, the deaf, the limbless and the legless . . .'

'Did she send anything to someone called Becky Marchant? I put her on the list.'

'Not that I know of. You'd better ask her.'

Mum is going through her mail. It's been already sorted by Vix so it's mainly fan mail. This is a well-timed moment. Fan mail always puts her in a good mood.

'Hi, babes! What is it?' She offers a cheek for a mumsy kiss.

'You know that friend of mine, Becky?'

'The one at the convent? Yes.'

'Well, she's not at the convent any more. She's at this special music school in London.'

Mum is reading a letter written on pink paper with a smile on her face. 'So?'

'Well, she desperately needs a proper violin. Like a Stradivarius. And she can't afford it.'

'Hollywood,' says Mum with a sigh, 'I'm not made of money, you know. Besides, that sort of gift isn't tax deductible.'

'But you did buy Marlowe a ranch.'

'Marlowe deserved it. Look what he did for me.'

'But Mu-um! Becky really needs this violin. She's up for a big competition and she doesn't stand a chance without it. So I thought seeing as you're always giving to deserving causes –'

'All right, I'll think about it. Now can Vix and I have a moment's peace? We have a wedding to plan in case you'd forgotten.'

'As if . . .' whispers Vix, rolling her eyes.

It seems that in our absence Vix has hired a wedding planner. A wise move. With her attitude to marriage she could well overlook something vital, like the preacher or something.

Our wedding planner is called Victor. He's told Mum not to worry about the teensiest little thing – he's in charge, it's all being taken care of. Vix had not anticipated that she would be expected to work for Victor, doing menial tasks like looking after the guest list. Naturally, she is SO NOT happy with this.

The plan is to have the wedding way up in the Hollywood Hills in the garden of a private house. An old friend of Mum's, Elwyn Jones, has offered his home.

'Elwyn Jones!' I exclaimed when I heard.

'Yes, babes, it'll be nice for you to meet up with your godfather.'

'I didn't even know I had a godfather.' (This must date back to one of Mum's Christian phases.)

'You had several. We stars do these things for each other. But Elwyn is the only one whose fame has really lasted. The others just kind of faded away.'

Elwyn Jones! I'd seen some old video footage of him when he was at the height of his punk phase. He had a red, white and blue Mohican and wore a skirt. Cool! Some godfather!

'Elwyn's place is totally isolated,' Mum continued. 'Not overlooked from anywhere. A really romantic secret rendezvous, just big enough for my dearest and closest friends.'

She turned to Vix. 'So how are you getting on with the guest list?'

'I don't know if you've given me a big enough budget to get all of them. Roma Sheriton is trying to push us up another thousand.'

'Mum, you don't mean to say you're *paying* people to come to your wedding?'

Mum pouted. 'It's really the only way to ensure you get the A-list. Honestly Holly, we don't want to be stuck with a load of nobodies.'

'But how are you going to keep it secret if you've got all these people coming?'

'Don't you worry your little head about it,' said Victor. 'No one's going to be told the actual venue until the very last minute.'

Victor picked up a pile of his papers and swept out of the room.

'It's a logistics nightmare,' muttered Vix as he left. 'I'm already having to do a daily traffic survey by helicopter just to fix the timings. Not to mention the weather . . .'

'What about Oliver's guests? Won't they be coming from England?' I asked.

'Oliver doesn't need guests,' said Mum. 'He'd only want to ask a load of those frumpy old relations of his, who'd ruin the photos.'

'But Mum, you can't just have young and beautiful people. I mean, you are going to ask Gi-Gi, aren't you?'

'She'll have to stand at the back, but of course . . .'

And then I had a sudden thought. 'And what about your mum? Anna?'

Mum put on her 'tragic abandoned' expression. 'I don't think she'd want to come.'

'But you ought to invite her all the same. She *is* your mother.'

'She never made it to any of my other weddings,' said Mum.

'She might've done, if she'd known they were on,' muttered Vix.

(Perhaps I ought to explain here. Mum's mum – my grandmother, Anastasia – abandoned Mum when she was a baby. She went off with the orange people – 'all shaven heads and sandals', as Mum puts it. Mum says that, according to her analyst, she has been deeply scarred by this.)

'The next thing you'll want is for me to invite your father,' said Mum.

'Yes, why not invite all your exes? We could charter a jumbo,' said Vix.

I frowned at her. Vix could have been more supportive.

'Well, there's no need to put Dad's name on the list. He wouldn't want to come. He loathes this sort of thing.'

Wednesday 25th June, 8.00 a.m.
The Plaza Residenza

Mum has taken to making unscheduled visits to my bedroom since our great bonding trip. (There are downsides to having a

195

loving mother.) On this particular morning she breaks into a very important dream in which I'm a really famous vet anaesthetising a race horse, and greets me with the news that Shug's new single has risen to Number 19 in the singles charts.

'So what?' I say as I turn over.

'I thought you'd be interested, that's all.'

'I can't see why you're his biggest fan all of a sudden.'

'He's *Oliver's* son, in case you've forgotten.'

'Ugghh! How could I?'

'And his father's very fond of him.'

'Yeah, I wonder how many millions of copies he bought of that sad little single?' With that I pull the covers over my head and try to get back to sleep.

Later, when I go and get my breakfast and carry it back to the salon, I have my peace shattered by Mum turning on the radio.

After a few bands, the first chords of 'Grab-Machine' ring out and Mum turns the volume up. She's humming and tapping her fingers to the beat.

I'm seething. Mum's seems to have totally *wiped* Shug's past behaviour. Now he's going to be official stepson it seems he can do no wrong.

In the shower I find the dumb tune is running through my head. Ugghh!

Later, when I turn on my TV, I find Contrôle Technique's on live. Shug's wearing this skin-tight T-shirt to give us all the treat of seeing his pecs, and he's wiggling his body round like it's the best bit of male flesh in the entire universe. What an ego-tripper! But the girls down below dancing in the front are lapping it up. They're waving their arms to the beat. If they get any closer, they'll get trodden on.

As soon as I turn off the TV I find I have a text from Becky:

Disaster!
William has gone off with first flute
E> broken
Bx

Well, what did she expect? Boy-hopping never works out. I reply with the classic:

rejection is character-building
HBШx

Almost immediately I get back the answer

b*ll*cks
B

Thursday 26th June onwards
The Plaza Residenza

Be warned: absolutely nothing is going to happen from now on apart from wedding preparations.

(PLUS 'Grab-Machine' slowly rising up the charts – uggh-grrr!)

Friday 27th June, 9.00 a.m.
The Plaza Residenza

Vix announces that the 'hardware' has arrived from Tiffany. These are two platinum bands, identical except for size, set with Mum and Oliver's birthstones and engraved with their star signs, their blood groups and their names in Sanskrit.

Why Sanskrit? Apparently it's the in-language this year.

('Grab-Machine' is at Number 17.)

Saturday 28th June, 12.00 noon

Mum and Victor are having a lunch meeting. I join them at the table. Nobody acknowledges my presence – they're far too busy to notice me. I manage to grab some salad as it's passed.

Mum is interrogating Victor about The Cake.

'I've been on to all known caterers in LA and found two who can do a ten-tier, but they're not so happy with the music bit.'

'Tell them to get on to Panasonic to put their sound engineers on the case,' says Mum. 'Doesn't matter how much it costs.'

'What music bit?' I ask.

Mum and Victor pause and realise I exist.

'It's a big secret,' says Victor, lowering his voice as if the walls are going to hear or something. 'You've got to promise not to tell a soul.'

'Victor's had this stroke of genius,' says Mum. 'When

Oliver and I cut the cake, it's going to play "Kandidly Yours". Out of all my singles, it's Oliver's favourite.'

Vix rolls her eyes at me from behind Victor's back, but I do not respond. I reckon this could make a truly romantic moment.

Sunday 29th June, 10.00 a.m.
The Plaza Residenza

Victor has put in an order for 30,000 Kandhi roses to be airfreighted over from Europe. It's a rose that was named after Mum at this massive flower show in Chelsea, London – they don't grow them in the States yet. Apparently to get them all to bloom on the right day they have to put acres of greenhouses into a mini eco-climate with timed misting and artificial daylight.

('Grab-Machine' is at Number 16.)

Monday 30th June, 12.00 noon
The Plaza Residenza

The first wedding gifts have started to arrive. I am allowed to unwrap them as long as I keep the cards really carefully so that Vix can send personal handwritten thank yous from Mum.

The first parcel I open is a set of sheets and pillowcases from Fortnum and Mason in London. They're in ivory satin with a deep blue embroidered monogram.

It's a pity about Oliver and Mum's initials. Having OK written on all your satin pillowcases kind of brings the tone down.

The second is an item so weird that I have to read the accompanying literature to make out what it is. It's a platinum-coated candle-snuffer, guaranteed to snuff out candles without endangering your health by inhalation of noxious substances or the risk of Repetitive Strain Injury. I guess some people must snuff an awful lot of candles.

('Grab-Machine' seems stuck at Number 16. Huh!)

Tuesday 1st July, 8.00 a.m.
The Plaza Residenza

Chaos! Gi-Gi has announced that she has managed to persuade the choir from the Russian Orthodox Church in Maida Vale to sing at Mum's wedding. I think Gi-Gi is under the impression the wedding is going to be a full-blown church affair, not an excuse for a lavish and horribly expensive party in a garden.

Mum is SO-OO not happy about this. She and Victor have already planned the music. There's going to be a medley of her early hits transcribed for organ as she makes her entrance. This will be followed by a truly emotional bit. Just as Mum and Oliver exchange rings, an entire string orchestra is going to rise from behind the rhododendrons on a motorised dais and provide the backing for Mum to sing 'Only You' (Platinum, 1998) to Oliver. Then, of course, there'll be 'Kandidly Yours' as they cut the cake.

A Russian choir is SO NOT going to fit in with their scheme of things.

Vix has been put on to the job of explaining tactfully to Gi-Gi that a Russian choir is going to be around fifty voices too many. Mum's is the only voice she wants at her wedding.

Gi-Gi is so shocked by this news that she says she won't come. So I guess she'll have to see the wedding later on video like all the other relations Mum says she can't fit in the garden.

Gift of the day: A diamond-encrusted camel saddle from the Sultan of Brindal. The camel is following by sea-freight.

(Grab-Machine has risen to Number 15.)

Wednesday 2nd July, 9.00 a.m.
The Plaza Residenza

Mum and Victor are going through the final details of the wedding programme before it goes to the printers. They're stuck on who is going to give the spoken addresses.

'Oliver's going to speak, of course. He's doing some French thing about a woman called Roxanne, but in English, of course. And then there's Shug. He has to say something because he's best man,' says Mum.

'Shug's going to be *best man*? You didn't tell me!' (Best man and bridesmaid – they're always thrown together.)

'Yes, isn't it sweet? He and Oliver, they're so close.'

'They've got a lot in common. Like the same *big heads*.'

Mum ignores this.

'And of course the preacher has to give his address,' says Victor, 'but we need another speaker from your side of the family . . .'

Mum and Victor now turn their gaze on me.

'Me? No way! You know how I hate doing anything like that.'

'But you *are* my daughter. And if Shug can do it . . .'

(Shug can do it. Sullen, non-cooperative Shug who wouldn't do anything for anyone?)

'He's making up his speech himself,' says Mum.

'You better check it for expletives then.'

'Nonsense!' says Mum. 'Shug's really turning into a nice boy. He's just misunderstood, that's all.'

I make no comment. Shug has clearly been sucking up to Mum like mad.

'But if you'd really rather not . . .'

I can just imagine the way Shug will gloat if he hears I'm too shy to say something. 'Chickening out' will be the least of his comments.

'Oh, I suppose if Shug's going to do something, I'd better.'

'Good. Now, what was that piece that you were doing last year with Rupert? That marriagey thing.'

'"Let me not to the marriage of true minds . . ."?'

'Yeah. I seem to remember it was by someone famous –'

'Shakespeare.'

'Shakespeare,' says Victor. 'He'll do. He's one of those

all-time classics. Like Elvis – never dates. So what's this number called?

'Sonnet number one hundred and sixteen.' (It was engraved on my memory.)

'Not exactly a zingy title, but it'll have to do . . .'

Thursday 2nd July, 2.00 p.m. The Plaza Residenza

Thierry is 'in conference' with Victor over the wedding menu. Now that Mum has eased up on her 'only raw food' regime since the salmon incident, his job should be easier.

However, according to Victor:

1) We can't have anything containing pork, ham or bacon as some of the guests are Jewish.

2) We can't have anything containing veal or foie gras as there will be other animal liberators apart from myself present.

3) We can't have any smoked foods because, according to the latest food safety scares, these could possibly be carcinogenic (same goes for soya sauce, black pepper, artificial sweeteners and anything with colourings e-numbered between 1000 and 5001).

4) We can't have anything with grapefruit in it, in case someone is on hayfever pills and goes into toxic shock. (The wedding is in a garden, after all.)

5) Same goes for anything containing peanuts or

peanut derivatives, unless we allergy-test all the guests on entrance.

6) Nothing with a high fat content because quite a lot of Mum's friends are on fat-free diets (same goes for sugar, and non-sugar supplements take you back to the no-carcinogens problem).

7) We have to danger-flag all non-pasteurised cheeses because some of the guests may be pregnant. Same goes for anything containing alcohol — at least half of Mum's friends are signed-up members of AA.

8) And we can't have any foodstuffs from countries where workers are a) exploited, b) under a politically corrupt dictatorship, c) under repressive religious domination, or d) communist.

'So what are we going to eat?' asks Mum.

'We-ell,' says Thierry, his shoulders going into a kind of automatic French reflex shrug, 'eef I was you Kandhi, I would simply prepare delicious food in my own way. Eef we kill the guests, let them sue. You can always pay up – you're so loaded.'

Gift of the day: An 18th-century Florentine baroque gilded love seat covered in its original hand-stitched antique petit point from Oliver's Italian director, Carlo Minetti. Mum's comment: 'You'd have thought Carlo would've known I'd gone minimal.'

('Grab-Machine' has slipped right down to Number 20, so there!)

Friday 4th July, 10.00 a.m.
The Plaza Residenza

Oliver's back. He flew in from Italy last night. They finished shooting early as the weather held and they didn't have to go into contingency time.

Mum has been out since dawn on essential body maintenance. She's gone for a mud massage and an algae body wrap, maybe waxing if they can locate a stray bodily hair that's been overlooked. Then she's having her tan resprayed in spite of the fact that she has a real tan from our vacation.

She panicked because Daffyd is still away on his honeymoon, but she has agreed to have her hair done by someone else as long as Daffyd is supervising on a video-link conference call and directing the scissors as they cut.

Question: Is Mum going to be able keep this standard up for her entire married life?

Gifts are now arriving by the hour. The doorbell has sounded and I have automatically pushed the Open button.

But it isn't a delivery. It's *Shug*.

'Hi!' he says to me. 'Where's your mum?'

'She's out. Why?'

'I've come to see her.'

'You've come to see Mum? Why?'

Close up, I can't help noticing he's slimmed down some since I last saw him. I become horribly aware that I'm dressed for bumming round the apartment. I'm in my least favourite tracksuit bottoms and I actually have my *pink fluffy slippers* on.

'How long's she gonna be?'

'I don't know. Why don't you come back another time?'

'No,' says Shug, turning away from me and wandering across the salon as if he's aiming to stay. 'I can wait.'

He sits himself down on one of the white leather couches. I hover. What am I expected to do? Entertain him?

I catch sight of myself in one of Mum's ceiling-to-floor mirrors. The mirror does NOT have good news for me. Shug may be my least favourite male in the universe, but he is male. And I do have my pride.

'I'll be back in a minute,' I say, shoving a pile of magazines in his direction.

I race into my suite and positively fall into the bathroom. Hurriedly, I fling on some make-up and scrape my hair into a ponytail band. I rake through my closet for my new flattering jeans. Where do clothes *go* when they know they're wanted? I can't leave Shug too long or he'll wonder what's going on. Only when I've thrown everything out on the floor do the jeans surface. I drag them on and force my feet into shoes, pulling-a-clean-T-shirt-over-my-head-as-I-head-back-into-the-salon – then . . . I saunter . . . slowly . . . back . . . into the room.

Shug looks up from the magazine he's been reading.

'Oh, you didn't have to change for me,' he says.

I can feel my face flaring bright red.

'I didn't change for you. I'm about to go out as a matter of fact.'

'Oh? Where?'

'Wouldn't you like to know?' (Wouldn't I!)

'Well, don't let me keep you.' He returns to his magazine.

I pause. He's really getting to me now. I can feel anger brewing up inside, but I'm not going to lose my temper. I want to show him that I'm a female worthy of respect. He can't simply walk over me like this. So I stand my ground and watch him for a while. I can tell he's pretending to ignore me. He's not really reading that magazine.

'Not going out then?' he asks without looking up.

'I can't go out now. What will Mum do if she comes back and finds you here alone?'

'Don't worry about me. I can handle older women. If she comes on to me, I'll just fend her off gently.'

His arrogance takes my breath away. I am about to lash out at him when he looks up. It's just an eye-flick from the magazine and back again.

He's kidding. Of course he is. I can feel a giggle surfacing. With difficulty I control my face. 'That was disgusting. Have you forgotten that my mother is about to marry your father?'

'How could I?' says Shug, spreading his arms wide at the mess of gift wrap and cartons spread over the floor. 'The whole world is waiting with bated breath to see if she turns up this time.'

'Oh, she'll turn up all right.'

'Yeah? How d'you know?'

'Improbable as it may seem, my mum really cares about your dad.'

'Does she?' There's another eye-flick at me, serious this time.

'Yes, she does. Believe me. I know Mum.'

'Good, because if she does anything more to hurt Dad I am personally going to throttle her,' says Shug.

I'm silent for a moment. It's kind of cute the way he cares about his dad, defending him like that.

'Is that why you came here today?' I ask in a calmer tone.

'Kind of. And I wanted to see you too.' There's a longer eye-flick at me this time. In spite of myself, I can't help noticing that Shug has nice eyes. I mean, *no way* near as nice as Rupert's – which are blue, pure sky blue – but nice-ish all the same.

'Me?'

'Is there anyone else in the room?'

'No.'

It's gone very quiet all of a sudden. I don't think the traffic has actually stopped rounding the corner from Fifth Avenue, it's just my heart pounding in my chest, drowning it out.

'Look, Holly . . .' he starts

I wait. I don't say anything. I just stand there. In some totally curious way I simply can't account for, I want to hear what he has to say.

'Don't you think it's about time we stopped fighting?' He looks up at me with that 'whipped Alsatian' expression of his.

I'm tempted, but I'm not going to let him off so easily. Not after the way he's treated me.

'I don't recollect *us* fighting. All I can remember is you being obnoxious –'

'Selective memory, eh?'

'No . . .'

'Each time we meet, you're like . . . like a she-cat with claws out.'

'No I'm not.' (But maybe he's right. Why is it Shug makes me so tense?)

'Yes you are.'

'No.'

'You know you are.' He gets up from the sofa and takes a few steps towards me.

'But I'm not.' (I'm backing off.)

'Just look at yourself right now.' (He's coming closer.) 'Look how you're on the defensive.'

'No I'm not.'

He's closing right in. He has nice white teeth – regular. His dad must've paid a fortune in orthodontics like my mum did.

I move back another step, which takes me right up to the wall. I can smell his aftershave. I can almost feel the heat of his body as he puts one hand up on the wall and – he can't be . . . he is . . . he's about to . . . his lips are approaching . . .

'Hi, you two!' Mum bursts into the apartment.

The two of us leap apart.

'Hi, Kandhi!' says Shug.

Mum goes to Shug first and gives him a hug. I watch fascinated. Not so long ago these two were out for each other's blood. Now they seem to have totally bonded.

'Sorry I wasn't here when you arrived.'

(She *knew* he was coming! She could've warned me.)

'Holly, be a babe and put some coffee on for us. Shug and I want to talk music.'

SAME but feels like YEARS later, 11.00 a.m.

I'm in the kitchen, staring at the coffee machine while my mind is doing whoozy whizzy things inside my head. What was going on in there just now with Shug?

Shug, I remind myself firmly, is the guy I loathe. No, heavier than that – *despise*. The guy who days ago I would have happily carved into bite-sized pieces and fed to my tropical fish.

Then I have a lightning flashback. I'm against the wall . . . He's leaning towards me and . . . NO! No way! I would not let Shug near me. Because I'm in love – truly, deeply, meaningfully IN LOVE – with Rupert.

I tell myself firmly to get a grip as I spoon ground coffee into the coffee filter paper. I turn on the filter machine and watch it as it slowly, in-fin-ite-ly slow-ly heats up. I want to dash back into the salon. I need to take another look at Shug. To confirm in my mind that he's not changed one bit. He's still that totally irritating, self-obsessed, arrogant, errm . . . and all those other things.

'How's that coffee going?' Shug is leaning in through the door.

'Coming.'

I pick up the coffee pot. Shug waits in the doorway so I have to kind of slide my body sideways past him. He's looking me straight in the eyes now with a kind of questioning look.

I DO NOT respond. I carry the coffee with complete composure to the table. Shug holds the door open for me as I go back for the cups. I get another eye-flick as I pass. I return with the cups and sit lightly down on the sofa beside Mum.

She hasn't noticed any of this. She's on the phone.

'Yeah Mike, I know, but if you could square it with *The Late Show* they could slot him in. They'd do it for me, I know.' She's nodding at Shug as if to say: 'Yes, you're on.'

Shug slides down on the sofa opposite me. His foot just glides ever so accidentally against mine under the coffee table.

I totally ignore it.

'Now who's for coffee?' I ask, cool, calm and collected. I pour three cups.

Shug takes a sip and chokes.

'What is this?'

'Coffee?'

'It's kinda sweet.'

Oh no I haven't! Yes, I have. I've absent-mindedly taken down a jar of pure dark demerara sugar and brewed a pot of it. It's Thierry's fault. The jars look SO-OO alike. It's a mistake anyone could've made.

Saturday 5th July, 10.00 a.m.
The Plaza Residenza

I wake and remember yesterday. Or to be more exact, I remember the precise moment just before Mum came into the apartment when I think Shug nearly . . . Oh my God! What nearly happened, but didn't because of Mum, was *my first kiss ever*! With *Shug* of all people! What an escape! Because I just know if he had kissed me – and I'm pretty sure he was going to – I would have totally messed up. Like banging noses or clashing teeth or having my tongue in

211

totally the wrong place or whatever . . . And then Shug would have known that I, Hollywood Bliss Winterman, have never been kissed before. I go hot and cold at the very thought. Imagine what would happen in September when I'm the new girl in his school! He'd probably tell all the other guys. How he would crow about it! He must *never, never* know.

Later, after a very long recovery process in the shower

I find Mum pitter-pattering around the apartment in bathrobe and bare feet, checking out the gifts and making little purring noises or sighs as appropriate.

She just loves the camel saddle – she's going to use it as a conversation piece. She's dragging it round the room, trying it in various locations, but none seems quite right. She's wandered out into the hallway with it.

Vix is on the phone to someone, enquiring about a delivery.

'Well, if you can't do a thousand I guess we'll have to take the five hundred and look around for more.'

She puts down the phone and calls over to me in an exhausted voice, 'Holly, you know about animals. Don't pigeons *eat* butterflies?'

'I imagine they do. They are insects. Why?'

'Well, Victor's got five hundred white fantail doves coming. But the thing is, your mum wants them let out simultaneously with a swarm of Giant Blue Ulysses butterflies. You know, kind of symbolic – her colour and Oliver's mingling . . .'

Hang on – my hackles are rising. Caged birds! Rare butterflies!

212

'But she can't!'

'That's what I said. Imagine the carnage.'

'No, but those doves – they'd have to be caged.'

Mum comes back at that moment, still dragging the saddle. 'That's the point, Holly. I'm *letting them out*. I thought you'd be *pleased*.'

'I know you're letting them out, but they have to be caged first.'

'But of course. How could I let them out if they weren't?' Mum's fast losing her cool.

'Mum, birds should not be caged *on principle*. And what about the butterflies?'

'Oh, they're OK. They'll be just hatched. Too young to know the difference.'

'I don't believe you! Using poor, innocent, just-hatched baby creatures to *decorate* your wedding.'

'Hollywood, if you knew what *people* are doing to get their hands on an invitation, you'd realise how lucky those creatures are.'

'Yeah, there are loads still bargaining for more cash,' Vix mutters evilly.

'Well, I'm going to get on to the National Ornithological Society and see what they say,' I threaten, reaching for my mobile.

'Don't you dare!' snaps Mum.

'You can't stop me.'

'And what about the butterflies?' asks Vix, giving me a sidelong look.

'Well, I guess they have a society too.'

'Oh Hollywood, you are being difficult,' says Mum.

'Mum, pigeons, doves or whatever *eat* butterflies. It's a totally dumb idea in the first place.'

Mum stares at me. 'Do they?'

'*Yes!*' Vix and I say in unison.

'OK, have it your own way both of you. Ruin my day.' Mum dumps the saddle on the floor. 'The one really important day of my life . . .'

She storms into her bedroom and slams the door.

Sunday 6th July, 3.00 p.m.
The Plaza Residenza

Just six days to go before the wedding.

Gift of the day: A set of sixty hand-etched monogrammed Venetian wine glasses with pure gold rims. The initials OK looks even odder surrounded by cupids and mermaids.

('Grab-Machine' has crept five places back up the charts. It's at Number 15.)

Monday 7th July
The Plaza Residenza

Shug was on *The Late Show* last night. I stayed awake to watch. It was odd how 'Grab-Machine' was starting to grow on me, because it was really pathetic. Shug came out with all this stuff about a guy who feels like the whole world is a game of chance. In the video he's standing buried waist-deep in trashy car parts and this great grab is coming down to get him. I mean, purr-leese? But I had to admit that Shug looked kind of OK in that tight white T-shirt. I mean, I can't remember Rupert wearing a T-shirt ever. Rupert was strictly of the shirt-with-long-sleeves-rolled-up type . . .

Tuesday 8th July, 9.00 p.m.
The Plaza Residenza

I got Abdul to drive me to Borders and I bought a copy of 'Grab-Machine'. I put it on as background music. The strange thing was that the more I listened to it, the more I realised that it had this kind of subtext. I guess it was about life really, and politics and the way the whole human race is helpless in the face of eternity . . .

But the really curious thing was, while it was on, a whole day went past without me thinking once about Rupert. It was even hard to picture him now. All I could remember were little bits which wouldn't stick together. And he was so far away – the other side of the world, in fact. And he'd only emailed me like *twice*. Did he really deserve the prime position as the love of my life?

I lay in bed a long time after that, wondering guiltily whether I was being horribly fickle. I mean, admittedly Rupert was unaware of my true, deep and eternal love, but it would be pretty hard-hearted to simply dump him.

Wednesday 9th July, 8.00 a.m.
The Plaza Residenza

I wake up with my mind running on the same theme. I wonder what Rupert is doing right now. Probably walking to the tap and filling his bucket with water which he's going to kind of sloosh over his perfect body. Back at the house, I imagine Juliette brewing coffee for him over a campfire. I wait for the familiar pang of jealousy. But it doesn't happen. Nothing. *Strange* . . . Surely I can't have stopped loving Rupert – just like that?

But he's got Juliette, hasn't he? You expect the guy you're passionately in love with to stay single at least. Look how he's treated me!

You know something? I reckon Rupert deserves to be dumped.

Having made the decision, I open my laptop.

Hi Rupert!

I followed this, with a ten-page email, in which I update him on everything that's happened since I've last seen him. No problem.

I can't think why I've been so hung up about it.

Later: Armando Mezzo's Private Clients' Suite

Mum and I go for the final fitting at Armando's. There are loads of press photographers camped outside the entrance, knowing that Mum's bound to come by.

Mum's doing her dark glasses, incognito, want-to-be-alone bit, but she still has time to pause in the lobby for a fleeting photo opportunity or two.

We are accompanied in the elevator by a guy with an automatic weapon. The Dress is having to be kept under round-the-clock armed guard in case anyone gets a sneak shot of it and publishes it ahead of time. Only Armando and two of his most trusted staff are allowed near it.

Armando pounces on Mum as soon as we're out of the elevator.

'Kandhi! Oh, I am so excited! You are going to be just such a dream in zis dress . . .'

(Mum recognises this for what it is – pure pre-sales softening up.)

'Yes Armando, sure I will. So where is it?'

'Ahhh . . .' says Armando. 'Zee moment has come . . .'

He walks over to an alcove which has been curtained off ceiling-to-floor with a long flouncy blind made of pearly satin. He presses a button. The blind slowly furls upwards to reveal a 'grotto' where The Dress is floating as if in a mist of metres of gauzy veil. It's beautiful. It's delicious. It's a dream of a dress.

'Hmm!' is Mum's only comment.

'But wait till you see it on . . .' says Armando.

Mum is swept into a changing room by two of Armando's assistants. I sit and wait on a little gilt chair.

Several minutes later she emerges looking totally amazing. Although she's tiny, Mum has a perfect figure (her cosmetic surgeon has seen to that), but Armando has somehow managed to give her top model dimensions (the three-inch-heel Blahniks may be helping). She positively floats into the room like a swan.

'Jeez, Armando!' she says in a very un-swanlike tone. 'There's a bone or whatever sticking right into my –'

'No!' says Armando. 'Impossible!'

'Right here . . .'

There is a great flap about the dress, which now has to be totally dismembered and resewn from scratch by Friday. When they've all recovered, I find I can get a word in to ask: 'What about my dress?'

Suddenly everyone remembers I'm there too.

My dress doesn't come out of a pearly grotto, it comes out of a box.

It's very nice really. It's pretty straightforward. Very straightforward. Very straight up and down. In short, I look like a column – a tall pearly-pink column. If you had three more of me, you could support a roof. But if Mum's a swan, I guess I'm child-of-swan – and we all know what they look like.

Thursday 10th July, 11.00 p.m.
The Plaza Residenza

Only two days to go before the wedding. Gifts are still arriving.

Gift of the day: The world's most uncomfortable chair made out of stag's antlers. Plus three more monogrammed bathrobe sets – they now have enough to clothe an entire Turkish bathhouse.

But along with today's deliveries comes a battered parcel wrapped in tatty brown paper and fraying string. For a moment I think Mum's relented and invited her mum, Anna, after all – the parcel looks homespun enough.

It's got a weird foreign stamp on it. But hang on – it's for *me*. That writing's familiar. My tummy turns over with a thump as I realise where I've seen it before – in red down the side of my essays. It's from *Rupert*.

I tear off the paper. (Oh, how could I have been so hasty and dumped him like that?) Inside, wrapped in newspaper, is the cutest little iguana made out of scrap metal – an old oilcan by the look of it – and there's a note and a photo.

I look at the photo first. There, in a dusty street, stands Rupert. He's wearing baggy khaki shorts and a *T-shirt*. And beside him – no, it can't be! Who is this woman who looks old enough to be his mother? I turn the photo over.

Me and Juliette taken in Blimii, it says.

Juliette! This is no sex kitten in faded denims, no raunchy babe in Army fatigues, no goddess in floaty *Out Of Africa* separates – no, Juliette is wearing the kind of outsize shorts that climb up the crotch and a sagging T-shirt that's tight in all the wrong places.

Oh Rupert, how could I have dumped you? I turn the photo back over. He's got a really fit body in that T-shirt. As fit or fitter than Shug's.

I read the note:

> *Dear Holly,*
> *When I saw this little iguana I thought of you.* (Aw. . . !)

It's long and skinny and has an expression on its face
a bit like you have when you're doing mental arithmetic.

I study the iguana. I guess it's quite pretty as iguanas go.

I was keeping it on my shelf. (My 'house' is now furnished
– I have a shelf.) But Juliette found it and threw it at me –
the little contretemps over the dinner still seems to rankle.
So I thought I'd send it to you.
How are plans going for the wedding?
How are you getting on with Oliver – and Shug!!!?
Love, Rupert x

And Shug! I think guiltily. How could I have been so untrue
to Rupert and had that totally out-of-character impulse
to . . . Yes, I have to admit it. Had Mum not come in at that
moment I might have had my first *precious, passionate* kiss with
Shug of all people!

Friday 11th July, 9.00 a.m.
The Plaza Residenza

Only one day to go before the wedding. Daffyd's back from
his honeymoon in the nick of time. He and Mum have been
up since dawn as he's had to do a total panic restyle. She
wants her hair tone matched to the dress. We're leaving for
LA at 12 noon. Oliver and Shug have gone on ahead. Mum
says she doesn't want to see Oliver again until the day of the

wedding – to make it more special. I think this is sweet – and SO-OO romantic. Vix says darkly that it's because she fears another blazing row and Oliver calling the whole thing off.

The apartment looks like a disaster area. Mum has had professional packers in to pack for the trip. All the wedding gifts are being rewrapped to take with us. They are going to be displayed for all the guests to admire at the reception (a neat way of shaming the people who have only sent, like, salad servers). My clothes are being packed just like Mum's between layers of crunchy tissue paper – my teddy and my PJs have never had such luxury treatment.

At 12 noon sharp a fleet of limos draws up in front of the Plaza Residenza. Mum and I get in the first one with Vix. After us come Daffyd and June and Sid and Abdul. The next one takes Thierry and Gervase. We're off to JFK.

First Class Cabin Flight AA 192 to LA, 2.30 p.m.

Mum is treating her entire entourage to a First Class Flight – she says she doesn't get married every day – although she does pretty often.

We're meant to have the whole First Class Cabin to ourselves, but as we take our seats I notice another person is already seated up front. By the look of it this someone is in total purdah, swathed in some strange orange robe from head to foot – not an inch of flesh showing.

I settle in my seat beside Mum but before I can ask her who this curious person up front might be, she's already tossed a couple of sleeping pills down her throat, put on her eye mask, inserted her earplugs and manoeuvred her seat into the reclining position. As usual she's going to use the flight to catch up on sleep.

I wonder whether I dare wake her. But now of all times Mum needs her beauty sleep. The flight attendants are passing round champagne and I'm given a juice. I notice that whoever-it-is in the front doesn't take any champagne. Maybe alcohol is against his or her religion.

The female flight attendant is doing the safety demonstration. Whoever-it-is doesn't appear to be watching as his or her head hasn't moved – obviously a seasoned traveller. That's when it strikes me. *Orange*. It must be. There's no other explanation. Mum has relented and asked Grandma Anna after all! She hasn't told me because she wants it to be a surprise. I want to leap out of my seat and run over to her and say, 'Hi, it's me Holly. I've been so longing to meet you.'

But I'll have to wait till the seat belt signs go off, so instead I sit in my seat fantasising about how brilliant it's going to be to have a real, live grandmother. I mean, I know Grandma Anna and I are going to have so much in common – according to Mum, she's really into nature and stuff. I have a brief and heady vision of the two of us, dressed in something silky and filmy, probably on horseback but maybe even on an elephant, fulfilling my dream, travelling across Rajasthan to visit the tigers in Ranthambore National Park.

But the seatbelt signs are not going off. There's a storm in the air and they're staying on because we're likely to encounter turbulence.

4.00 p.m.

They're bringing round trays of food. Basically I'm too excited to eat. I'm imagining all the things Grandma Anna and I will have to tell each other in order to catch up. I notice that she doesn't accept the food either. But she probably has brought her own supplies of that special macrobiotic stuff that orange people eat. I experience a slight negative twinge here. I mean, you expect grandmothers to be into stuff like milk chocs and layer cakes so they can kind of indulge you. She's not exactly a bundle of energy either. She's got her head down, probably asleep.

I watch a movie for a while. It's one I've seen, but I'm really into it when I find Daffyd is nudging me. The seatbelt signs are off and he's on his feet and stretching: 'Aren't you going to eat your food Holly? If not I'll have it,' he says. I pass it over to him.

'Daffyd?' I ask. 'Do you know who that person is up there in the front?' I point out Grandma Anna who seems to have slumped somewhat in her seat.

'Person?' says Daffyd screwing his eyes and looking in that direction.

'Yes – wearing orange.'

'Oh that's not a person Holly, that's the dress.'

They could have told me. All that excitement and anticipation over *nothing*!

I make my way up the aisle to check for myself. Sure enough the seat is occupied by a vast orange nylon zipper-bag with AM for Armando Mezzo embroidered boldly across the front. Apparently a First Class ticket has been bought for the wedding dress, so that it can have a seat to itself and travel with us in the cabin and not be packed up and creased in the hold. Great!

223

5.00 p.m.

I'm feeling totally let down. Not only have I NOT met the grandmother I've been longing my entire life to meet, I've also missed out on my first First Class meal. Daffyd scoffed the lot. I have to console myself with the most spectacular view from my First Class seat instead. The storm has cleared and we are flying through a totally clear sky over the Grand Canyon. I can see right down into it and it's a wonderful rare roast beef colour with the tiniest trickle of muddy river like gravy running along the bottom.

After the Grand Canyon we pass over a not-so-grand canyon and then several more which aren't grand at all, and suddenly we're out over open flat land. We're flying over what looks like some mad seamstress's love-quilt design. There are patchwork squares of green and brown and beige with odd green circles in between, threaded with silver where rivers are catching the light. Occasionally, there's a lone road drawn ruler-straight, stretching infinitely towards the far horizon.

This is the great empty interior of the US of A.

Same, 7.00 p.m.

We've made the trip from The City that Never Sleeps to The City that Never Walks. LA has been stretching out beneath us for quite some time. (It's 100 kilometres across, for your information.)

Mum has woken up, ordered three glasses of her usual still spa water (no ice), consumed them, and is now ready to disembark.

For some reason we are kept on the plane until last. 'Why aren't we going with the others?' I ask.

'Security,' says Mum. 'They promised to find a way for us to dodge the press.'

Below us on the tarmac is a van with a ventilator on top and 'VIP Pet Chauffeurs' printed on the side.

'You mean to say this is the best you could come up with?' complains Mum as we climb into the back.

The van is air-conditioned but smells faintly of the place where I got Brandy.

Mum sits herself down on one of the wooden benches. 'The things I've had to do to keep the venue secret!'

I can't tell you much about the journey. There were no windows in the van. All I can say is that the first bit was kind of straight and the last bit was kind of bendy.

8.00 p.m., Elwyn Jones's residence

We climb out of the van to find we are high up in the Holly-wood Hills. The sun is sinking in the sky, turning everything a kind of molten gold colour, and the view is mind-blowing.

And then, as I turn and scan the horizon, over in the distance I see my name written up fifty foot high:

HOLLYWOOD

in slightly wonky letters. And I feel welcomed and famous in a funny kind of way.

9.00 p.m., Elwyn Jones's garden

Elwyn's place is awesome. Totally, totally awesome. The steps running up to his front door are made of glass with a waterfall running underneath. (They're a perfect copy of the ones at the Wessex Hotel.) The garden is full of statues which would be copies too, if they weren't Elwyn's – according to Mum, these have been shipped over from Italy and they're all originals.

Elwyn's not there to greet us. He's in one or other of his houses in Cap Ferrat or Monte Carlo or wherever. But there's a housekeeper and a load of guys in uniform who sweep down the stairs and take charge of our luggage.

Elwyn's not going to arrive till tomorrow, in time for the ceremony. I'm a bit relieved by this because I know if he'd been here he and Mum would have ended up in a long reminiscence session and I'd be left out. But as it is, we'll have time on our own.

Mum and I are shown to our own private mini-mansion in the garden. There are two suites inside, one for me and one for Mum, plus a great big living area with double French windows leading out on to our own private terrace where a hot tub is gently bubbling.

The sun is sinking fast and the lights of LA are coming on, twinkling as far as the eye can see in the hazy evening light. A cold supper has been laid for us in the garden – all the things Mum likes best. They've obviously been briefed by Thierry.

Mum comes out behind me and leans on the balcony rail. 'Heaven, isn't it?

'Mmm.'

'Can you imagine anywhere more perfect to be married?'

(I can, in fact – like underwater with dolphins in atten-dance. Or in the rainforest in a cloud of tropical butterflies, or on a kind of tree-platform in a safari park with lions down below. But I say 'no' anyway to keep Mum happy.)

10.00 p.m.

We've had our supper and we're now lazing in the hot tub. Mum stretches out and closes her eyes.

'You do think I'm doing the right thing, babes, don't you?' she asks.

'Marrying Oliver? But of course I do.' (She could hardly change her mind at this late date.)

'You don't. I can tell you don't by the way you said it.'

'Mum, it's you who's marrying him, not me.'

'I know, but . . . maybe I've rushed into it a bit fast.'

'But you're crazy about him! You said so.'

'He can be quite difficult at times . . . and I think his hair is starting to recede, just a bit . . .'

'What does it matter about his hair? At least it's not grey.'

'You don't think he dyes it, do you?' Mum's eyes are wide open now.

'How should I know?'

'Oh my God! What *am* I doing?' Mum was staring at me with a scared look on her face.

'Mum, you can't have second thoughts *now*. The wedding's tomorrow.'

'What if I can't stop myself?'

227

'But it's too late to back out –'

'There are twelve whole hours before the ceremony.'

'What about all the guests and the presents and –'

'Oliver isn't the only man in the world, you know.'

'What d'you mean?'

Mum bit her lip. 'Well, Marlowe was very sweet to me . . .'

'*Marlowe*?'

'There's no need to take that tone.'

'Mum, Oliver is a thousand times better than Marlowe. I mean, he's got a brain for a start.'

'Oliver can be so condescending . . .'

'He's not too condescending to want to marry you.'

'But is he right for me? Truly, what do you think, Holly? You've got to tell me. Straight.'

(It was now or never. Mum was teetering on the brink. One word from me could push her over and the marriage tomorrow would not take place.)

I took a deep breath.

'Well?'

'Mum, you are so lucky. Every girl in the world worships Oliver, even Becky, and she's really hard to please.'

'That little friend of yours in England?'

'Mmm. A date with Oliver Bream – it's Becky's ultimate wish. It's right up there top of her Wish List – Number One. She wants it more than a Stradivarius. And she wants that really badly.'

'Mmm?' Mum was smiling now. 'Why does she want the Strad so badly?'

'I told you. She's going in for this big international competition, but she can't win unless she has a really good violin.'

'And she wants a date with Oliver more than this fiddle?'

'Yes.'

'Oh, that's really cute. I guess he is pretty wonderful, isn't he?'

'And he's a brilliant actor. I mean, let's face it, Mum. Who else could someone as famous as you marry?'

Mum leaned back and closed her eyes again.

'You're right. Of course you're right. It was just last-minute nerves, I guess.'

Saturday 12th July
The actual day! Elwyn Jones's residence

During the night I'd slept restlessly. My windows were open and I was subconsciously aware of something going on secretly, like a guerrilla army on the move, in the garden. I woke at one point and went to the window to check. In the moonlight, crates of Kandhi roses were being delivered from a refrigerated van, a magical forest of gilt chairs was on the move up the pathway, and a ghostly mist of snow-white tablecloths was being spread between the trees.

8.00 a.m.
I've overslept! Only two and half hours to go. I stumble into Mum's room to find the dress displayed on a dress

stand, swathed in transparent gauzy stuff to keep off the dust. Beneath it a pair of Manolos stand at the ready, and above it – the veil. All it lacks is Mum.

I find her in her bathroom, which is so crammed with people you can barely move (and it's a pretty large bathroom). June and Daffyd are there working on Mum's hair and make-up. There's an aromatherapist on each foot and a manicurist on each hand. The rest of Mum's body is having a panic last-minute re-oxygenation and tone-up in a hyperbaric suit. Her head is sticking out from it as if decapitated and presented on a plate.

'Hollywood, babes, come and give me a kiss and wish me luck,' she says. All her doubts of yesterday seem to have evaporated.

I lean over and kiss her. 'Good luck, Mum.'

'Now, Hollywood, you have gone over that piece you're reciting, haven't you?'

My heart does a minor somersault and thump at the mention of it. But curiously enough, I'm not totally panicking. I think it must be true what they say about phobias. Like people who are phobic about flying start by standing on chairs and jumping off and then move on to stepladders and tree houses until they can handle a thirty-minute round-the-city sightseeing flight. Well, now I've been on TV and survived I guess I've kind of got over the worst.

'Mum, I know it by heart. And anyway, Victor's put everyone's text on autocue, so I've only got to read it.'

But I go back to my room to practise all the same.

8.30 a.m.

Vix is in charge of texting the venue to all the different people involved. Because of the high level of secrecy required, this needs split-second timing. Each guest is being notified of the address leaving just enough time for them to make it.

9.00 a.m.

An army of caterers arrives in an unmarked coach. They are now seething around the tables like black ants.

9.15 a.m.

A refrigerated hearse arrives and the seafood is delivered in a coffin. (I'm not going to touch as much as a prawn. To my mind, this is taking secrecy that bit too far.)

9.30 a.m.

A car horn is sounding angrily. Elwyn has arrived to find he can't get his car into his garage. The hot-air balloon which is going to fly overhead and release two million scarlet rose petals (a panic last-minute replacement for the doves and butterflies) is being inflated under camouflage wraps and blocking the way.

I lean out of the window, trying to get a sight of him. I regret to tell all his past fans that all I see is a slightly tubby balding man in a perfectly ordinary white tuxedo. If this is the punk hero you all worshipped way back, you're in for a big disappointment.

9.45 a.m.

A furniture removal van draws up and the musicians file out, carrying their instruments. They disappear from sight behind the bank of rhododendrons.

9.50 a.m.

Panic attack! Apparently Mr Blackman has spotted a loophole in the pre-nup and Mum has to sign an amendment *before* the wedding takes place. Only trouble is, he's in court downtown and it has to be signed in his presence.

I am instructed to stay put and Vix and Victor are sent out to cover for her. (Mum can't admit to Oliver she's doing him out of another billion dollars, should they split.)

I catch a glimpse of her dressed in her wrap, running down the steps to a waiting car.

10.00 a.m.

Oliver and Shug arrive in a laundry van. Oliver tries to drop by and say 'hi' to Mum. I cover for her by telling them it's bad luck for the groom to see the bride before the wedding (even if they've been like cohabiting on and off for yonks).

10.30 a.m.

The guests have begun to arrive. There's a little trickle at first, and then more and more cars draw up. From my vantage point I can see Elwyn and Vix and Victor, plus Oliver and Shug out greeting them. They're being shown to their places on the little gilt chairs. They don't seem to suspect that one vital element of the wedding is currently *absent*.

232

10.31 a.m.

I zip myself into my pearly pink column and put on my satin shoes all the same.

10.45 a.m.

I reckon all the guests have arrived. Even Daffyd and June have taken up their places. All the little gilt chairs seem to be filled. *Still no Mum.*

Behind me I can hear the house phone ringing. I pounce on it. It's probably Mum caught in the traffic.

'Hello,' says a voice. 'Is that Elwyn Jones's residence?'

'Yes, it is.'

'Well, thank God we got you! This is the patisserie. We're still waiting to be notified for delivery of the cake.'

(The cake! The high point of the ceremony. The cake which is going to play 'Kandidly Yours' when Mum and Oliver cut it!)

'That is the Kandhi/Bream wedding location, isn't it?'

'Oh, it's here all right. You want the address?'

'Don't worry. We know where Mr Jones lives. We're on our way.'

I put the phone down. Good thing I answered it. How could Vix have forgotten the cake of all things? I knew she couldn't be trusted . . .

10.55 a.m.

The preacher arrives. I can see him standing and talking to Oliver and Shug. *Where is Mum?*

11.00 a.m.

The piano starts up with a medley of Mum's hits. A respectful silence has fallen over the guests. I can see Vix and Victor casting anxious glances down the driveway. There's still no sign of Mum. The pianist gets to the end of the medley and there is a slight hesitation before he begins at the beginning again.

11.06 a.m.

A car skids into the drive and does a half-turn practically on two wheels. Mum leaps out before it's even drawn to a halt and runs up the steps two at a time.

'Oh my God, Holly! Help me!' she pants. 'If Oliver thinks I've stood him up again he'll walk out. I know he will.'

Somehow with shaking hands we get her into her dress. She shoves her feet into her shoes and I clamp the veil to her head.

She turns for a moment and stares in the mirror and then turns back to me.

'How do I look?'

Mum is flushed from the panic, her make-up is running a bit, and the veil is a trifle lopsided. But I've never seen her looking more radiant.

'You look stellar, Mum. In fact you look *supernova*!'

'OK, let's go.'

11.21 a.m.

I don't think anyone has ever seen a bride go down an aisle at quite such a speed before. I had to run to keep up.

She nearly toppled Elwyn when she grabbed him by the arm. Oliver turned and smiled and said, with his typical cool, 'What kept you?'

Shug turned too and raised his eyebrows and winked at me. He was wearing a tux and he'd had his hair cut. It wasn't like a stegosaurus any more, it was more like a tyrannosaurus rex. They have smaller spikes.

The preacher kept his intro short – I reckon he must be used to marrying stars and knows they don't like being upstaged.

After that Shug moved up to the podium and took the mike to make his speech. I have to say, dressed up like that in a tux, he suddenly looked kind of young and shy. He cleared his voice as he cast his eye over the congregation.

'I have to admit,' he started, 'that when my dad first told me he was going to marry Kandhi, I thought I was in for the stepmother from hell.'

A gasp like a little gust of wind went through the audience.

'But since that day, through their little ups and downs . . .'

The congregation laughed knowingly.

'. . . I've grown to respect this incredible woman that Dad's marrying. I know I'll never call you Mum, Kandhi – but all the same, welcome to the Breams.'

And with that he looked over to his dad with kind of tears in his eyes, which was SO-OO unlike Shug.

I was so taken off my guard that I had completely forgotten that it was my turn to speak next. Mum was nudging me.

I stepped into place on the podium and took the mike

from Shug. The first line of the sonnet came up on the autocue:

> 'Let me not to the marriage of true minds
> Admit impediment . . .' I started.
> 'Love is not love
> Which alters as it alteration finds . . .'

And then, suddenly, standing up there in front of everyone, I *knew* what Shakespeare was on about. I mean, Rupert had explained what the words meant and everything, but this was a different kind of knowing. Somehow, although he'd lived like aeons ago, Shakespeare told me why I'd dumped Rupert. He was right. '*Love is not love which alters* . . .' I hadn't really been in love with Rupert, though I'd fancied him like mad. No, love was something deeper and far more important:

> 'Oh no it is an ever-fixèd mark
> that looks on tempests and is never shaken . . .'

Love was more like what Mum and Oliver had. They'd lived through tempests and survived, hadn't they? Suddenly I felt I had to belt out the words because at that precise moment the meaning was crystal clear to me.

When I ended the sonnet there was total silence. I looked up, embarrassed. I mean, maybe I'd like totally overacted or something. And then the applause burst out. I caught Shug's eye – he was clapping with a kind of slow smile on his face. Mum was drying her eyes.

I watched in a haze as Mum and Oliver went through the 'I do' bit. And right on cue, as Oliver put the ring on Mum's finger, the string orchestra rose majestically over the rhododendrons and the intro bars of 'Only You' flooded out.

Mum took a deep breath and took Oliver's hand, then she turned towards the congregation . . .

'O-only . . . Y—' she started.

I guess this would have been the ultimate *truly romantic moment*, had it not been for a totally out-of-line helicopter practically grazing the heads of the people in the front row and drowning out Mum, deafening us with umpteen decibels.

That first helicopter was followed by another, then another. And then I saw why. Each helicopter had zoom lenses protruding from every orifice and they were all trained on Mum.

'How the hell did the press get wind of the venue?' Oliver shouted at Mum. He was shaking his fist and taking totally useless swipes at the circling helicopters.

'How should I know?' screamed Mum above the din. Her veil was being caught in the updraught, practically taking her hair with it.

'Don't give me that!' roared Oliver at Mum. 'You must've tipped them off . . .'

Mum was so speechless with anger she snatched off one of her Manolos and threatened Oliver with it.

The preacher had got between them and was holding them apart, vainly trying to keep the ceremony going by shouting: 'You may kiss the bride!'

'Kiss the bride? You must be joking!' Oliver hurled back at him.

The arrival of the fifth helicopter unfortunately coincided with the launch of the hot-air balloon. It rose splendidly above the garage and then, caught in the downdraught of the chopper blades, it was thrown wildly off course. I watched helplessly as it spiked itself on the finial of the marquee . . .

All of a sudden the air was filled with bits of slashed balloon. Mashed scarlet rose petals rained down on the guests, giving the unfortunate impression that a massacre was taking place.

Later – still Elwyn Jones's residence unfortunately
I guess it could have been worse. I mean, Oliver could have stormed off and had the marriage annulled or something. It was only when I saw the cake standing there on the head table, and Vix confirmed that it had been there all along, that I realised who had tipped off the press.

Me.

Inadvertently, of course, as I tried to explain over the din of the helicopters and the full-on row between Mum and Oliver.

But you couldn't really blame me for the fist-fight that broke out between the security guards and the photographers who had cut their way through the perimeter fence.

Or the clash between the television crew and the armed police who had parachuted in. There was only one guy hurt and his injuries were minor – he didn't have to be hospitalised.

But it was kind of sad the way it ended with the police using water cannons like that. Unnecessary, really, because as soon as the shooting broke out (and it was only over the heads of people, not straight at them) Mum and Oliver drove off in the limo which had been standing by waiting to take them off on their honeymoon.

And the press set off in hot pursuit.

Even later (amid the carnage)

The place is very quiet now. Elwyn and all the guests have gone off to some other place where they can party. I could've gone too but I'm feeling too bad about the way things turned out. I want to do something to make amends, so I've changed out of my dress and into my jeans and I've come to see if I can help clear up the mess.

I walk between the soggy tables covered in chopped rose petals and disembodied bits of banquet which have been hosed around the place.

The cake still stands on the top table, leaning over slightly. It took a full-on water cannon blast to its east side. It never did get cut, so no one ever got to hear it play 'Kandidly Yours' in that truly romantic way it should have done.

A voice breaks the silence. 'Holly?'

I turn. It's Shug. What's he doing here? He's the last person I want to see right now.

'Why haven't you gone with the others?' I ask him.

'I've got to be down at the recording studios in half an hour. Why haven't you?'

'I didn't feel like it.' I can feel myself about to cry. I know my nose is going red.

'Look, none of this is your fault.'

I'm taken off guard. He's being nice. Shug is *actually being nice to me*!

'Yes it is. I'm the one who gave the location away.'

'Nah, those press guys have had their helicopters circling the city since dawn. They just homed in on the place where they saw the most hats.'

This makes an enormous lump appear in my throat. 'You think?' I manage to croak.

'Yeah. It was a dumb idea to have the wedding in the open air in the first place.'

'But it's all ruined. They didn't even cut the cake.' (Snuffle.)

'Hey, it looks pretty intact. Why waste it? I'm starving, aren't you?'

'No, we shouldn't, it's –'

'Oh, come on, it's only going to get chucked.'

Before I can stop him Shug has thrust the knife into the cake. Instantly, 'Kandidly Yours' starts playing and the little bridal couple on the top tier do a stately pirouette together.

'Jeez! That is SO-OO naff!' says Shug.

'No it's not.' (But I have a sneaking feeling that maybe he's right.)

'You know what? I reckon this whole marriage thing is pretty off. Veils and dresses! I mean – give me a break – they've been like having it away for months.'

'It was all going to be really, really . . . romantic.'

'Rubbish. It was false and tacky. You know what? I thought

the water cannons were the best bit. All those designer outfits getting trashed. I thought that made a statement.'

'But think of all the preparations! And it's all got spoilt.'

'Come on, cheer up. Have a slice of cake.'

I take the plate he offers despite myself. The cake is full of fruit and fresh cream and layers of hazelnut meringue, so I can't help cheering up . . . *a little bit.*

'You know what?' says Shug.

'What?'

'You've got cream on your chin.'

'No I haven't.'

He flicks a bit at me. 'Now you have.'

I flick some back at him. 'Not as much as you have.'

Then he flicks a big sloppy lump. 'Well, you have now.'

After that cake and cream flies. I give as good as I get. At the end of the fight, I reckon Shug has more cake on him than I do.

Sunday 13th July, 7.00 a.m.
Thinking back on yesterday

OK, you can stop right there. *Nothing* happened in the garden apart from a food fight. You should've seen what a mess we were in at the end.

But I did discover a fundamental truth about human relationships – it's really hard to loathe someone you've covered in whipped cream.

So anyway . . .

I'm currently lying in the hot tub recovering from the stress of the whole disaster, planning what I am going to say to Mr Jones. I shudder at the thought of that horrible gash in the side of his Lamborghini. It slid sideways under a water cannon blast and slammed into one of his Italian Renaissance statues. But I guess they can stick the head back on – it looked like a pretty clean break.

And I am going to have ample opportunity to apologise because I'm due to have Sunday lunch with him today. *Just the two of us*.

By twelve o'clock I am dressed in a suitably apologetic skirt and proper shoes with tights and my hair dragged back into a penitential ponytail band. A chauffeur-driven limo has been sent to fetch us because Mr Jones's Lamborghini has been hoisted up on to a carrier and taken off to the menders. We are both very quiet in the limo. I stare out of the window, horribly conscious of the fact that he's really angry with me. I can almost feel him seething.

The limo takes us to a hotel called Chateau Marmont on Sunset Strip. It looks a bit like a castle – the kind of castle that has dungeons and things below where they imprison people like me who've done terrible deeds.

I follow Mr Jones inside and find it's reassuringly plush, all panelling and cushy sofas, so I guess it wouldn't be *too* much of a punishment to be a prisoner in here.

We are shown to Mr Jones's usual table in the window. It's all a bit old-fashioned – not a bit what you'd expect for the King of Punk.

Mr Jones orders a Campari for himself and I ask for a Coke. I reckon that apology time has now come.

I clear my throat and say in my clearest and most apologetic voice: 'Mr Jones, I just want to say I'm so sorry. About your tux . . . and the garden and all the plants . . . and your car, and the statue – and everything else that got damaged. But please, whatever it costs, just send the bill to Mum . . .'

He looks into his Campari and sighs.

I can see I'm going to have to lay it on thick. 'Really, Mr Jones, don't be too hard on me. It really, truly wasn't my fault. I totally thought that the person who rang was the caterer with the cake –'

'Holly,' he interrupts.

'Yes, Mr Jones?'

'I've got the most almighty hangover from yesterday. Do you think you could talk a little more softly?'

'Of course.'

'And there's something else . . .'

'Yes?'

'Do you think you could call me Elwyn? It's tough enough being, you know, old and out of it and somewhat passé. But you don't have to rub it in.'

'But you're not so old, Mr – I mean Elwyn.'

'I feel pretty old today.'

'You must be really, really mad at me . . .' I say as softly as I can.

'To tell you the truth, Holly, I thought the end of the wedding was the best bit. It was kind of like a happening . . .'

'Really? You don't have to be nice about it.'

243

'Holly, I am never nice. You know what my ideal wedding would be?'

I shake my head.

'I'd give all the guests paintballs and let them fight it out.'

'That is so cool. Have you ever been married, Elwyn?'

'More times than I care to remember.'

'So where are all your wives?'

'New York. Cannes. Puerto Rico. Oh, and I think there's one in Wales – the blonde. At least she was then.'

'Have you got kids?'

'Only one godkid. And that's more than enough! Come on, drink up. Let's have lunch.'

Over lunch Elwyn came out with all these stories about what he and Mum had got up to in the music business way back when they were on tour together. He had me in fits of laughter. I hardly noticed the food in spite of its scrumminess because I was so into what he was telling me.

'Anyway,' he finished, 'you're going to catch up on it all tomorrow.'

'Tomorrow?'

'It's your mum's premiere. *Supernova*. Remember?'

In all the excitement about the wedding I had totally, totally forgotten about it.

Same, 3.00 p.m.

After our lunch, during which I made a real pig of myself because Elwyn insisted I had everything I liked best – including extra double-chocolate topping on my Divine

244

Dark Dessert – he suggested that as my godfather he should treat me to a tour of Tinseltown.

I guess the afternoon was a bit of a blur, but if you want me to list the High Spots, these are the ones I remember (listed in order of appearance):

1) A Great Dane wearing sunglasses in Rodeo Drive.
2) A post office with valet parking!
3) An LCD sign that updates you on how many McDonald's hamburgers have been consumed world-wide to date. For your information, the total at the time recorded was 99 billion 12 thousand and 29 . . . and still rising
4) Twin chihuahuas wearing identical pink velour designer hoodies at Venice Beach
5) A psychic who told me I'd realise my dream! So I am going to be a vet
6) My photo taken between two Mr Universes on Muscle Beach
7) Endless avenues of palm trees
8) Acres of blue sky
9) Having a henna tattoo of a python done right up my arm
10) Eating a corn-dog watching the sunset on the beach at Malibu
11) A Pussyfoot cocktail big enough to drown in at the Viper Lounge

Monday 14th July, 9.00 a.m.
The day of the Supernova premiere

I have absolutely nothing to do until 5 p.m., when I'm due to meet Mum and Oliver at Mann's Chinese Theatre for the *Supernova* premiere.

They're flying back for it, direct from their secret honeymoon destination. Stars apparently only have mini-break honeymoons – they can't admit to being able to fit anything longer into their schedule.

Elwyn has appointments all day but he's insisted on giving me a large stash of dollars to make up for all the godfather presents he hasn't given me to date. He has also given me the use of the chauffeur-driven limo. So I do what any self-respecting person does in LA – I go shopping.

But I'm not shopping for me. I'm shopping for Brandy. If LA is famous for anything, it's shops for dogs – although not many of their customers are the size of Brandy.

Elwyn's chauffeur says he knows all the best places and he takes me on a tour of stores with names like Poochi, Wag and Barkers.

My favourite is a really stylish one in West Hollywood called Dogue. But it's kind of tricky finding anything for an extra-outsize German Shepherd cross. I've checked through a load of Kenzo military-style dog jackets, but frankly I can't really picture Brandy in one. They've got epaulettes and he's already kind of heavy round the shoulders. And the Chanel dogstooth check coats are way too girly.

'You being helped out?' asks a voice.

It's a lady assistant with a poodle-dog hairstyle with a pink bow in front.

'Oh – well, no. I'm looking for a present for a really big dog.'

'Well, our new winter season's stock has just come in. How about a K9 overcoat? We have these vests in red or blue ballistic nylon. They're lined with fleece, so great for sloshing around outdoors.'

'Well, actually this dog is more of a city dweller. He lives in New York.'

'Something smarter then? How about something from our designer collar range?'

'Maybe.'

She takes me through a selection of collars with studs and false gems and ones on which you can have the dog's name embossed in diamante. But nothing seems quite Brandy's style.

'Seems like he's a pretty tough customer to please.'

We move on to the Dining area, where I ponder over an aerated, charcoal-filtered dog fountain. Or a special dog bowl ergonomically designed so that your dog can eat without the strain of bending down. In the Sleep-eezy section there's an air-conditioned massage dog bed. Or a tartan pet sleeping bag which comes in extra large and is kind of cute . . .

It's in the Petfotec section, after pondering over the selection of Neva-Lone Pet Videos, that I find the perfect present: The Pet-U-Love Vu-Cam.

It's a neat little camera that you set up close to the pet-u-love, and it sends live Tru-Vu pictures to your PC.

Which means I can check on Brandy whenever I like and find out if Dad is taking him for his walks or not.

I am having a demonstration of how it works when I notice Elwyn's driver is hovering and looking at his watch.

'But we've got ages before it starts,' I point out.

'Depends how popular the movie is. Traffic's not looking good.'

5.00 p.m., Gridlocked!

Seems like the whole world is going to Mann's Chinese Theatre. The traffic is stop-start all the way up Wilshire Boulevard.

Elwyn's driver is trying all the back-doubles but we're still getting snarled up in any route leading to Sunset Boulevard.

'Sure looks like your mother's fans are out in force,' he comments.

At last we're in Sunset, but the traffic's practically at a standstill. My heart sinks as I watch the minutes ticking by on my watch. I'm meant to be meeting Mum on the red carpet outside the theatre. She's going to kill me if I'm late.

5.10 p.m.

I've had enough. We're only five or so blocks down from the theatre but nothing is moving. Everywhere there are people in Kandhi T-shirts promoting the movie. There are guys selling *Supernova* balloons and Kandhi posters and facsimiles of signed photos. Wherever I look there are pictures of Mum. And all of them are staring back at me reproachfully as if to say: 'How could you be late for my premiere?'

'OK,' I tell the driver. 'This is where I get out and walk.'

'But they'll never let you in if you arrive on foot,' he objects.

'Rubbish! I'm Kandhi's daughter.'

'Don't rely on it . . .' he says warningly.

'Goodbye and thanks,' I say, slamming the door.

I start to run along the sidewalk and I'm swallowed up by the crowd. Running soon ceases to be an option as the crush of people builds up. Within minutes it's so thick that I'm forced to push my way through.

At last, between massed bodies, I spot the barrier. There's the red carpet stretching away beyond the cordon, but my route forward is totally blocked by people.

Suddenly a scream goes up – as if the whole place has been set on fire or something. By jumping up and down I catch a glimpse of Mum, lit up by the strobelighting of camera flashes. She's being handed out of a stretch limo.

The screaming goes up a few more decibels as Mum is followed by Oliver. The crowd is going crazy.

There's nothing else for it. I go down on my hands and knees and crawl the last hundred metres, forcing my way between the legs of the crowd.

I emerge by the barrier. I've made it!

'Hi!' I gasp to the security lady who's manning the cordon.

She doesn't seem to have heard me. 'Hi!' I say louder. 'I'm meant to be in there. Will you let me through please?'

'Your pass?' she says.

'I haven't got a pass. I'm meant to be with Mum.'

'So where is your mother?'

'She's through there.'

'Yeah, sure. Which lady is it?'

'It's Kandhi. I'm *Holly*, her *daughter*.'

The security lady gives me a sideways look. 'Sure, and I'm Pope Pius the Twelfth. Now will you get back with the others? I'm trying keep things moving here.'

'No, but I am. I really am.'

'Look, if you're going to be difficult . . .' she says threateningly, unhooking her mobile. She speaks into it in an undertone, 'We've got a fan here, Arnold. One of the crazy type. Not sure if she'll go quietly.'

I shrink back as I spot two massive guys detaching themselves from a huddle of security guards.

I go quietly. Very quietly. And fast. In fact I disappear like magic into the crowd.

Clearly there's no way I'm going to get past that lady guard. I stare over to the other side of the street. This is where the main body of fans is congregated, opposite the entrance to the theatre, where you get the best view of the stars. I can see a solid press of people thrust up against the security barrier. If I could get over there and out front, maybe I'd be able to attract Mum's attention.

I wait with a clump of crowd that wants to cross the road and when the lights change, I scurry over.

The crush of people is even heavier on this side. I edge along behind them until I'm level with the entrance to the theatre. By jumping up and down, I can make out that Mum and Oliver are lingering for the benefit of the press. They're making a kind of 'royal progress' down the red carpet, stopping here and there to have a word with a journalist they know or to have their picture taken.

Frantically, I start elbowing my way through to the front. There are protests from all sides as I break every form of fan etiquette, but at last I'm up against the barrier. From where I'm standing the people on the carpet look like another species – bright, glittering, untouchable – caught in the blitz of camera flashes.

'Mum!' I shout. But my voice – one voice in a million – is lost in the general screaming. Mum's eyes slide over the crowd. I leap in the air waving. 'I'm here, Mum!'

There's a chubby little girl squashed in beside me, holding a handmade sign. She's stuck on pictures of Mum and written 'I love you, Kandhi – Melanie' in wonky felt-tip letters with glitter and flowers round them.

'Why do you keep calling Kandhi, "Mum"?' she asks. 'That's really dumb.'

'Because she is my mum.'

'As if . . .' she says, rolling her eyes.

'No, she is. She really is.'

'If you say so . . .' she says. She pulls at her mother's sleeve and says something in her ear. I can tell her mum doesn't believe me either. But she kind of humours me all the same.

'Keep screaming,' she says. 'They come over sometimes. I once saw someone actually get an autograph.'

'Mum!' I try again.

Mum's reached the end of the carpet. She's turning to face our side of the street. This is my chance.

251

'Mum!' I scream fit to burst a lung.

For a moment I think she's heard me. She's stepped off the far pavement. She's walking over the road towards me. Oliver's following.

'Mum! Oliver!' I scream, waving both arms in the air. But I guess this kind of makes me blend into the crowd because everyone else is screaming and waving.

Mum and Oliver are over on our side of the street now. They're out of my sight line further down the barrier. Pens and books and scraps of paper have appeared out of nowhere and are being thrust towards them.

I lean over the barrier. I see Mum sign a couple of autographs and accept some flowers. Oliver is following, signing too.

But just as I think she's coming within earshot, Mum seems to lose interest.

'Mum! Oliver!' I croak. I'm going hoarse now. But it's no use. My heart sinks as they turn. Oliver puts an arm around Mum and the two of them walk back across to the theatre.

The chubby little girl is crying because she hasn't had her poster signed.

'Oh, give me that,' I say, crouching down and taking it from her. 'I've done Mum's signature loads of times. No one can tell the difference.'

Her tears dry in amazement as I scrawl on it 'For Melanie with love and kisses from Kandhi'.

That's when I hear a voice out of nowhere, saying: 'What the hell are you doing down there?'

It's Shug. I hadn't noticed him in all the panic of trying to

252

attract Mum's attention. He must've come up behind the others.

Instantly, the autograph books are thrust in his direction.

'I didn't have a pass. They wouldn't let me through,' I shout at him.

'Silly you,' he says, casually signing an autograph.

'Oh, for God's sake! Please tell someone I'm me. Mum's going to be so mad if I miss her premiere.'

Shug gives me an arrogant grin and moves further down the barrier, signing autographs all the way.

'*Shug!* You *can't* just leave me here.'

'Wanna bet?'

'Oh Shug, honestly. *Please!*' I'm hopping up and down with frustration.

He saunters back grinning: 'OK. Put your arms round my neck . . .'

Suddenly I find I'm being lifted bodily over the barrier. Strong arms are round me and *that whoozy whizzy feeling has come back again with a vengeance.*

6.00 p.m.

The film has already started when we get in. That's why I have to sit at the back of the theatre with Shug, when I should have been sitting at the front with Mum.

'This is nice,' whispers Shug, sliding down in his seat. 'Just the two of us. Like a date.'

'As if!' I whisper back.

'Oh, come on. If it wasn't for me, you'd still be outside.'

People in front are shushing us.

'Will you hush up and watch!' I hiss at him. Because I really want to concentrate on the film. It's kind of unique being given the opportunity to watch your very own mother's life – I don't want to miss a crucial bit.

We've come in at the place where Mum's still a kid of around five or six. She's living with her grandmother, who is my great-grandmother – played by this all-time famous actress who doesn't look a bit like Gi-Gi. At this point Mum (or Candice, as she's called) is behaving in a very un-Mum-like fashion, doing classical ballet classes and learning the piano.

Shug is making 'omigod' noises beside me as the miniature Mum is doing all her neat little pirouettes and pliés. I kick him to shut him up.

The film moves on to the part where Mum is around my age and suddenly it's Gina – a girl I know from London – acting the part of Mum. I nudge Shug. 'Isn't she brilliant?'

Gina has to play the difficult bits – screaming, rebellion, refusing to go to school – and she does it really well. She's made up to look a true nightmare of a teenager – raggy things tied in her hair, big holes cut into her tights and a lip ring and everything.

'She certainly has attitude,' says Shug.

'Don't overreact – Gina's not like that really.'

It isn't until the bit where Mum becomes a groupie and starts trailing around after Dad's band that Shug sits up and really starts to take notice.

'Your dad's not bad,' he says, as if it's the most amazing thing ever.

'Naturally,' I whisper back.

It's kind of hard to believe the bits that follow. Mum and Dad are living in a trailer park. Dad's struggling to write music and Mum's six months pregnant. She's doing things undreamed of by Mum, like hanging out washing. And there's *no way* she ever peeled a potato – she simply wouldn't know how to.

Then all of a sudden we're cutting to real photos of Mum. She's coming out of hospital carrying a closely wrapped bundle – that's *me*.

'Glad you got rid of those wrinkles,' whispers Shug.

After that comes Mum's amazing rise to fame. I can tell Shug's dead impressed, by the way he's stopped fidgeting and gone all quiet. There's loads of footage taken direct from Mum's early concerts with the Popsicles. And then they screen the bit we've actually witnessed shooting in New York.

Shug nudges me.

I nod. My mind goes back to that morning. I remember Shug barring my way and how I had to brush up against him to get by. And the way I caught him looking at me when I turned back. I sit through the rest of the film very much aware of the warmth of his shoulder just inches away from mine.

10.00 p.m.

There's this massive party after the premiere. Predictably, Shug goes off to talk to loads of important people and there's no way I can get near Mum or Oliver. Even Elwyn is surrounded by a little group of ageing fans.

I'm feeling really out of it when suddenly someone bounces up to me.

'Gina!' (It's the girl who played Mum when she was my age. I met her when they had the auditions for the part way back in London.)

'Hi! I knew you'd be here,' she says.

'Did they fly you out specially from London?'

'No, I was here already, filming something else.'

'Brilliant!'

'Who was that boy I saw you with?'

'Oh, him. That's Shug, my stepbrother,'

'Isn't he in a band?'

'Mm-hmm. And doesn't he know it!'

'They're really good.'

'Oh, don't you start.'

'No, but they are.'

'Don't tell him – he's got a big enough head already.'

'Hey, won't you take me over? I'd like to meet him.'

I pause. What is this strange feeling? There's no reason on this earth why I wouldn't want to introduce Gina to Shug.

'Yeah, OK.'

I led Gina over to where Shug was standing with a load of guys who looked as if they were from the press. It took a minute or two to get his attention.

'Shug, this is Gina. Gina, this is Shug.'

The minute they set eyes on Gina the press guys wanted to take her picture with Shug. I turned to them, putting on my best press smile.

'Can you two get closer? Do you mind standing to one side, honey?' asked one of the guys.

'Me? Oh yes, sure.'

I stood aside. I watched as Gina and Shug had photos taken. Loads of them. I didn't want to be in the photos. No way. But that odd feeling came back again. It was stronger now. Why should I mind if Shug had his picture taken with Gina?

'So, guys, what are we going to do now?' asked Gina.

'We're all going out to eat later. Let's stick together,' said Shug.

I looked from one to the other of them, not sure if this invitation included me.

But Gina said: 'Yes, let's.' Then she put an arm through mine and whispered: 'I'm going to, as you say here, *freshen up*. You coming?'

'OK. Sure.'

I followed Gina to the Ladies Room.

'You OK?' she asked.

'Sure. Why?'

'You were looking as if you were about to chuck or something.'

'It's hot in there, that's all.'

'Uh-huh?' she said, leaning into the mirror and applying more mascara. 'You know something? Your stepbrother. *He's* hot.'

I shrugged. 'He's OK, I guess.'

'OK? He's more than OK.'

'Well, I'm kind of getting used to him being around.'

'He can be around me as much as he likes.'

'Whatever.'

I took out my hairbrush and started brushing my hair.

Gina stared at me in the mirror. Her eyes narrowed. 'You've got the hots for him, haven't you?'

'No I have not!'

'Holly, admit it. You have. Look at you.'

I was not blushing – truly I wasn't. I slapped more foundation on my face.

'Would I want to go out with my own stepbrother?'

'You're not actually related.'

'Well, I wouldn't. So there.'

'OK! In that case, there's no reason why I shouldn't,' said Gina.

'None in the world,' I agreed.

11.00 p.m.

We didn't go to a restaurant. We were driven in a convoy of cars up into the Hollywood Hills. Gina and Shug and I were squeezed into the back of a car. Shug was in between.

Miles out of town, in the middle of nowhere, our car was met by a masked horseman. He escorted us from the valet parking to a mansion hidden away in the trees. Long tables had been set out in a courtyard, and there was a banquet that looked like a medieval feast – everything on silver platters and lit by flaming torches. As a mark of recognition to Mum and Oliver, there were little blue and white lights everywhere – in all the trees and floating in the pool. There were even little LEDs in the ice buckets which kept switiching from white to blue.

Mum and Oliver were already seated with Elwyn and a load of people who I'd seen in all the celebrity magazines. Gina was loving it. She kept nudging me and pointing people out, which I wished she wouldn't do – practically everyone was famous.

People were seated kind of in pecking order. Like the truly famous people at the top of the table with Mum and Oliver, then the less famous people like the other actors. And then right at the end were Shug and Gina and me.

Everyone seemed to be talking at once and there was loads of toasting the newly-weds. Great gales of laughter kept coming from their end of the table. If you wanted to hear what anyone was saying, you had to sit really close. If Gina sat any closer to Shug, she'd be on his lap.

I sat toying with my food. It was kind of late to eat.

Shug kept glancing across at me. I could tell he and Gina were talking about me by the way she was laughing. I bet he was telling her about all the dumb things I've done. Like how I loused up Mum's wedding and nearly missed the premiere.

When we'd finished our main course, Gina leaned over the table to me.

'You OK?'

'Yes, fine. Why?'

'Nothing. You want to do something tomorrow? I've got the day off.'

'OK.'

'Shug wants to meet up at a diner on Sunset Strip.'

'Oh. Right. Are you sure you want me too?'

'Of course!'

After that someone put on a smoochy number from one of Mum's early albums. Mum and Oliver got up and started slow-dancing. With that, everyone got to their feet clapping. Then Mum started dragging people on to the dance floor.

Gina leapt up right away and grabbed Shug by the arm. 'Come on,' she called over to me. 'Let's dance.'

She flounced off ahead to the floor. I didn't get up – she was just being nice. It was Shug she wanted to dance with.

Shug came round to my side. 'Don't you want to dance?'

I shrugged. 'Why don't you dance with Gina?'

'We can all dance together, can't we?'

'Not if it's a slow dance.'

I could see Gina waving and beckoning to us.

'Go on, dance with Gina,' I said, hoping maybe he wouldn't.

'OK,' said Shug. 'I'll do that.'

I watched as he threaded his way on to the dance floor and started dancing with Gina.

Why was I feeling like this? Shug could go out with Gina if he wanted to. Why not? He was only my stepbrother, after all.

Tuesday 15th July, 8.00 a.m.
Elwyn Jones's residence

I wake up to hear footsteps going back and forth in my room. I peep over the covers and find there's a maid in my room taking everything out of my closet and packing it in my suitcase.

'Hello. What's going on?'

'Oh, sorry to wake you, Miss Hollywood. But your mother's said to pack all your things.'

'Pack? Why?'

'I'm told you're leaving today.'

'Leaving?'

We can't be leaving. I'm meant to be meeting up with Shug and Gina.

'By the midday flight. But don't you worry about a thing. Would you like your breakfast served in your room?'

I'm wide awake now. What's Mum up to? I reach for the phone. Mum and Oliver's number's engaged. Elwyn's given them an even bigger suite in the main house now they're married. I fling on my robe and stumble through the garden.

30 seconds later, inside Elwyn's house

The main house is filled to bursting with Elwyn's priceless collection of Chinese antiquities. Between two life-size porcelain horses I find Mum seated on a couch made to look like a reclining dragon. She's on the phone. She waves at me to sit down and wait. This call is clearly important.

'But I know there are two free. I saw them with my own eyes. Between Fred Astaire and Charlie Chaplin. You go take a look for yourself.'

'. . . . .'

'What do you mean, further downtown? No way!'

261

'. . . . .'

'What if I make a bigger donation?'

'. . . . .'

'Yeah, you do that. Look into it.'

Mum puts the phone down with a frown.

'What was all that about?'

'The Walk of Fame, babes. Now we're married, Oliver and I want our plaques side by side. And for some reason these City Council people are being really difficult about it.'

'Maybe they want to see how long it lasts.' Vix's voice comes from behind a lacquer cabinet.

Mum's eyes narrow. 'Vix, this is important. I want you to get down there straight away and sort it out. Now, babes, what was it you wanted?'

'There's someone in my room packing my things. Nobody told me we were *leaving*.'

'Oliver got a call this morning. He's had to fly back to Rome. And I just had this brilliant idea. Why not go after him? It would be a really good trip for you too, babes – educational. You know, the Colosseum – all those ruins and stuff.'

'But I've got things planned!'

'Planned? What could you possibly have planned?'

'I was meeting up with some friends and –'

'Babes, you can see friends any time.'

'Not if I'm in Rome and they're in LA I can't.'

But Mum's lost interest. Vix wants to know the exact location where Mum's set her heart on having the plaques. I try to interrupt.

Mum turns to me. 'Hollywood, this is important. These plaques are going to be there like for *eternity* . . .'

Later, Flight AA 945 to Rome

So I'm flying to Rome with Mum. Vix and Daffyd and June and Thierry and Abdul and Sid and Gervase are flying to New York. I've given Sid the Pet-U-Love Vu-Cam with strict instructions to install it at Dad's the minute he gets there, so I can keep an eye on Brandy and check whether Dad's walking him. Shug is staying in LA *and so is Gina*.

I spend the flight imagining how Shug and Gina are spending their day:

a) They're having a burger together in this really cool diner on Sunset. They're sharing a large-size French fries and their hands kind of touch . . .

b) They've gone down to Venice Beach and they're cycling – no, rollerblading together. Gina's kind of wobbly and Shug has to put his arm round her . . .

c) They're at Malibu walking on the beach into the sunset hand-in-hand . . .

Gina has kindly said she'll keep me texted. *I can't wait to hear how they're getting on.*

9.00 p.m., Rome Airport

There's a car waiting at the airport to meet us. No one is expecting Mum to arrive so we don't have to run the gauntlet of the usual frantic paparazzi. Mum climbs into the front and I'm just settling into the back and checking my mobile to see if Gina's texted me about her *brilliant* day with Shug, when I find I have a text from Becky.

> **it's the awards**
> **tonight**
> **wish me luck**
> **you will watch**
> **won't you?**
> **Bx**

I text back immediately

> **of course!**
> **break a string or whatever**
> **love**
> **HBWX**

It's The Young Musician of the Year Awards tonight! I've got to get to a TV somehow to watch it.

10.05 p.m., The Palazzo Albrizzi Hotel, Rome

The Palazzo Albrizzi is a really old palace up in the hills overlooking Rome. The entrance hall is all marble and gilt mirrors and tapestries, but I don't have time to linger over the decor.

The minute I'm in my suite I zap on the TV. After channel-switching through enough programmes to send the Albrizzi's motorised satellite dish into pirouettes, I find the channel I'm looking for. Phew! There is the uneasy sound of an orchestra tuning up in the background.

I fume through flashbacks of two other performers, wondering if I've missed Becky's bit. But no. Now it's her turn. For a moment I hardly recognise her. She's wearing a really grown-up black dress and has her hair tied back.

One of the interviewers says: 'Tell us something about the violin you're playing, Becky.'

Becky looks at the violin lovingly. 'It's a really strange story. I've always dreamed of owning a Stradivarius, then, out of the blue, this violin was delivered to me anonymously – as a gift.'

She's got her Strad! Brilliant! I'm so knocked out I feel like yelling! But who could have sent it? Someone pretty rich. Becky doesn't know anyone rich apart from us. Mum! It must be from Mum. She didn't just give a donation, she bought it outright! Oh, that is SO-OO kind of her – and not letting on to anyone either.

I'm about to grab the phone and thank Mum when I think better of it. No. If Mum wants to be generous and keep it a secret, I think I should respect her wishes. I won't mention it unless she does.

Becky's started playing. It's a piece I can remember her practising when we were at school together. For a moment this takes me back. I'm standing in the grounds beneath the practice room, wondering how much longer she's going to be. But it seems like all this practice has paid off. She plays better than I've ever heard her. She must be right about the Strad. I wait in an agony of anticipation while the two presenters go into an endless rigmarole summing up the performances of the finalists.

I have my fingers crossed and my toes crossed and my hands are wet with the suspense. At last the finalists file on to the stage for the verdict of the jury.

I now have my hands over my eyes. But I take a peek long enough to see that Becky's come FIRST!

I'm practically crying with excitement as I watch her accepting a cheque for the prize. It's for five thousand pounds – the kind of money Mum wouldn't even pick up a mike for. But Becky is totally, totally knocked out about it.

I text her instantly:

!!!!!!!!!! x a million!
HBWXXXXXX

Wednesday 16th July
The Palazzo Albrizzi Hotel, Rome

Soon as I'm awake I check for a text from Gina. There isn't one. I lie in bed staring up at my ceiling, which is painted with a scene of goddesses and cherubs being kept barely decent by a load of flimsy clouds. I wonder whether this is good news or bad.

No text could mean:

a) She's having such a brilliant time with Shug she hasn't had time to think of texting me.
b) She's not having such a brilliant time and doesn't want to admit it.

266

I order up my breakfast in my room. It comes on a silver tray with antique china and a coffee pot with a knob shaped like a dolphin. I eat little curled Italian rolls with ace black cherry jam. After that I fill the bathtub with really hot water and loads of bath foam. It's a massive affair standing on four gilded lion's feet so it takes ages. Then I have a soothing soak.

Hang on – my phone's ringing. I leap out of the tub. It could be Gina!

'Hi?'

It's not. It's Mum

'You OK, babes?'

'I was till you got me out of the bathtub. Now I'm dripping all over the floor.'

'Oh babes, I'm sorry.'

'It's OK. I've a grabbed a towel.'

'Now, listen. You'll have to get moving. Carlo wants you and me to be on the set by eleven.'

'Oh, I thought maybe we could go sightseeing and check out the Colosseum and –'

'But that's where they're shooting, babes.'

'Oh? Are we going to watch Oliver?'

'Kind of.'

11.00 a.m., in a dank smelly bit at the back of the Colosseum

I don't actually see much of the Colosseum, just a gloomy corner with a few arches which has been roped off behind sheets of tarpaulin. It's a typical film set – people everywhere looking bored out of their minds drinking coffee out of paper cups and one tiny little bit of action going on under the lights.

'There's Oliver,' says Mum, pointing to where all the attention is focused.

Oliver's in a passionate clinch with a girl who looks as if she's just swept off the Ancient Roman equivalent of a catwalk. She's wearing this flowing robe thing that's kind of half torn off at the top so it's *just* decent. Oliver is in full centurion costume. God, he looks a plonker in that plumed helmet!

When they finish the take, he comes over and gives Mum a big kiss and then turns to me.

'Hi, Holly! Glad you could make it. This is really good of you.'

'Hello, Oliver.' I give him a kiss too.

'Carlo will be over in a moment to go through what you have to do. But maybe you should get over to Wardrobe first.'

'What?' I stare at Mum.

'OK, listen, Hollywood. There's this girl about your age. She doesn't have to do a lot – nothing really. And the girl who's playing it has fallen sick. And since you're here anyway, I thought –'

'Mum! You are NOT going to get me in the movies.'

'No! This is just to help out. And Carlo was so impressed by the way you delivered that sonnet at the wedding.'

'Mu-um!'

'It's only one incy wincy little scene.'

11.30 a.m.

The thing I have to act has an official name. I'm being 'impaled'. It's kind of like being stabbed but more dramatic – the spear has to come out the other side. So what I'm doing in Wardrobe is having half a spear stuck on my front and the other half stuck on my back. They're going to slosh the blood on afterwards.

It takes for ever, which gives me time to learn my lines, or rather line, which is: 'AAAAAAAAHHHHHHH!'

It's a good thing I mastered that sonnet. All that studying will really come in handy.

12.00 noon onwards, starring as a Christian virgin

I'm on set at last. *I* don't look as if I've just stepped off a catwalk. I have a long matted wig and loads of hair stuck on to my legs so it looks like I've got fetlocks.

I'm tied to this pole in the boiling sun and Oliver's getting ready to do his bit. He's on horseback and he has this massive spear which is just like the one 'going through' me. He's getting geared up to 'impale' me. But they have to use a body double for the actual charges because Oliver doesn't ride that well. I sure hope this body double knows what he's doing.

First charge – I'm practically sick with fear.

Second charge – I'm cowering.

Third charge – I'm flinching.

Fourth charge and after – I've become so blasé I'm not feeling scared at all.

So it takes six takes before I get the 'AAAAAAHHHH!' to sound convincing enough.

6.00 p.m.

I've been released from the set and had my wig and fetlocks peeled off and I'm looking round for Mum. Apparently she's gone shopping. She wasn't even watching when I did my 'AAAAAAAHHHHHH!'

9.00 p.m., Emilio Bianchi's in the Piazza delle Sirene

Emilio Bianchi's, apparently, is the most fashionable restaurant in Rome. It's in a square which has an all-time ancient fountain in the centre. It's decorated with naked ladies and bearded gods and dolphins which have cascades of water sloshing over them.

We're in an open air bit that's fenced off from the square with a little hedge of scented plants. It's refreshingly cool after the heat of the day. The air is filled with the whistling sound of swallows and half of Rome seems to have come out to stroll. I sit watching all these young Italian people going by. They all seem to be in couples, walking hand in hand.

There's a boy and a girl sitting on the edge of the fountain. They're eating watermelon. She's feeding him segments and they're killing themselves laughing as the juice drips down his neck.

All the leading members of the cast are with us. Carlo and Mum and Oliver are sitting together. On the far side of Mum there's this Russian girl, Svetlana, who we saw this morning in the clinch with Oliver. She's amazingly beautiful with green eyes, glossy tanned skin and long blonde hair to die for. She keeps leaning over to speak to Oliver and kind of swooshing her hair over Mum.

My eye keeps going back to the boy and girl. He's splashing water over her now and she's shrieking with laughter. Suddenly I'm back in Elwyn's garden. I'm screaming with laughter as cake and cream is flying . . . My train of thought is interrupted by the strident sound of Mum's voice.

'Can you just *not do that?*'

It seems Mum has been swooshed enough. She's on her feet. Svetlana's standing too. She's a good foot taller than Mum. Oliver's getting to his feet and trying to calm things down.

Carlo's called a waiter over and there's a lot of fuss with plates and knives and forks and glasses being repositioned. Mum is now reseated next to Oliver and Svetlana is sitting beside Carlo.

I glance over at Mum. Uh-uh! I've seen that thunderous look before.

Thursday 17th July, 7.00 a.m.
The Palazzo Albrizzi Hotel

I wake up early. The hotel is very quiet – no one's around yet. Which is not surprising, because I discovered from Mum yesterday that she's booked the whole hotel. There are no other guests apart from us.

I log on on my laptop and check whether Sid has installed the Pet-U-Love Vu-Cam. He has. When I dial up the address the Vu-Cam provides me with a tiny square up in the corner of my PC screen with a very small Tru-Vu of Brandy.

He's lying asleep on the rug. There's a glimmer of light coming from under the music room door, so I guess Dad's working.

7.10 a.m. (1.10 a.m. in New York), edited highlights from the Pet-U-Love Vu-Cam

There's movement in the corner of the screen. Brandy is twitching and wagging his tail. He must be dreaming.

7.30 a.m. (1.30 a.m. NY time)

Brandy gets up, yawns and shakes himself, then lies down again.

(Sorry about this – as a medium the Vu-Cam is rather low on plot.)

7.45 a.m. (1.45 a.m. NY time)

Brandy is on his feet again. Dad's feet have emerged from his music room and gone towards the bathroom.

7.50 a.m. (1.50 a.m. NY time)

Dad's feet, now naked, go back in the direction of the bedroom. Brandy spends some time standing outside the bedroom door with his tail wagging.

8.00 a.m. (2.00 a.m. NY time)

Dad's feet, now in outdoor shoes, make for the front door followed by Brandy. Dad's walking Brandy at 2.00 in the morning!

I'm intrigued. After breakfast, I take my laptop with me down to the Albrizzi pool so I can keep updated. *Three whole hours go by.*

11.00 a.m. (in New York this is 5.00 in the morning!)

The loft door opens. Brandy and Dad return. *Some walk!*

12.15 p.m.

Mum hasn't appeared yet. We're meant to be going sightseeing. I'd better ring her and find out what she's up to.

'Hi, Mum! Everything OK?'

'Fine.' I can tell from her voice that things aren't.

'Only fine? What's wrong?'

'It's just that Oliver's got to spend all day on the set. I'll hardly see him.'

'Well, what did you expect?'

'I know. I guess I shouldn't have come. But maybe it's a good thing.'

'Why?'

'That Svetlana girl. Didn't you see the way she looked at him?'

'Mum! You can't be jealous. You only just got married.'

'Oh, I'm not jealous. I know I can trust Oliver.'

'Sure you can.'

'But they do spend a lot of time together.'

'Well, they're bound to. They're working together.'

'Look, I've got to go now. My car's arrived.'

'But aren't we going sightseeing?'

'No, I'm going to the set. I feel I ought to be there.'

'What about me?'

'Oh babes, you can have a nice time by the pool till I get back.'

6.00 p.m. (9.00 a.m. LA time)

I get a text from Gina at last:

> **Guess what**
> **we're meeting up at the**
> **recording studio**
> **Shug's going to introduce me**
> **to his band!**
> **Gina L. x**

So that puts me in a *really* good mood. This means that she and Shug are most definitely an item.

I vow to totally ban all thoughts of Shug and Gina from my mind. TOTALLY.

Friday 18th July
The Palazzo Albrizzi Hotel

I wake up to find that this total ban doesn't apply to dreams.

In my dream, Shug has invited Gina to do a duet with him

– I know for a fact she can sing really well. They sing this number called 'Gina' that Shug has specially written for her. *The song goes straight to Number One.*

9.00 a.m.
Mum rings down to say she plans to spend another day at the set. So, great, I get to spend another day at the pool.

I've now got to know the Albrizzi pool in all its fascinating detail.

For your information:

> It's 2 metres 50 in the deep end.
> One length takes precisely 2 minutes doing breast stroke, 1 min. 45 crawl.
> If you leave your sunlounger for more than thirty seconds, you get fresh towels.
> They don't serve Coke. They serve Pepsi.

11.00 a.m. (5.00 a.m. NY time), further edited highlights from the Pet-U-Love Vu-Cam
It's a precise repeat of yesterday. Once again Dad and Brandy have returned at 5.00 in the morning NY time – after *three whole hours*. You can't walk a dog in the middle of the night for three hours. Where have they been?

7.00 p.m.
They should be awake by now in LA. I might as well know the worst so I text Gina. I make it really casual to show I don't care.

> **Hi Gina!**
> **so how did it go with Shug?**
> **HBWx**

I get a text back almost immediately.

> **Shug who?**
> **Gina L.x**

Weird!? I text her again.

> **But I thought you two**
> **were an item**
> **HBWx**

Her text comes back:

> **we were till**
> **I chucked him.**
> **Gina L.x**

> **why?**
> **HBWx**

> **he kept on going on**
> **about this other girl!!!!**
> **Gina L.x**

Another girl! Typical! That's Shug all over. Men!

7.30 p.m.

I am brooding over this when Mum comes storming along the poolside looking for me.

'Holly, we're leaving. We're going back to New York.'

'*What?*'

'I've had enough of this!'

'What's Oliver done precisely?'

Mum bends down so that no one can hear what she's saying. 'That Svetlana girl. He's bought her this massive present behind my back.'

'So? Maybe it was her birthday or –'

Mum looks at me pityingly. 'Hollywood. Don't be naive.'

'But Mum, I've hardly seen any of Rome yet.'

'Hollywood, as far as I'm concerned we've done Rome. Period.'

'But –'

Mum turns on me with glaring eyes.

'If you say so,' I mutter.

'Your things have been packed. They're already in the car.'

I knew better than to try and argue with Mum when she's in this sort of mood.

'OK, I'll get dressed.'

So that was Rome. Nice. As far as it went. I did see a bit of the Colosseum. And a fountain with statues. And the Albrizzi pool. I saw a lot of the Albrizzi pool.

I follow Mum as she staggers into the apartment with her 'tragic' look on her face and slumps on the sofa.

Vix comes out of the office. 'OK, tell me about it,' she says.

'You think you know a guy. You trust him. And then behind your back . . .' Mum smothers a sob.

Vix raises her eyebrows at me from behind her back with an 'I-told-you-so' look on her face.

'Do you want to talk about it?'

Mum shakes her head, too stricken to go on. She takes herself off into her room and closes the door.

'So what happened?' Vix asks me.

'I don't know. There was this girl who was acting with Oliver. I guess she was kind of flirting with him, but I don't think it was serious.'

7.00 p.m.

Mr Bateman arrives even though it's out of office hours. When I open the door to him, he says 'Hello, Hollywood' and strides past me. Mum emerges from the bedroom. She looks all blotchy as if she's been crying. She shuts herself up in the office with Mr Bateman and Vix.

If Mum is going to pay a lawyer to work out of hours, it's serious.

9.00 p.m.

Mr Bateman has left, but Vix and Mum are still holed up together. It seems Mum is going to throw herself into her work in order to get over this.

As I pop in and out doing sympathetic dutiful daughter things, like bringing aspirin and cups of camomile tea and finding Mum's pashmina for her, I hear exotic names like Bombay ... Tokyo ... Buenos Aires ... It seems Mum is continuing with her Heatwave tour. Well, I guess she does have the rest of the world to cover.

10.00 p.m.

But enough of Mum. I have other things on my mind. I do have two parents, and I'd like to know what the other one is up to.

I check my stock of blueberry jelly beans and then I call up Abdul.

He arrives jangling his keys.

'It's late, Holly. Where do you want me to take you?'

I shake my head. 'Nowhere right now. Sit down, Abdul.'

He sits and catches sight of the jelly beans.

'Uh-uh!'

'This is a case of surveillance. I want someone followed.'

Abdul raises his eyebrows. 'And who would this person be?'

'My dad.'

Abdul leans over and dips into the bag. He takes a jelly bean and chews on it thoughtfully.

'Now, I've heard of dads surveilling their daughters. Doesn't happen that much the other way. What's he up to?'

'That's what I want to find out. Every night at 2.00 a.m. precisely he walks the dog.

'Yeah? So?'

'*For three whole hours.*'

'I see,' says Abdul. 'Doesn't sound much like your dad.'

1.45 a.m., South Mercer

Abdul and I sit parked a block down from Dad's and wait.

At two o'clock, sure enough, out comes Dad with Brandy.

Abdul waits till they round the bend then follows at a safe distance. We track Dad and Brandy to the gumball machine. Dad puts in a coin and gives Brandy his dog treat.

'Sure is tense so far,' says Abdul.

I ignore his comment. Dad has turned back and is crossing the park. He's outside Al's. Al's come out. He's shaking him by the hand and slapping him on the back and they've disappeared inside.

Abdul stares at me. 'OK, so he's gone for a meal. You want me to creep in and check what he's ordering?'

'No one eats at this hour.'

'So . . .' says Abdul, 'we better take a look-see inside.'

2.30 a.m., Al's café

Abdul and I are down in the cavern under Al's. The place is packed – so packed we have to stand at the back. I notice Abdul and I are the only ones not wearing beanies – unless you have an Afro, that is.

Through the haze of smoke I can see Dad up front playing keyboard. Brandy is lying under the keyboard as

280

if he owns the place. There's a guy with a bass and another on drums and another who comes in from time to time on a sax.

They're playing the kind of music you come across on the car radio when you can't get it tuned right, or in those films they play in art movie cinemas. Stuff I don't understand. But the people round us seem to. Every so often there's a pause and they're all nodding their heads and saying things like 'Yeah!' and 'Ni-ice!'. So I guess it must be pretty good.

Abdul is nudging me. There are some seats free. We slip into them.

They've started another number. It's made of smudgy sounds that make me think of fog over the Hudson River and deserted streets at night. Lonely places like the streets around Mr Herman Matlock's clinic. And sad things, like lost animals maybe wandering round with no place to go.

When Dad comes to the end of a riff it's clear that everyone else feels the same. They're applauding and stamping their feet on the floor like it's the *best* thing they've ever heard.

Dad's taking a break and he's shouldering his way through the crowd to the bar. People are slapping him on the back and shaking him by the hand.

As he reaches the bar he comes face to face with me.

'Holly?' he says. 'What are you doing here? It's the middle of the night!'

'It's OK, Dad. I just got back from Rome. It's only the afternoon there. And I came with Abdul.'

'Yes, sir, we were just passing and we saw you with the dog,' says Abdul (which is kind of true, I guess). 'Holly won't come to any harm when I'm around.'

Dad looks Abdul up and down and seems reassured.

'No, I guess not. All the same, it's late.'

'Dad,' I interrupt. 'That music. It just knocked me out. Is that what you've been writing?'

He looks at me and his face kind of softens.

'You liked it? Didn't think it would be your sort of scene.'

'Nor did I, till now.'

'Promise me, Holly, you won't tell your mum. OK?'

'Why not?'

'Can you imagine what she'd say? This isn't exactly the Carnegie.'

'Who cares what Mum says?'

Dad shrugs.

'Dad, you know, some day you've got to get over what happened when Mum got famous.'

Dad looks at me oddly, and for a moment I think I've really overstepped the mark. Then a slow grin spreads across his face. 'You know something, Holly? I think maybe I just did.'

Saturday 19th July, 10.00 a.m.
The Plaza Residenza

I check for a text from Gina. Nothing. I can't bear it any longer. I really *have* to know about this girl that Shug's going on about. I bet she's gorgeous. She's probably an actress, someone really famous, starring in a soap. Or the presenter of a teen show maybe. Or a model. I bet she's a model with ten metre legs.

I text Gina:

Hi Gina!
you've got to tell me
who is this girl?
HBШx

I wait for a text but nothing comes. I bet Shug's made her promise not to tell.

Sunday 20th July, 10.00 a.m.
The Plaza Residenza

Vix has scheduled a press conference at the Wessex Hotel. Mum comes out of her room dressed in tragic black. She even has a veil pulled down over her face.

I search my mind for something to say to cheer her up.

'Is there really no way you and Oliver could make up?' I ask gently.

'Not after the things Oliver said to me.'

'What did he say?'

'He said I was selfish and self-centred. That I never do anything for anyone if I'm not going to gain from it. I don't know, maybe he's right.'

'But that's not true, Mum. Look what you did for Becky.'

Mum looks at me blankly. 'What did I do for Becky?'

'The Stradivarius. There was nothing you could gain from that.'

'Holly, I don't know what you're talking about.'

'But I assumed – I mean, I told you how it was practically top of her Ultimate Wish List. After a date with Oliver . . .'

'A date with Oliver . . . He thought that was so cute. Oh my God!'

'What is it?'

'That explains it!'

'Explains what?'

'That massive cheque he paid out. He wouldn't say what for. So I kind of assumed he'd bought me a little present.'

'Mum, *what* are you going on about?'

'A million dollars.'

What?'

'That's what it cost. The present I thought Oliver had bought me. Which he hadn't. So I thought he'd bought someone else a present. Like that 'bitch' who's starring with him . . .'

'You mean, it's *Oliver* who gave Becky the Strad!'

'It must've been. I couldn't think what he could possibly have spent that much on, not in some *musty old Viennese music shop*.'

Mum is scrabbling in her bag for her mobile.

'Oh my God! Cyril was right.'

'What's this got to do with Mr Bateman?'

'He said, "Marry the man if you must, but never have a joint bank account." '

Tuesday 5th August, 6.00 p.m.
En route to Mum's Greek island

Mum and I are in a helicopter. It's currently circling Kandhiki – Mum's Greek island. Mum's out for the count as usual with her eye mask on and her earplugs in but I'm trying to wake her. We've actually begun our descent. There's an island down below us, looking like a tiny rock glowing golden in the evening sun. And we're spiralling down towards it, closer and closer.

Mum's planned this big family holiday to make up for everything that's happened lately. It's going to be just her and Oliver and me – and Shug.

7.00 p.m.
We've touched down. This is a big moment for me as I've never been to Mum's island. Nor has Mum, but I guess she's used to not going to places she owns. She's got a Tudor mansion in Kent and a castle in Scotland she's never been to either.

There are all these people lined up to greet us.

'Mum, who are these people?'

'Staff, babes. An island can't run itself, you know.'

There's a lot of ducking and bobbing and saying stuff like 'kalisperasas' as we are led down to a speedboat moored below the helicopter pad.

'Cool, isn't it?' says Mum. 'No roads, no airstrip. It's so hidden away – no one can bother us here.'

7.30 p.m.

Our speedboat is rounding a headland and Kandhiki Bay comes into view. A perfect arc of sandy beach lies below three white marble terraces carved into the hillside. A line of Grecian columns leads up to the entrance of the villa.

'Spiro always did overdo things,' says Mum as we disembark, 'but I guess the location's OK.'

The location is more than OK. Limpid blue water laps the beach. The water is still warm from the sun. I want to linger on the beach, maybe have a swim, but Mum is fussing about getting inside and sorting out our rooms and stuff.

I follow her up the path between the columns and switch on my mobile. I have a text from Gina.

You, you dope
Gina L. x

It takes me a moment to realise what she means. *Me?*

Oh my God! That girl Shug was going on about. She's not an actress starring in a soap. Or the presenter of a teen show. Or a model with ten metre legs. She's a perfectly ordinary girl who wants to be a vet.

ME!

That whoozy-whizzy feeling has come back again!

10.30 p.m.

I'm lying in bed listening to the waves lapping gently against the shore. The sea is ink-black and the moon is casting a long beam of light across it. It's so quiet I can hear the fishermen's voices from way out to sea. There's the scent of some plant hanging over my window – white stuff.

I stretch luxuriously in bed. Tomorrow Oliver will arrive. *And Shug.*

Wednesday 6th August, 11.00 a.m.
Still heaven

I've spent the morning lazing on this raft. It's about fifty metres from the beach and it rocks gently to the rhythm of the waves. I wait until the umpteenth moment when I'm really hot and then plunge into the water.

12.30 p.m.

A speedboat is rounding the headland and I can see two figures standing in the back. It's Oliver and Shug!

I raise myself on one elbow and wave.

But Shug's too busy to notice. He's taking his jacket off. But hang on, it's not just his jacket he's taking off – it's his shirt . . . and wait a minute . . . there go his jeans. Shug's climbed up on the hull of the speedboat in nothing but his boxers . . .

And he's dived off!

12.31 p.m.

Shug's head has appeared right beside the raft.

'Hi!' I say.

But he doesn't say anything. Instead, he hoists himself up on the raft and all of a sudden cold wet arms are around me.

We don't bump noses.

Our teeth don't clash.

Don't ask me what happened to my tongue. I simply can't remember.

Wow, Shug! Some first kiss!

We're so involved that we don't notice the head of a guy in a scuba diving suit that pops up out of the water right by the raft. There are all these camera flashes. And BLOOP! he disappears.

Which is how my first totally personal private kiss got spread across the front page of every single tabloid in the world.

Why is life is SO-OO unfair?